Michael –

PLASTIPOCALYPSE

A Novel

DOUGLAS CORNELL

Enjoy!

Douglas Cornell

For Carol

We were cold as hell.

It hadn't always been like this, but it was hard to remember when we took things like heat and running water for granted. Oh, to go back to the days of Walmart, red lights, and smart phones!

At this point, we haven't been in a car for months. There aren't any that are left that still run. Funny thing, when I was fixing my customers computers, I used to tell them that they should prepare for a time when the grid would melt down, which I guess *did* happen. It just didn't happen like I thought it would.

It was worse.

The Beginning

I woke around 6 am on a normal Sunday in March. Since I hurt my neck I quit sleeping much anyway. Our dog Annie, a big yellow lab, was sound asleep on the old carpet that covered the wood flooring. She stirred as I closed the bedroom door and stood to follow me downstairs. The old girl didn't move as quickly as she used to, probably bad hips. Someone told us all labs eventually have bad hips.

I grabbed the coffee from the cupboard and put water on the stove. I used to be quite the coffee chemist. Heat the water, grind the beans, soak the ground coffee in cold water, take the water off the stove at exactly 180 degrees, pour it on the coffee, let it steep —dang, what a stupid, wasteful process! It was the sort of useless crap that modern people did to convince themselves they were doing something useful.

Annie nudged my leg, and I gave her a soft pat on the head. She was not the world's most intelligent animal, but she was loyal and that meant a lot to me.

The old house was cold. We kept the furnace set at a barely tolerable 65 degrees during the winter. Propane cost too much, so we got used to wearing long underwear and having cold feet. I slipped into my Merrill hiking shoes and jacket and walked outside with Annie to get the Sunday papers from the box that was out by the road.

A stiff wind blew from the northwest. Piles of snow lined the driveway, half melted but still resisting the certain coming of spring. Annie sniffed around, looking for a dry spot to do her business. Mornings were always my favorite time of day out here. I could hear an occasional car or truck out on the state highway that was just a mile away across the fields. We had a few neighbors, people we barely knew but probably would have liked just fine if we'd taken the time.

I remember looking up at the sky that day and thinking that it was going be a typical, blustery late winter day.

March in Michigan can be a real bitch. Everyone is sick of winter, but March just hangs around for 31 nasty, windy days. Oh, a few years ago we had a warm spell - all of the trees budded early and then everything froze again and we had no fruit that year.

As I grabbed the newspaper from the box, I was wondering what Trix and I would find to do to occupy ourselves for the day. When it is dry we enjoy hiking and bicycling, but today we'd have to find something else to do instead. Maybe we'd go catch a movie in the afternoon.

Annie rumbled over to me and I picked up a stick and threw it across the yard. She seemed to smile as she ran to retrieve it and bring it back to me. My eyeglasses seemed dirty so I pulled them off and cleaned the lenses with a handkerchief that I kept in my jacket pocket. For some reason the lenses were smeared, but I forgot about it for a moment and walked back inside. Annie would stay in the yard – we had an invisible fence to keep her from running off.

Back in the house, I ran some hot water on my eyeglasses to clean them. They just got more smeared.

What the heck? It was like I'd spilled some solvent on the lenses. I can see okay without the glasses, but out beyond ten or fifteen feet things get fuzzy. I set the glasses down on the kitchen counter, poured myself a cup of coffee, and went out to the living room to read the newspaper.

Trix came downstairs a little later and put on a pot of oatmeal for breakfast. She wasn't a coffee drinker, but she did enjoy a hot cup of tea in the morning. The microwave oven beeped when her water was hot and she came out to the living room. I handed her the parts of the paper I'd already read or didn't want to read (mostly the ads), and said "Good morning."

After all of these years we were beyond having to say much to each other. We'd been married for over 30 years but we still liked each other fine. Trix was an easy person to live with. She worked hard at her job as a midwife, but she really was most happy when working in her flower garden or out hiking in the backcountry with me. We had a couple of kids who were grown and living lives of their own. Our daughter and son-in-law (a guard at a juvenile detention center), a 3 year-old grandson and newborn granddaughter lived about 35 miles away. Graham, our youngest, had just graduated from college and was getting started in his career as a food scientist in South Dakota. He frequently sent us fresh beef jerky from the factory where he worked.

I told her that something was wrong with my glasses. They were smeared and I couldn't clean them. She replied that the glasses were probably fine but that my eyes were probably screwed up. I ignored the comment and continued looking at the paper. There wasn't much interesting going on, except that March Madness would be starting later that week. I looked over the tournament bracket and told Trix that MSU had a good chance at making the Final Four. She said she hoped so.

A little later Trix went out to the kitchen to check on the oatmeal.

She yelled from the kitchen – "Greg! What *did* you do to your glasses?"

"Nothing! I think they were okay when I put them on this morning. I went outside with Annie and noticed they were all smeared."

"They are worse than smeared. It's like you spilled solvent on them. "

"I know. I'm not happy about it."

She dug around in a junk drawer and pulled out my last pair of glasses. We never throw glasses away, because you never know when you might need a backup pair.

"Here. Try these."

I put on the old pair of metal-framed eyeglasses and looked out the window and saw Annie walk across the back yard, sniffing the ground, probably smelling the scent of a rabbit or other local critter.

"That's better. Thanks."

We each got a big bowl of oatmeal. I turned on the TV and we sat down to watch the morning news. It had been a quiet night, with just the usual problems. The opposition wouldn't work with the president, there was flooding in Missouri, and gas prices were expected to go up. As we watched in silence, I remember thinking that we didn't have it so bad. We had good jobs, our house was paid for, and we were both healthy and fit.

Trix and I were often considered eccentric by our coworkers and friends because we tried to live life on our own terms. Since I was a self-employed information technology consultant, I had a lot of freedom in my work schedule. Trix worked for a local OB/GYN, but as a midwife, her schedule wasn't nearly as hectic as it would be if she were a doctor. She usually supervised 100 births each year, and the OB doc covered her if an emergency came up while we were out of town.

We went backpacking several times each year. Just last autumn we spent a week in California hiking a section of the John Muir Trail. We were quite happy being out in the wilderness together. We could cover about 15 miles daily, and we seemed to really need the time away from technology and the craziness of modern life. When we weren't hiking, we were avid bicyclists. We had a custom tandem touring bike that we rode 5 or 6 times each week, riding 20 to 30 miles each trip. During the winter months, Trix walked on her treadmill and I cross-country skied. We were always active and we didn't take being healthy for granted.

Neither of us had ever had any serious illnesses. A year ago I had a pinched nerve in my neck – and it hurt like crazy. Fortunately, I had access to good physical therapy and got it mostly fixed. It only hurt now when I slept on it wrong.

After breakfast we both went outside to pick up sticks that had blown onto our yard from the March winds. Even though it was currently about 40 degrees, it might get warm enough to go for a bike ride after lunch. Annie jumped up from the back porch and joined us as we walked around the yard and filled our arms with tree debris.

I told Trix that the road was pretty wet from the snow melting. Maybe the wind would dry it up.

She replied, "It's still pretty chilly. We'd have to bundle up if we do go out."

I watched her remove her eyeglasses and absent mindedly wipe them on her undershirt.

"Dang," she said. "My glasses are smeared too."

*****

A few minutes later we were standing in the kitchen laughing at how strange we both looked wearing our old, outdated eyeglasses.

I told her that it must have been some fluke. We both must have gotten into something that affected the polycarbonate lenses.

She laughed. "Polycarbonate? How did you know that word?"

I shrugged. "It's just the sort of stuff I remember."

"Did we get sprayed or gassed with anything while wearing our glasses?"

"No," I replied. "But we do keep them on the bed stand at night. Maybe something leaked in from the attic?"

We had a back stairway that went from the kitchen to the attic. We didn't use these stairs because there was another attic doorway in our son's old bedroom. But we did store paint and paint thinner and other household chemicals on the stairway.

She took a big sniff. "I don't smell anything."

I grabbed a flashlight and walked up the creaky stars, stepping over the paint cans and other junk stored there. Shining the light around in the gloom, I didn't find anything that was out of place. There were boxes of books, old clothing, and the other usual junk one keeps in one's attic. I retraced my steps and returned to the kitchen, where Trixie waited.

"What did you find?" she asked.

"Nothing. Not a thing out of place."

I scratched my head as I walked into my office. I turned on my computer to see if anyone else was reporting smeared glasses. The social media sites were quiet - nothing but photographs of other people's breakfasts or comments about the weather.

I even checked Google, using the phrase "smeared eyeglass lenses," but came up empty.

I walked back into the kitchen and told her that we must be the only people with the problem.

9

*****

We never did make it out for a bike ride that day; it was just too cold and windy. Instead we went into town to see a movie. We'd always been fans of good filmmaking, and there was a new Wes Anderson film playing at the multiplex. A couple of hours later, we left the theater and climbed back into the car.

"Good movie", I said. "Wes Anderson has an amazing imagination."

"I thought it was overly complicated," she replied. "He always crams his film with so many characters! But I did enjoy Bill Murray."

"Yeah," I said. "He's the best."

As I drove out of town towards home, I noticed that my hands were slightly sticky. I brushed my hands together and wiped them on my jeans.

"There must have been something sticky on the arms of my theater chair."

She was quiet for a moment, then asked, "How well can you see out of your glasses?"

"Now that you mention it, not too great. This pair is smeared again."

"Mine are too," she replied.

It's only a brief drive home. As I pulled the car into the garage, I saw that the plastic trim on the steering wheel was sticky. The wheel itself was also sticky. I stopped the car and sat there for a moment, thinking.

"Look," I said. "The trim – it looks like it's... dissolving?"

I rubbed my finger across it and some dark gray residue clung to my skin.

Trixie rubbed her hand across the dashboard and held her hand up to the light. It was also gray. There was a slight smear left where her hand had been.

I asked, "Is your hand sticky?"

"Uh-huh. Sort of."

The faux-chrome shiny trim in the car interior was fine. But the softer interior plastic looked like it was beginning to melt. It was subtle – unless you ran your finger across the surface, you wouldn't know anything was wrong.

After getting out of the car, I walked around it for a moment and looked at all of the exterior plastic. There was a lot of plastic on this car. The bumpers, front and rear fascia, and door trim were all molded plastic. I poked the rear bumper with my index finger and was amazed at how far it sunk into the material. It was as if the plastic was melting, yet it wasn't hot at all.

"Trix," I said. "This is not good."

She watched as I poked another hole into the bumper.

"You ought to check your car too."

Her car, which was parked next to mine in the garage, also had plastic bumpers. She easily pushed her finger right through and made a hole.

"Dang! My car's messed up too!"

I muttered under my breath, "What the heck is going on?"

Trix had a worried look on her face. "Look at your jacket – it's falling apart!"

I looked down - the fabric was beginning to shred, as if it was just disintegrating into the air. I pulled gently on the fabric and it just fell apart. The threads that connected the insulation baffles were simply gone. The insulation inside the remaining fabric was also disintegrating or evaporating or whatever the hell you want to call it.

I looked at Trix's jacket, which was essentially the same as mine - a North Face that we purchased in Yosemite when the weather turned colder than we'd expected during a week of hiking in the park.

"Yours is failing also!"

I looked at her other clothes. She had on blue jeans, and they seemed all right. I suddenly needed to sit down and think for a minute. I needed to figure out what was happening.

I backed up against the wall and sat down on a bench we keep by the back door. I looked down at my shoes and noticed that the laces were nearly gone. The shoe fabric, which was a durable synthetic

11

material, was also beginning to fall apart. The soles looked fine though.

Trix and I walked inside. We walked into the living room and turned on the TV. It was late afternoon, and all of the major networks were broadcasting sports. We sat down and Trix watched as I channel surfed, looking for any news that might be related to the strangeness that was happening around us. After about 15 minutes of finding out nothing at all, I pulled my cell phone out of my polar fleece sweater. Neither the phone nor sweater had any visible deterioration. At least we had that much going for us.

I called my brother, Jeff. He lived just 10 miles away and we frequently relied upon one another for help when we really needed it.

He picked up on the third ring. "Hey Jeff," I asked, "Have you noticed anything weird today around your place?"

"What do you mean?"

"The plastic on our cars is..." I paused "... melting?"

"What?" He almost laughed. I can imagine how stupid I sounded to him at that moment.

"No, really," I said. "You can push your finger right through the bumpers. Also, our jackets and shoes are falling apart!"

He paused for a moment. "That's messed up!"

I walked around the house with my phone pressed to my ear. "It looks like everything inside is okay. Have you been outdoors today?"

"No," he said. "I've been playing around on the computer and watching TV all day. "

"Did you see anything on the news about this? Was there a chemical spill or something?"

"No, not that I know of. "

"Okay. I'll call you later if I figure this out." I disconnected the call and put the phone back into my pocket.

I went into my office and opened the Internet browser to look at the social media feeds. None of the 250 or so people on my social media feed had anything important or interesting to report.

I walked back into the living room, where Trix was sitting, watching the TV. She said, "Still nothing on the news."

We sat in silence. I could tell she was worried. "There's got to be a simple reason for what's happening, I'm sure everything will be okay."

A moment later Trix's phone rang. It was our daughter, Emily.

"Really?" Trix said. "Your car is melting? What? Try to make it home!!"

Just then Trix looked up at me. "The phone just went dead."

Then the power went out.

Chapter 1

Fortunately, we owned a nice gasoline-powered generator. It was out in the garage, just waiting for a power outage.

Since my replacement eyeglasses were smeared, I just took them off and decided to go without them. My polar fleece sweater, which just moments ago was in perfect shape, was also beginning to fail. I absentmindedly reached for my jacket, and suddenly realized that it too was useless. Fortunately, a nice wool lumberjack shirt was hanging on an adjacent hook. I quickly threw it on over my long-sleeved cotton t-shirt and sat on the stool in the back room to put on my shoes.

"Son-of-a-bitch!" The shoes were almost totally disintegrated. They couldn't have looked worse if they were 1000 years old. I rummaged through a cupboard and pulled out a pair of leather work boots. They looked fine – the leather was dirty but solid. The Vibram soles were also OK –and I had no idea why plastic would disintegrate but Vibram would be all right. Must be the rubber content.

The boot laces were also holding up, although the plastic tips were gone.

I walked out to the garage, where Annie was snoozing on her rug – lucky for her the rug was made of natural material! She barely noticed as I walked by and climbed over a wheelbarrow to access the generator.

The PowerStroke 6000 had set us back nearly $1000 last December when we bought it the day after an epic ice storm. We had always planned on getting a generator, but to tell the truth, the power rarely went out in our part of Michigan. I always figured we could tough it out for a few days if it came to that, but that ice storm was the worst we'd ever experienced. With Christmas just a few days away, I decided to spend the money and get some backup power – only to find out that everyone else had the same idea. Fortunately the good folks at Home Depot got a delivery of generators that very day. I was first in line and counting my blessings that we would have some power, however marginal, for the holiday.

It turned out that we were off-the-grid for 8 days. The generator burned about 10 gallons each 24 hours, but we were able to heat the house, cook with the microwave, pump water, and watch TV.

I looked down at the generator and smiled. It was nice to be prepared for an emergency.

I moved the wheelbarrow out of the way and tipped the generator backwards to pull it out of the garage, not realizing right away that the cars were in the way.

No problem, I'll just back one out.

I pulled my car keys out of my pants pocket and opened the door to my car. I remembered that the car's abundant plastic was falling apart (melting?) but I wasn't ready for what I found. The entire dashboard had slid down to the floor, completely covering the gas pedal, the brakes, the transmission shifter, everything! The inside of the roof was also shredding and hanging in tatters. It took me a moment, but I also realized that the car key was disintegrating. The plastic that makes up the remote locks was literally falling apart in my hand. The metal was OK, and after a minute or so, all I was left with was a thin piece of metal that made up the actual key.

Now I was getting worried. Think, Greg. What the hell is happening to all of the plastic? I looked around the garage and it didn't take long to realize how many things were made from plastics. Some garden tools were all metal and wood (axes, shovels, rakes), but all of the power tools had plastic housings and structural components. I also owned three five-gallon plastic gas cans — each full of gas — that still looked all right, but were probably going to fail within the next few hours.

The PowerStroke 6000 was no different. The starter controls, gas tank, wheels, and pretty much everything but the engine and frame were made from plastic.

This was not going to be an easy problem to solve.

*****

15

I suddenly realized that something was very, very wrong, at least in our little corner of Michigan. Maybe there had been a chemical spill on the highway? Something was in the air and it was melting plastic. Fast.

I ran inside and shouted at Trix, "Quick, take all of the food you can out of plastic containers and get it into glass!"

She stood there, looking at me like I was crazy.

"I'm serious! We are going to starve if we don't find a way to store food."

"What are you talking about? Starving?"

"Yes!" I suddenly had another realization. "Water. We can't run water and I don't think the power will be on any time soon."

"We've got some in bottles in the refrigerator."

"Plastic bottles?"

She looked at me for a moment. I could tell she was fighting tears.

"This is serious, Trix. I could be wrong, but just in case I am right, we need to get moving!"

"Okay, okay! I'll find something to pour it into."

While Trix began to pull metal and glass bowls out of the cupboards, I thought for a moment about our situation.

I opened our pantry and surveyed the contents. Lots of canned soup, tomato sauce, condiments... not a lot of nutrition. We also had pasta, cereal, and a small cache of Clif Bars that we used mostly while bicycling and camping. If we could save the food that was stored in plastic packaging, we might last a couple of weeks.

"Trix, there isn't enough food here to last us very long."

"But we'll get help from the government? Won't we?"

Concern was visible upon her face – and even though I was trying hard not to show it, I was getting worried.

I replied, "Government help? We can't count on it. At least not for a while."

"What about Emily? Declan and Cora? Jory? Graham?"

Our daughter, grandchildren, and son-in-law lived 35 miles away. Our son lived out of state. "We'll find a way to help them later."

After a moment's silence, she said, "We have some more camping food stored upstairs."

"Good. Most of that stuff is in foil packaging. What about the freeze-dried meals?"

We had about a week's worth of freeze-dried dinners on hand in case we decided to take a spur-of-the-moment camping trip. It suddenly felt like we were going to be on a permanent camping trip.

"That food is in some sort of foil packaging too. I know it doesn't fully burn when we put it on a campfire."-

"Maybe it will hold up. I think I need to run to the nearest store and see what I can get."

"Do the cars still work?" she asked.

"No, when I said 'run' I meant it literally. Unless our bikes still work."

"Okay. You get going; I'll get things squared away as best I can here."

I quickly ran upstairs to grab a backpack. As I walked across the wood flooring, I felt my shoes stick to the polyurethane finish.

Most of the backpacking gear was beginning to fall apart. Our backpacks, tent, sleeping bags, and all of our backpacking clothing were made of synthetics. I needed something to carry food in, and quickly found a large old cotton clothing bag. It would have to do.

Just a year ago we went to California and spent a week hiking in the High Sierra. We had become very competent backpackers, confident in our ability to find our way in the backcountry. We had all of the best gear, but most of it would be useless now.

I found our stash of energy bars, locked tightly inside a bear canister. The canister is used while camping in bear country to store food. It was made of plastic, but so far it hadn't deteriorated very much. Fortunately, the lid wasn't screwed on too tightly and I was able to dump the contents onto the floor. We had about a dozen Clif Bars, eight Payday candy bars, an assortment of Tootsie Roll Pops, and some hard candy, which was wrapped in plastic. I put the food back into the canister and picked it up to give to Trixie.

On the way out of the room I remembered that I had an excellent backpacking knife. I found it on top of a small bookshelf and it looked serviceable. Since it was new just last year, it had a lot of rubber in the handle. I looked it over carefully and concluded that it would hold up. For some reason, rubber was not disintegrating. Yet.

I found Trixie in the kitchen. She had found a lot of non-plastic containers. All of the breakfast cereal had been poured into one big metal bowl. She had chips and crackers in another bowl.

"This stuff is going to go stale in a hurry," She complained.

"Yes, but we can eat it if we have to."

I handed her the canister and showed her the bag I was going to use to carry stuff in. "Both of our backpacks are shot."

"Dang," she replied. "I'm having trouble getting my head around this. Every time I reach for something, I find it's made out of plastic. It's like when you keep trying to turn the lights on when the power is out."

"Me too." I gave her a hug and said, "I've gotta get to the store."

"Ok. Hurry, and be safe."

Chapter 2

I quickly left the house. Annie looked at me with anticipation as I walked past her as I entered the garage.

"You'll have to stay here for a bit, girl."

Lucky for her, the dog food was stored in a 30 gallon rubber garbage can. I popped the lid and was glad to see that the can was mostly full. I carefully pulled out the plastic scoop and set it on a shelf. The scoop still had just enough life to still look like a scoop. In an hour or so it would look like a scoop blob.

I grabbed a couple of handfuls of food and threw it into her metal dish. She still had a little water left, but she would need more before the day was over.

I looked over my collection of bicycles. Maybe there would be one that would still work.

My newest bike, a carbon fiber racing bike with all of the latest technology, looked like it was holding up. I put my weight on the frame and it felt stiff. The composite pedals also looked like they might last. Unfortunately, the saddle had a plastic frame under the thin leather cover, and I knew it wouldn't work for long. The shift and brake cables all had metal interiors, but the housings were plastic. I looked into the corner of the garage where I keep old bike parts and spotted an old saddle. It was a classic Brooks seat, which was entirely made of metal and leather. I had quit riding it because of it was heavy compared to the new composite saddles.

Without hesitation, I found a wrench and swapped the saddles. Now the bike was road-worthy.

I didn't bother with changing into cycling shoes, because they were certainly not going to hold up. I looked at them as they lay on the shelf, and for now they looked okay. But I knew that if I touched them, they'd fall apart.

I wheeled the bike out of the garage and thought, "Thank God rubber isn't disintegrating. "

At the last minute I remembered that I had left some leather gloves lying on the seat of my car. It was by now late in the afternoon but it was still pretty nippy out. I wanted those gloves.

I ran back into the garage and carefully opened the passenger door of my car. The gloves lay on what used to be the center console. As I carefully picked up the gloves, bits of console adhered to the leather. I stepped away from the car and gave the gloves a quick shake and the console bits fell off, looking like clumps of dust that just disappeared into the air.

As I was finally beginning to leave, I spotted an old wool hat on a shelf. It would do fine to keep my head warm as I rode to the store.

With my cotton clothes bag stuffed inside my wool lumberjack shirt, I pulled from my dirt driveway and nearly crashed as soon as the bike's front tire reached the paved road. The road was a sticky mess.

"Sonofabitch!"

I pushed the bike over to the gravel shoulder and hopped back on. As long as I didn't ride on the pavement I would be okay. I had to be careful though, because with skinny tires I could easily puncture a tube.

The Valero gas station and party store was about 3 miles away, at a busy intersection of a state highway and a main county road. I rode the gravel shoulder to the highway and slowed to a stop, my jaw dropping in amazement at the scene in front of me.

Even with my slightly blurred vision, cars were stopped on the road in each direction as far as I could see. People walked, most nearly naked as their clothing deteriorated while it was still on their bodies.

One elderly lady looked at me and tried to cover her flesh with her hands and what remained of a tattered, rapidly disintegrating blanket.

As much as I wanted to try to help, I knew that my first responsibility was to my family. I'd get Trixie squared away, and then find my children and grandchildren.

A few trudging, nearly naked pedestrians walked on the highway shoulder. None of these people had any idea what was going on. These were good people, all doing the sort of things people do on a Sunday afternoon in March. They were returning from the mall or from a movie. They were going to visit their relatives. They were going to get groceries. Maybe some were going to a late Sunday church service.

Cars were left abandoned, doors open. The vinyl or velour upholstery was unrecognizable. The shoulder here was quite wide, so I was able to ride to the very far right side and avoid running into anyone.

A group of three young men were walking on the opposite side of the road, trying not to hurt their bare feet on stones and road debris. Two of the men were wearing cotton undershirts and underpants. The other was naked.

"Hey!" one of them yelled. "You, on the bike. Stop!"

I didn't know what they had in mind, but I certainly wasn't going to stick around to find out. I pedaled faster and saw the naked guy begin to run towards me across the 2-lane blacktop. He was a big man, standing over 6 feet tall, possessing a physique that would serve him well as an interior lineman on a football team.

He made it three or four steps across the blacktop before he realized that his feet were sticking to the asphalt.

"Fuck!" he yelled. "Fuck fuck fuck fuck fuck!"

I am certain that he wouldn't believe for a second that I totally agreed with his choice of words. This was the sort of day that was made for cursing. The big guy looked like he was stuck to the road for good, or at least until the tar completely lost the molecules that made it sticky.

I left the threesome behind and rode the last mile to the store without incident. The problem I had now was that the store was on the opposite side of the road – which I wasn't sure I could cross.

I looked in both directions, and other than a lone walker heading away from me, there was no one else in sight. Just a bit ahead, an older Ford pickup truck sat in the roadway, its owner already gone. I pedaled over to the truck and looked in the box to see if there was anything in there I could use to cross the road. Leaning the bike against the truck, I saw a couple of two-by-fours, each about four feet long, a pile of water-softener salt (the plastic bag was long-gone), and an undetermined length of rope. I leaned my bicycle against the truck and grabbed the two pieces of lumber.

Working quickly, hoping to avoid contact with any other like-minded scavengers, I ran back towards the store. As soon as I was directly across from the store I reached out across the road and carefully placed the two by four out away from me, perpendicular to the roadway. This would get me almost to the center of the road. It took a bit of a stretch, but I was able to walk out onto the first board. I placed the second board the same way. I jumped over to the second board and nailed the landing, but nearly wobbled off as my momentum carried me forward.

I walked to the end of the board. I had about four feet of sticky roadway between me and the gravel shoulder. I couldn't jump that far from where I was balanced, so I backed up as far as I could and made a running jump and landed squarely in the middle of the gravel shoulder. The return trip would be more difficult, so I made a mental note to look for another piece of wood or cardboard that I could use to close the four foot gap.

A deep ditch was all that remained between me and the store. I slid down into the ditch and jumped across the remnants of dirty winter snow. I climbed up to the paved store parking lot and was not surprised to find I would again have to find a way to cross the sticky surface. At this point I was wishing that contractors used more concrete to build roads and parking lots!

As I walked around the perimeter of the lot, I spotted the store dumpster. Leaning against the dumpster was a wood pallet. I needed about 12 feet of material to use as a bridge. I knocked over the pallet and looked into the dumpster and was relieved to find a substantial amount of cardboard.

I grabbed as much cardboard as I could hold and spread it before me, creating a walkway that took me right up to the store's cement sidewalk.

The front of the store was a mess. The store's vinyl siding looked okay – was vinyl immune? Shards of glass lay everywhere, as the windows casings had failed.

I pulled on the front door, but it was locked. At least the hired help locked up when they left that morning!

Carefully, I climbed through the front window. It was dark in the store and I regretted not bringing a flashlight until I remembered that all of my flashlights were made of plastic.

I yelled "Hello!" to an empty room. The interior wasn't looking too bad yet, and I began to think about the sort of things I could grab here that would help Trix and I survive until the authorities got everything back to normal.

The first thing I wanted was high-calorie food. One of the interesting developments of the 21st century is that nearly every party store has a row of high-protein energy foods. Since this was just a rural gas station and party store, the selection was limited.

On the shelves were a couple of dozen Balance nutrition bars, all caramel nut flavored. There were also 30 or 40 Clif Bars (chocolate fudge and blueberry crisp). This would last us a few days – but we would need more if we ever hoped to reach our daughter and grandchildren, who lived just 35 minutes away – by car. I could only barely consider ever seeing my son again. Maybe this plastic virus hadn't hit South Dakota. Maybe he was all right.

I rummaged around for a bit and found some boxes of matches. I stuffed all of the available stock into my bag but kept out some matches to use for light. I walked to the rear of the store and looked for the storage room. Peering into the darkness, I found several unopened cases of Clif and Balance bars. I wouldn't be able to carry them all home, but I figured I could stash them somewhere where they wouldn't be found by someone else. I could always return to get them later.

I suddenly realized I was very hungry. Where else would I find such a convenient place to have a snack?

A showcase of donuts caught my eye. One of my favorite joys in life is to enjoy a weekly fresh nutty or glazed donut. The donut case must have been made from glass, because it was retaining its form and function. The donuts all rested upon wax paper, which was also a good thing.

Just as I sank my teeth into an apple fritter, a body stumbled through the window and fell to the floor.

Chapter 3

I wiped bits of fritter icing from the corners of my mouth. "Hello!"

My hand subconsciously reached into my pocket and felt the rubber handle of the backpacking knife.

A young woman, no, let me correct that... she was in her late teens, stood before me, wearing only a cotton t-shirt. Her private parts were only just barely covered. Her feet were filthy – I could tell she had walked on the melting blacktop highway.

"Fuck, I'm freezing!" she cried.

At this exact moment the concept of "sacrifice" wasn't foremost in my thinking, but my mom always said, "Greg, you really need to be more considerate."

So I took off my lumberjack shirt and handed it to her. "Here, put this on." I quickly forgot about the knife – this poor girl wasn't going to be a threat.

She looked up at me with a hint of suspicion, but I must have seemed harmless so she took the shirt and muttered a week "Thanks."

A moment later she was reasonably covered up and slightly warmer, due to my precious wool shirt (where would I find another one?).

She made a beeline for the store's candy row and quickly devoured a Snickers bar. While she was eating I sauntered over to the beverages section and pulled out a couple of cans of Coke. I handed one to the girl and then popped the top and took a deep swig from my can.

"Damn, I didn't know I was this thirsty!" I exclaimed.

She was a pretty girl, with short brown hair and lovely green eyes. She stood just over five feet tall, but her build was athletic.

"Are you very close to home?" I asked.

She took another bite of her candy bar and replied, "I live in Owosso. What's that – eight or nine miles? Might as well be 80 or 90 miles."

She looked me over and realized that I was fully dressed. "What's your story? How come your clothes haven't melted like everyone else's?"

I sort of laughed, "They did, but I was still at home when it happened. I only live a couple of miles away. So I had time to find some clothes that would work."

We each took a drink from our pop cans.

"What the fuck is going on?" she asked.

"All I know is that plastic is disintegrating."

"I wonder if it's just happening here or all over the country."

"Me too. It could be local, it could be global."

She took another swig. "So you came over here to scavenge some food and whatever?"

I nodded yes. "I didn't see any other way. I wanted to get here before everyone else had the same idea."

I really wanted the girl to leave so I could go about my business. There were a lot of 24 packs of canned soft drinks here, and if we ran out of water, soft drinks would keep us hydrated. I could hide provisions out in the weeds where no one would find them.

"It's going to take you about four hours to walk into Owosso," I stated. "Maybe longer since you're barefoot."

"I know." Finished with her Snickers, she grabbed a Baby Ruth and pulled off the wrapper. "I'll eat this and then get going."

I can't begin to explain how much this next sentence pained me, but I replied, "You can keep the shirt."

"Thanks."

"Oh, and one other thing: Watch out for two or three guys who are also walking towards Owosso. They didn't look like friendly types."

"Great," she groaned, as she chewed on the Baby Ruth candy bar.

Since she obviously wasn't a threat to me physically and she wasn't likely to return to this store any time soon, I began to carry boxes of soda outside. The store was surrounded by barren fields, with corn stubble as the dominant theme. A lone stand of trees stood about 200 yards away. I lugged a couple of cases of Coke across the field, stepping over the rows of corn stubble. It was tedious going, but

I reached the trees and set the boxes of pop behind a pile of rocks that the farmer had left there. I went back for another load of pop and protein bars, but didn't make it too far before the glue holding the boxes together failed, spilling the cans and energy bars to the ground.

"Shit," I muttered. I returned to the store and began to look for something to carry my survival stash in. I found some paper grocery bags behind the counter that would do the job. I had to replace bags as the glue holding them together failed.

Eventually, after multiple trips, I managed to stash most of the energy bars, soda, tea, and energy drinks under the tree. Hopefully, woodchucks and mice wouldn't find the food. The pop and other drinks were all in cans or bottles.

As I was returning to the store, I saw the girl walking down the shoulder of the road, heading west towards Owosso.

She turned and gave me a wave.

*****

With a bag full of energy bars, matches, rope, and spaghetti-o's (canned), I crossed the road (with the help of more cardboard) and returned to the pickup truck where I'd left my bike.

My bike was gone.

"MOTHERFUCKER!!!" I screamed.

I was mad as hell at whoever stole my bike, but madder at myself for leaving it alone. Heck, I probably would have taken it myself if I'd spotted it while walking down the road.

Without any other option, I turned around and headed home on foot.

*****

I seethed with anger as I marched west towards home. The bag of food hung over my back awkwardly. That bike had cost me almost $3000. I purchased it five years ago after the frame cracked on my previous ride, a titanium racing bike. Now my baby was gone, and with it the only saddle I owned that didn't have a plastic seat frame.

27

Gravel crunched under my feet as I walked upon the shoulder of the road. Looking ahead, there were cars scattered on the roadway. Some were on the shoulder, others were on the road. Without my eyeglasses things in the distance were blurry but still identifiable. About a quarter of a mile ahead of me I could see someone else walking west, in the same direction I was heading.

A cold wind blew in my face and made my eyes sting. I thought about our situation and wondered if we would be able to survive this bizarre plasti-pocalypse.

Who ever considered that such a thing could happen? Many people believed that the human race would be wiped out by a virus like Ebola or destroyed by an asteroid. I even told Trixie a few times that "Mother Earth thinks human beings are a virus. She's trying really hard to get rid of us."

But what was making plastic disintegrate? Was it a destabilization in the molecules? I was never any good at chemistry, but in the few hours since this all began, I know for a fact that nylon, polyester, hard plastics, soft plastics and vinyl were all in some state of decomposition. For some reason rubber was not affected – or maybe it just took longer to deteriorate than plastic. Carbon fiber seemed to be holding up, not that I owned much of the stuff other than my bike and a couple pairs of high-performance cross-country ski poles.

I hoped that the plastipocalypse was limited to plastics. What if this started happening to metal, wood, or glass? What if the stuff that holds all molecules together was failing – and even human flesh and bones and hair....

I shook my head. Physically I felt fine. Even though the calendar said I was in my 50's, I felt much younger. So my body probably wasn't going to begin to break apart in the next 24 hours. I was a bit less confident about my emotional condition. Even though I possessed some skills and talents that would give me a fighting chance to survive, I would still have to adapt, at least for the short term, to living without modern conveniences. Like most people living in the 21st century, I was a creature of comfort. I liked my house to be warm in the winter and cool in the summer. I watched TV. I drove a car everywhere.

Suddenly, in the last 10 hours or so, everyone has been thrown into the 1800's, except very few people alive know how to make stuff without plastic. If this catastrophe wasn't just a local event – and the human race is going to survive – we would all would need to learn how to do things the way our great-grandparents did them.

We will have to figure out how to make things with steel, wood, and natural fibers. Remnants of our past technologies would remain visible for decades, reminders of how wasteful we all were.

We wouldn't have smart phones and computers and DVR's and fancy hybrid cars. If we could make it through to summer we might be able to find a way to make it through the next winter. I knew it wouldn't be easy or fun, but it *was* possible. We'd take it one season at a time.

Nearly lost in the silence of my thoughts, I almost didn't hear the sound of gravel crunching behind me.

*****

As I turned I was shocked to see a man, wearing nothing but underwear and socks, riding a blue carbon fiber racing bicycle! He was clearly uncomfortable, because my bike was set-up for my 31" inseam. He appeared to be much shorter. Plus, the bike was in a very hard gear, which made him strain to turn the pedals.

As he rode up to me I blocked his path and put my hands firmly on the handlebars, bringing him to a stop.

"Hey, let me go!" he yelled.

"Sorry my friend, but you are riding my bike."

"It is not!"

"It most certainly is. You found it back a ways, leaning against a pickup truck, didn't you?"

He looked at me sheepishly as he dismounted. "Yeah, that's where it was."

I was so relieved to have my bike back that I found it hard to be mad at the guy.

"Look, no harm, no foul. I'm happy to have it back."

He stood there, shivering, and said, "Now how am I going to get all the way to Grand Rapids?"

I shook my head in amazement. "Jeez, that's more than 80 miles away. You would have had one hell of a time getting there, even on my bike!"

"It was better than walking," he replied. "The gravel is hard on my feet."

"Most everyone is in the same predicament."

He looked me over and saw that I was fully clothed. "Not you. You look like you are doing all right."

"I'll get by. I've got someone at home waiting for me, so I've gotta go."

I took the bike from him, lifted the rear wheel, and rocked the right break leaver to the left, which shifted the chain into an easier gear.

He looked at me like I had just performed magic. "So that's how you change gears!"

I smiled.

His ignorance is what probably responsible for me getting the bike back.

I wished him "Good Luck" and rode off towards home.

Moments after turning onto the country road from the highway, a massive "Whoosh!" exploded from behind me. I turned and looked back and saw the highway exploding into flames! Fire reached high into the sky, burning furiously. What the hell?

While I stood staring at the fire, the flames quickly began to head in my direction. The flames shot 50, then 100 feet in the air. Reacting by instinct, I pedaled the bike furiously, trying to outrun the approaching fire. I turned onto my road and quickly steered my bike onto a wet farm lane, getting as far from the road as possible. The skinny tires on the bike sunk into the mud and I fell to the ground. As the fire roared down the road surface I buried my head in the damp grass and cold mud. The flames roared past and burned for several minutes until the tar in the road was totally consumed. All of the remaining tar in the road had evaporated or burned – it had all disappeared. All that was left were stones and dirt.

"Whoosh!" I looked towards the sound and saw a nearby house completely explode. All of the windows blew from the modernish ranch home. In the distance, I heard another explosion, and as I looked across the horizon, I could see smoke rising into the sky.

It took quite a while for the road surface to cool enough that I could walk on the shoulder. As I passed one of the houses that exploded, I saw that a home with a paved driveway had exploded. Evidently the fire had followed the driveway right up to the house.

Chapter 4

Something in the plastic disintegration was causing explosions. I pedaled my bike furiously and was relieved to see that the houses on my road were all still intact. My neighbor, Connie, was standing in her front yard, looking at fires raging across the field.

I yelled, "Don't light any matches! Don't let anything spark!" and pedaled the remaining eighth of a mile into my driveway.

The house was still there.

I ran inside, where I found Trixie standing on newspapers in the kitchen.

"Oh, Greg! You are all right!"

"Get out of the house! Now! Before it explodes!"

I grabbed her arm and we both ran outside, heading for a stand of trees near the rear of our property.

We watched and waited. The sky was heavy with black smoke. The trees blocked us from the wind, but it was still quite chilly, especially since neither of us wore jackets. I gave Trixie my hat and gloves.

We crouched under the trees and looked at our house. Everything looked all right from outside.

Trixie asked, "When do you think we can go back inside?"

"I have no idea. I don't think there is anything in the house that could cause a spark. But I wonder – is the air safe to breathe?"

"What do you mean?"

"I think that the plastic isn't just dissolving." I struggled for the right word. "It's...gasifying."

"Holy crap."

Suddenly I had another thought. "The gas tanks... on the cars..."

Trixie looked at me, clearly not grasping my meaning.

"The tanks are affected by this phenomenon," I explained. "But the gasoline inside the tanks might not be. The garage floor might be covered in gasoline."

I looked off across the barren fields and saw a black smoke in every direction across the horizon.

"You stay here," I commanded. "I am going to go open some windows. Maybe we can let the gas escape outside."

"Be careful!"

I walked across the lumpy, late-winter yard and cautiously re-entered the garage. I was immediately struck with the powerful smell of over 20 gallons of spilled gasoline. Fortunately, the garage floor had a drain and the gasoline was pooling near the center of the structure. I covered my face with my arm to block the worst of the smell and carefully opened one of the windows on the east wall. By leaving the front door open, the fumes should be able to ventilate. Next, I entered the kitchen through the interior garage door. I saw that Trix had laid newspapers across the wood floor so her feet wouldn't stick to the dissolving polyurethane finish. I reached down and touched the hard maple. The polyurethane had completely disappeared.

I gave a sniff but could not smell anything that wasn't normal. I left the back door open, then went to the front of the house and opened another door. A cold wind blew into the house, but it was fresh air and as far as I knew, the air outdoors was still breathable. But what if the gas emitting from the decaying plastic got into the atmosphere?

I tried to open a window, but quickly realized that the storm windows, which are installed from the outside of the house, would not allow air to enter or escape.

But there were windows in the two unused bedrooms that I didn't bother to install storm windows on. I ran upstairs and opened them. "There," I said to myself. "That should let the gases out."

I walked back outside and found Trixie sitting on a wood box, with Annie at her feet, next to our old granary building.

"Hey, we can wait inside the granary until the house is safe to re-enter," I said.

"You think the granary is safe?"

"It's a drafty place," I replied. I looked at the windows, which were old and made from wood. One of the panes in the back had been broken years ago and I'd never replaced it. The roof was also in bad shape. Cedar shakes had blown off and there were a few visible openings. I had always been reluctant to put any money into fixing the building because I was hoping to eventually tear it down and replace it with a new garage.

I swung the front door open wide and we climbed up into the shelter. The building hadn't been used for at least forty years, yet wheat was still scattered in the cracks.

We sat on wooden fruit boxes and watched the house.

I told her about getting to the store, the girl, getting my bike stolen, and retrieving my bike.

"The good news," I continued, "Is that civilization hasn't turned into roving bands of thieves and murderers."

She looked me in the eyes and replied, "Yet."

Of course, she was right. In a week or two, those who were still alive would fight for every scrap of food. Right now, everyone was in a state of shock. By my estimation, a third of the homes in our county would go up in flames. Possibly another third of the population would die in their sleep, unaware that the air was full of deadly gasses.

"I hope that girl at the store is okay," I said. "I hope the flames didn't get her."

I retrieved the cotton bag of food that I'd looted from the store and dumped it on the floor.

She looked at my pile of energy bars, sodas, and matches and said, "So this is all you managed to get?"

"It should keep us from starving for a few days. I stashed a bunch of other stuff under a tree where no one will find it."

"How much water were you able to save?" I asked.

"I was able to fill the tub about halfway." Fortunately, our antique bath tub was made from cast iron. It would remain long after everything else was long gone.

I stood and looked around the granary. In the corner stood a 10 gallon metal milk can. There were also four old Surge stainless-steel milking machine tanks.

We lugged the milk containers to the house and positioned them under the aluminum rain gutters.

"We should be able to capture quite a bit of water now," I said, as we finished the task.

Darkness was now fully upon us, and it was getting very cold. Carefully, we entered the house. We walked around and sniffed the air.

"I don't smell anything," Trixie said.

"Me neither. But the gas must be odorless – because I was on the highway just minutes before it went up in flames and I never smelled a thing."

"I don't think it would be safe to sleep inside tonight," Trixie replied.

"Me neither."

We each scrounged around for a bit and found some more warm clothes. We now wore two wool sweaters each, plus had warm wool hats. I found another pair of leather gloves too.

We spent the night huddled together in the cold granary, sharing all of the wool blankets we owned. At dawn we stood and rubbed our arms to restart the circulation in our cold, stiff bodies.

"Let's check out the house."

*****

We entered the silent house. There was no familiar hum of the furnace or refrigerator.

The floors were no longer sticky. The living room rug had completely disappeared. Otherwise the inside of the house didn't look too bad. The plastic stuff had dissolved, leaving behind the metals, screws and wires that were housed inside the plastic exterior. We'd have to pitch what was left from the TV, the computer, and the telephone. Most of our home was furnished in wood and metal, and while there were odds and ends like lamp cords that were plastic, the mess was manageable.

"Look," I said. "The couch is still in good shape!"

"It should be," she replied. "We paid enough for it."

"I just had a thought," I told Trixie. "Wait here for a minute."

I ran back upstairs and retrieved our backpacking stove, a can of iso-butane fuel, and our aluminum backpacking pan.

"Would you like a hot drink for breakfast?" I asked as I showed Trixie the gear.

"Sure!"

To be safe, we took the stove outdoors and set it on the cement in front of our garage.

"I wonder if it will burn," I muttered as I held a match to the stove and turned on the gas.

The flame looked as strong as it ever had.

Trixie put two cups of water in the pan.

"You have about 10 packets of instant coffee or we can have tea."

The days of drinking freshly ground coffee were over. I decided to save the instant coffee for a future celebration.

"I'll have tea," I replied, lacking enthusiasm as I went to the garage to check on Annie. I let her outside to do her business and then filled her food dish with half the usual ration. "Sorry girl," I muttered. "This will have to do." Her water dish was getting low, but I decided to let that pass for the time being.

*****

Back in the kitchen, Trix sat upon an oak chair, staring at her nearly empty mug of tea.

"What do you think happened?" she asked. Her eyes looked at me with concern and the expectation that I would have the answer.

I thought carefully for a moment before replying. I had been so busy with our immediate survival needs that I hadn't really considered the full impact of our situation.

"I have an idea," I answered, "But we may never know the true answer."

Her brown eyes fixed upon mine as she waited for me to continue.

Trying to buy another moment to frame my answer, I walked around the kitchen and found our stash of energy bars. I rummaged through the bars and picked one out for each of us to eat.

"I think some scientists might have let something bad out of their laboratory."

"Like a virus?" She asked.

I nodded in agreement. "Sort of. More like a microbe – maybe developed to clean up oil spills or even the mountain of plastic floating out in the Pacific Ocean."

For years, photos had been showing up on the television news that showed the floating island of plastic that lay a few hundred miles from the west coast. To my knowledge, nothing had ever been done to clean up the mess.

"Maybe the scientists were working on a solution to cleaning up oil-based pollution and somehow their chemistry got out of the lab."

"That could be it," she replied. "But what about terrorism? Do you think Al Qaida or ISIS could have caused this to happen?"

"I suppose. But hell, we live in Michigan for God's sake. How could it have gotten here?"

I took a bite of my Clif bar and pondered my question.

"Maybe...," I began. "Maybe the biologists or scientists or terrorists created this plastic destroying microbe and it became airborne. Maybe it's self-replicating, but they hadn't figured out a way to turn it off. So somehow it got into the air and now all of our modern stuff is now evaporating into the air. Maybe it's turning into methane – which will take a long time to dissipate in modern buildings. We have to deal with the consequences of someone else's fuck up and find a way to carry on. We have to survive so we can find our kids and help them survive."

Fighting back tears, she said, "I pray that the fire didn't get them."

I looked at the floor, suddenly aware that I had said more that I had intended. I did not want to scare Trixie. I needed her to be steady and positive – just like she was in her work at the hospital. She didn't panic easily. I needed her to be strong. Our kids needed her to be strong.

Without hesitation, she stood up and said, "Okay. We've got a lot of stuff to do today."

*****

After each eating one Clif Bar for breakfast, we decided to walk to our nearest neighbor's house to see how they were doing.

The Foster's, who were younger than us, still had two young children at home. I was friendly with Mike, and we watched over each other's home when we were away on vacations.

As we walked the quarter mile to their house, Trix remarked, "Amazing how quiet it is this morning."

"No cars," I replied. "Or planes."

I sniffed the air. "It smells bad out here."

We could both smell the strong scent of smoke as the smoldering remains of buildings and cars blew towards us on the prevailing wind.

We entered the Foster's yard and were greeted by their chocolate lab watchdog, Radar, which promptly began to lick my hands as I reached to scratch her ears.

"Hi girl! Where's your people?"

The house was very quiet. I knocked on the front door and after a moment or so, concluded that there was no one home.

I gave Trixie a shrug and said, "No one here. Maybe we should take a look around and see if there is anything we can use?"

"No," Trixie said, scolding me. "Mike wouldn't do that to us. Leave their stuff alone."

"Okay, okay! You are right."

As we turned to leave the front door opened and Connie Foster appeared. She looked like she hadn't slept in two days. Here two children lurked behind her, acting as if they were afraid of us.

"Thank God it's you!" she exclaimed. "We survived the fires!"

Trixie replied, "Have you been here all alone with the kids?"

"Yes. Mike didn't come home yesterday. He was up north, checking on his trap lines."

Mike Foster was an avid hunter and trapper. He'd be the kind of guy you want around during an apocalypse. I hadn't mentioned it to Trixie yet, but I was hoping to make an alliance with him. With Trixie's nursing experience and my backcountry and engineering skills, combined with his woodland and hunting skills, would make up a formidable survival team.

"Dang," I replied, with a grimace.

"We are so sorry, Connie!" Trixie stepped forward and gave her a hug. "Greg and I will help you out."

"Really?!?!"

I laughed as I looked around Connie and spotted the kids. "We'll have a blast teaching these two scamps how to live like pioneers!"

Trixie winked at me, knowing full well that the road ahead would be tough, especially now that Mike was gone.

"Come on outside with me kids, while your mom and Aunt Trixie visit for a bit."

As the women disappeared into the house, the two children joined me in the yard.

"Let me think," I said with a wry smile, "You are Hansel and Gretel?"

The two looked at me like I was a total idiot. Evidently they had never heard the story of Hansel and Gretel (which I would certainly rectify as quickly as possible).

"No, silly," the daughter, who was the older of the two replied. "I'm Hailey, he's Josh."

"I knew that!" I lied. "My name is Greg Bowman. You can call me Uncle Greg. We are going to be great friends and help each other a lot around here."

I asked the kids to show me their dad's hunting gear.

Josh took me by the hand to their small pole barn and paused at the door.

"We're not supposed to go in here without dad."

"I think he'd make an exception this one time," I replied.

I could see the concern on the boy's face. He was a smallish 10-year-old, but then his dad wasn't a large man either. He was dressed in blue jean and layers of cotton shirts. His feet were covered by leather moccasins. His sister, who stood a few inches taller, was dressed similarly. Even though the morning was brisk, neither child showed any sign of discomfort. I took this as a good sign, since physical toughness would be vital to our continued survival.

It took a few moments for my eyes to adjust to the barn's darkness. I held back a startled yell as I spotted a fully stuffed fox resting on a workbench.

"This is cool," I said to the kids.

"My dad is a great hunter and trapper," replied Josh with pride.

I looked at both children and said, "I am interested in his hunting gear. Where does he keep his guns?"

Josh looked at his sister, who thought for a moment, then nodded "yes."

He grabbed my hand and took me to locked door. "Daddy doesn't ever want us to go in here."

"But you know where the key is," his sister taunted.

He struggled with his desire to please his father with his need to help another adult.

"Yeah, I know." He ran over to a large MasterCraft tool box and pulled out one of the drawers. Reaching way into the back, he found a key and brought it to me.

"Here you go, Uncle Greg."

I unlocked the door and looked into a very dark room.

"Dang," I said. "It's dark in here, but we don't dare light a candle yet. Do you know why?"

Hailey replied, "Because it will cause an explosion!"

"That's right," I answered.

I waited for my vision to adjust to the dark. A cardboard box was blocking the light from the room's sole window. I set the box on the floor and now had enough light to see.

A variety of bows hung on the wall. I ignored the composite compound bows, since they certainly used plastic components. Fortunately, Mike owned a classic wood bow, which was probably the sort of weapon his father had owned at one time. A collection of hunting and target arrows all rested neatly in a tube beside the bows.

After looking around a bit, I found some bow strings. The majority were made of Dyneema, which appeared to be synthetic.

"This stuff will melt as soon as we take it outside," I explained to Josh, who was watching every move I made. "We need some natural bow string."

I looked in the assortment of strings again and found some that were made from linen or hemp.

"Did your dad make these?"

Josh thought for a moment and replied, "Probably. He's always doing stuff out here."

Besides the bow, arrow, and string, I found a metal canteen, a WWII-era belt, a really nice hunting knife and sheath, and a lot of cotton camouflage hunting garments. I chuckled to myself thinking about the camo – it would be too small for me but the women could wear it.

As happy as I was with Mike's archery equipment and other accessories, I was really after his firearms. If the times ended up turning violent, I wanted to be prepared.

"Do you know where your dad keeps his guns?"

Hailey, who had been standing by, watching, replied "In the safe."

She pointed towards a dark corner, and there stood a massive gun safe.

I laughed, "It would have bit me if I'd been any closer!"

The kids looked at me like I was stupid, which was something I would eventually get used to.

The safe, which stood at least 6' tall, had the words "Browning" printed in script across the top. A three-handled unlocking mechanism rested square in the middle, just below the combination lock.

I scratched my head and looked at the kids.

"Do either of you know the combination?"

******

41

I found the Foster's kitchen – which was a complete disaster zone. All of the dry food was piled upon the kitchen table.

Trix looked up at me as I entered the room.

"How are they doing here?" I asked.

"Not too great. Connie did what she could to salvage her food, but she didn't have any water stored."

"Crap." I looked at the piles of Oreo cookies, potato chips, Fruit Loops, and Pop Tarts that cluttered the table and shook my head in dismay.

"I know," Trix replied in a whisper. "Connie just went downstairs to see if she had any more glass jars. We need to find a way to keep this dry food from going stale."

Shaking my head in agreement, I replied, "Yeah, but there still isn't much nutrition here."

"They do have a lot of dried meat stored. Venison, mostly."

"Good. We will all need as much protein as we can get." I looked around. "Where did they sleep last night?"

"Connie said that after you warned her about fire and sparks, she figured that something about the decomposing plastic was flammable. So they all slept in the back sun room, with the doors and windows open."

I wandered through the living room and found the sun room. It was made from glass and screen. Most people only use these rooms in warm weather, but it would have ample ventilation for explosive or noxious gas.

*****

I heard the sound of clinking glass as Connie appeared from what must be the basement doorway. "This is all I could find," she explained, as she entered the kitchen.

She had a box of old Mason jars and an assortment of lids. "I used to do some canning, but stopped when I went back to work full-time."

I took the box of jars from Connie and set them on the floor.

"We have some peaches and tomato soup canned," Trixie said. "We'll share what we have."

I nodded in agreement. If we were going to last more than a few weeks we would need to combine our resources.

"Connie," I asked, "Do you know the combination to Mike's gun safe?"

Connie, who had a slight frame and stood about 5'6", brushed as strand of dark brown hair from in front of eyes that were threatening to burst with tears and replied, "No, Mike doesn't share that sort of thing with me."

I wasn't surprised. Mike probably kept the details of his hunting hobby to himself, just as I didn't share the minutia of my Nordic skiing obsession.

"That's okay," I replied, not wanting to upset her more than she already was. "I'll figure something else out."

Trixie grabbed a quart jar from the box, blew out the dust, and began to fill the jar with cookies.

I chuckled and said, "I can't believe what I just saw. Two days ago you would have washed each jar out in the sink."

Trix just looked up at me and shrugged. "I guess things have changed."

*****

After an hour or so of helping Connie get her food situation under control, Trixie and I set off to recover the food and drinks I'd cached under the tree by the Valero gas station and party store.

Before our hike to the store, we'd scrounged around my workshop and found a large duffel bag, the sort you'd use to haul camping equipment. The bag was old and dirty, but it was still intact.

"Must be made of cotton," I muttered as I shook the bag in the breeze, raising a cloud of dust.

The plan was for us to hike undetected to the store, grab our stash, and get back home. Hopefully without encountering anyone.

We got out to the State highway easy enough, walking on the road shoulder as a cold wind blew in from the northwest.

"Looks like a zombie film," Trixie said as she saw the highway for the first time.

"You should have seen it yesterday. At least the naked people are all gone."

We stayed on the shoulder, warily passing the torched metal bodies of what used to be Ford Escapes, Chevy Impalas, and Dodge Ram pickups (foreign cars are rare in this part of Michigan). Metal frames, engines, and transmissions sat on the remnants of the burned-out highway. The worst thing was the smell. The stench of burned tar and vehicles was unlike anything I'd ever experienced.

I looked in the skeletal remains of a sedan. The burned remains of two people sat upon the metal springs of what used to be car seats.

"Oh my God!" I exclaimed.

Trixie looked and gasped – "Oh..."

I put my arm around her and steered us away from the carnage. "Those poor people," she said.

We walked the rest of the way to the store without looking into vehicles.

Soon we reached the spot where I'd used cardboard to cross the highway. Quietly, just in case anyone was lurking in the store, we snuck up to the store. I slowly raised my head and looked into the open front window. The store was ravaged. The shelves were all bare, the refrigeration units were empty.

"I don't think we need to go in there," I whispered. "There's nothing left."

I lead Trix around to the back of the building and towards the lone tree that held vigil over the empty cornfield.

I was anxious that our stash might be gone. If anyone had seen me head out here, the food and drinks would certainly have been taken.

I picked up the pace and jogged the final hundred yards to the tree, and exhaled in a sigh of relief. The food was still there. The packaging had dissolved, but the energy bars were still edible.

"Good thing an animal didn't find this, "Trixie stated as she caught up with me.

"We didn't bring anything to put the food in," I said. "Normally we'd use a Zip-Lock."

We collected the food and just put it in the duffle unwrapped with the cans and bottles of soda and energy drinks. There really wasn't any other option.

Just then, I heard a strange voice say, "So what do we have here?"

Looking up, a large man stood over us. He was holding onto an axe, which means he was either cutting wood or using the tool as a weapon.

He looked at me with malevolent intent. "Just back away from the bag and leave. Now."

Trixie and I stood, and before I could speak, she said "No way. This stuff is ours!"

I took a moment to assess our adversary. He stood over six feet tall and weighed over 200 pounds. He wore cotton Carhartt coveralls, work boots, and an old John Deere stocking cap. If I had to guess, I'd say he was a local farmer.

"Is this your property?" I asked.

"Maybe. What's it to *you*?"

"I wondered if you'd thought about how you might get a food crop planted. This stuff we have in the bag will only last us week or two at best."

His stance softened a bit, but he was still a threatening sight.

"Are you one of my neighbors?" he asked.

"Yes." I didn't want him to know exactly where our house was, in case he had an ulterior, unfriendly motive. "We live just a mile or two away."

He set down the axe and smiled. "I thought you was some city people who didn't belong out here. Go ahead and take your bag, I have enough of my own food at home."

Cautiously, I relaxed. "It looks like you made it through the fires."

He nodded grimly. "My mother lived alone in a mobile home across the road. Before we had any idea what was going on, it exploded."

"Oh, I am so sorry." Trixie replied.

"We spent the night in the barn, which is mostly cement anyway. Not a lot of plastic crap out there."

"You need to be wary of gas," I added.

"Gas?"

"Yeah. When the plastic evaporates, it releases invisible gas. Probably methane. You need to make sure that anywhere you sleep is well ventilated, at least for a few days."

"Shit." He took off his hat and scratched his head absentmindedly. "I had no idea."

"What I said about crops. Do you have any way to feed anyone besides your own family?"

He considered my question and replied, "I don't know. I've got a few head of beef. The kids are raising some hogs for the County Fair. The wife and I always have a garden. We love sweet corn, green beans, squash, and melons. But out here in the big fields, we usually plant soy-beans, corn, or wheat."

I nodded to show I understood what he was telling me. "If we could get our hands on enough seeds, do you think you could find a way to work the ground and get them planted?"

He looked me over carefully. I knew that in my current state I wasn't a very impressive figure. But he must have seen something in my eyes that made him trust me.

"What have you got in mind?"

*****

I explained my plan to Trixie as we trekked back to our home.

"Do you know of any place that would have vegetable seeds?" I asked.

"Maybe the grain elevator has some. They had quite a selection of garden seeds last year."

"Right." It was a ramshackle place on the south side of town. "If they haven't been looted, there might be seeds there."

"Might?" she asked.

"It's officially not spring yet. They might not have received any of this year's shipment yet."

"Oh. Dang."

"Or they might not have much of anything at all."

I thought for a moment and asked, "You do the gardening around here. What are seeds packaged in these days? Paper or Plastic?"

"I'm pretty sure that the seeds I bought last year were in paper envelopes."

"Good, because if they have anything, it would help if the seeds weren't scattered all over the floor."

We walked on towards home. "We've got a few weeks before we can plant anything anyway," she replied.

"So what do we do until then?"

We walked quietly for a bit. If you forgot about the dire situation we were suddenly thrust into, the walk was refreshing. The day was pleasantly brisk and the wind was now at our backs. Here and there a bird fluttered past, but it was still too early in the season for Michigan's true harbinger of spring, the Robin.

Eventually I formulated an answer. "I think I need to get to Lansing and see if Emily and Jory and the grandkids are okay."

"I want to go with you."

I expected this answer. "Are you sure? It's about forty miles one-way. You could stay here and help Connie and the kids get their act together."

"We can help them get squared-away over the next day or two – but then we will both go and find our daughter and grandchildren."

Her jaw was set and she walked with purpose. There was no dissuading Trixie when her mind was made up, so I didn't bother. Besides, I really did not want to make the trip alone. I would worry about Trix the entire time I was away, and I am sure she would worry about me as well.

"All right. Let's get Connie into survival mode and leave tomorrow morning."

*****

Connie took the news of our imminent departure better than I thought she would.

"If my kids were out there somewhere," she said, "I don't care if it was forty miles or four hundred miles, I'd go find them."

I went out to Mike's barn to see what I might use for our journey. I grabbed the bow, string, and arrows that I'd inventoried the day before. I also took his hunting knife and sheath and attached it to the leather belt that I'd remembered to put on that morning. At the time I was more worried about my pants being too loose than about strapping on a weapon, but you've gotta roll with the times when things get tough. I hoped that I'd only use the knife to cut up food, because if I had to protect Trixie and myself in a fight for survival, we'd be screwed. I had little experience with fighting during my life, but concluded that my survival instinct would probably take over if it came to that.

Trixie entered the barn and found me looking through Mike's supplies.

"Does he have anything here we can use?" she asked.

I showed here the bow, arrow, and knife. "We might need these to get some food."

She laughed. "When have you ever shot an arrow at an animal?"

It was true that I wasn't a hunter. That set of skills went to my dad and brother, who seemed to spend nine months each year killing stuff. I was more into the quiet side of being in the wild – walking wilderness trails, summiting mountains, camping beside isolated lakes and rivers.

"I shot a deer once when I was 14. It was enough for me."

She laughed. "And who's going to gut the food you kill?"

I cringed. "We'll do *that* together."

Trix told me that Connie and the kids were all set for the time being.

48

"They have enough food and water to last a week or so."

"Hopefully, Mike will be back soon," I replied.

She nodded her head in agreement. "Oh, and I have this."

In her hand she held a foil-wrapped package.

"Venison jerky. It's actually pretty tasty."

"Good! We'll need it."

I suddenly remembered that I was hungry. But I also remembered that humans did not need to eat as much food as we had become accustomed to in our cushy, over-indulging American lifestyle. I would learn to be hungry. I would revel in having an empty stomach. My senses would become tuned and I would be alert to the smallest danger.

I chuckled at my cockiness.

"What's so funny," she asked.

"Nothing much. Other than I expect you never realized that I am one bad-ass mofo."

She rolled her eyes and smiled. "Okay, Rambo, let's get home and get packed."

*****

"This isn't anything like how we *used* to pack for a backpacking trip," I muttered as I surveyed our meager possessions.

Trixie emerged from the closet, carrying a dusty old canvas daypack. She also held two pair of ancient eyeglasses – one's that we had both worn over 20 years earlier.

"What? I couldn't hear you."

Looking at the eyeglasses in her hand, I repeated, "We don't have much to take with us."

"But maybe," She replied as she handed me a pair of eyeglasses, "We will be able to see where we are going."

"These must be made of glass!" I exclaimed. "I immediately put the glasses on and was relieved to find that my vision was considerably improved. The nose pieces were a rubbery substance – and if they failed I'd just go without.

I looked at Trix and began cracking up.

"What!?!?"

"Your glasses are ridiculous!"

"You should look at yourself in a mirror." She began laughing too, and for just a moment we found humor in our situation.

Spread out on the floor was a backpacking stove, two half-empty cans of iso-butane fuel (I always bought a new can before a trip, so we seemed to accumulate a lot of partially-used canisters), a light-weight aluminum cook kit, a coil of rope, a small can of lighter fluid, wooden matches, and some aluminum tent stakes.

"That's it?" she asked.

"Yup. I guess we are going lightweight for this trip."

Normally we'd carry goose-down sleeping bags, a lightweight tent, sleeping pads, Kindle e-readers, and lots and lots of food. We were efficient backpackers who liked to travel light and fast.

"What are we going to do about sleeping?" she asked.

"Grab the wool blanket from the bed. We'll figure the rest out later."

There was the possibility that we might get all of the way to Lansing and find no one there. They could walk here – only to find us gone as well. I found some paper and a pencil and rafted a note:

Dear Emily and Jory:

If you are reading this it means that you are probably OK. Mom and I hiked to Lansing to find you and help you get back here. We must have crossed paths and missed each other. Please stay put and we'll be back as soon as possible.

Love,

Dad and Mom

Chapter 5

Feeling that the house was now safe, we returned indoors to sleep.

"We can't use the bed," Trixie stated. "The mattress is failing."

So we improvised, making a sleeping pad from as many wool and cotton blankets as possible. Fortunately, our pillows were made from all natural fibers and stuffed with goose down.

After an uneventful evening and without much fanfare we left our house. I took a look back and hoped we'd see the place again.

In the brief time since the plastipocalypse began, the road surface had transformed into an odd stone and dust conglomeration. It was firm and surprisingly easy to walk upon. We headed east, Annie loping along beside us. I carried the old backpack. While it was fairly light, it wasn't exactly comfortable. The unpadded straps would probably rub my shoulders raw.

Trixie carried the bow and arrows. I hadn't yet tried shooting it, but figured I'd have plenty of time to practice while we camped. She also had an old canteen that I'd remembered at the last minute. It had hung on a nail in the corner of the garage for decades. We were both surprised to find it was in pretty good shape.

We also had all of the energy bars we could carry, and a couple of bottles of juice. The rest was stashed in the basement at home, well hidden from any possible looter.

The hunting knife was still attached to my belt, and Trix carried the backpacking knife in her pocket.

The morning was overcast. A damp mist hung in the air, and a cold breeze blew from the north. We each wore comfortable wool sweaters and wool stocking caps. Trixie had on some knitted mittens and I wore an old pair of leather work gloves. We wore cotton long underwear under our jeans. Fortunately, we each had serviceable leather boots, but I sure did long for my Gore-Tex hiking boots. We would certainly get wet on this hike – after all it was still mid-March, one of the wettest and most unpredictable seasons in Michigan. In a single day it could be sunny and rainy, or five inches of wet snow could fall.

As we walked down the road, we passed a house every quarter-mile or so. It was odd that there wasn't any sign of human activity. Two houses were smoldering heaps of wood and metal. But most were intact.

"Where are the people" Trix asked.

"I hope the gas didn't kill everyone."

Trixies eyes watered with tears. "The kids..."

Stopping, I gave her a hug. But there weren't any words that would make either of us feel better.

We reached the intersection and headed south. These roads were all very familiar to us, as we travelled them each day on our commutes to work and on our bicycle rides. We wouldn't need a map or have any difficulty with finding our way to Lansing – we would just hike the back roads all of the way there. I figured we could make the 40 mile trek in about three days. We did have one stop to make before leaving town: The grain elevator was on our route. Hopefully we would find vegetable seeds.

Annie kept pace with us as we quietly walked down the middle of the road. Before the plastic melt-down we would be passed by cars ever few minutes. Now we walked in eerie silence, with only the sound of our footsteps reaching our ears.

After an hour we reached the river, where there was a small roadside park. An old Ford Explorer SUV was parked under the trees. We walked by quietly, hoping to avoid any chance of discovery.

Annie sniffed the ground, did one of those strange 360-degree turns that dogs do, and sat down on the ground.

The SUV's owner was long gone. "Come on, Girl." With reluctance, Annie stood and followed us.

We headed away from the river and climbed a small hill. We passed the farm where we bought our Christmas trees. There was someone there – smoke billowed from the barn's chimney pipe.

Evidently, the gas had dissipated enough that in some places it was safe to start a fire.

It was reassuring to know that people were surviving. The same was probably true of the other houses we passed; people were hunkered down, hoarding what little comfort they still possessed. The story would be different in week or two, as starvation would force them out of their homes and out into the world to forage for food.

*****

It only took a couple of hours to walk the six miles to the outskirts of town. We had come in the back way, avoiding the big box stores and franchised fast food joints. If there were dangerous people lurking about, that's where they'd be. Besides, we already had all of the supplies we could carry.

We passed a party store. The front windows were smashed. As we walked by a row of houses, I spotted someone looking out the window at us. It was a younger person, wrapped in a blanket. They just stared at us as we continued on our journey.

"These houses are in pretty good shape," Trixie commented.

But just a quarter of a mile later, we encountered an entire city block that had been burned to the ground.

"Just one match, one cigarette..." Trixie whispered.

"It's spooky quiet." I kept my head on a swivel, cautious of approach by anyone with malicious intent.

To say it was a strange experience – walking down the middle of a main street in a half-burned ghost town – would be an understatement. The quiet was unnerving as we walked by the occasional decayed pickup truck or car. We had both been down this street countless times as we drove our kids to school or just wanted to avoid the busy commercial district. The houses here were old, probably built in the 1930's. We passed a commercial building that once sold horse-hauling trailers, but until a couple of days ago was an Evangelical church.

Our boots crunched upon the pebbles and dust that now made up the road's surface. As we reached an intersection, the non-functioning traffic light hung limp and dark. We turned left and immediately saw the grain elevator silos just ahead.

A flash of color briefly flickered past my peripheral vision. I stopped in my tracks – listening and looking. The street was lined with old maple trees – maybe I had just caught a glimpse of something blowing in the wind?

"Did you see something?" asked Trixie.

I continued to study our surroundings for a moment. When I was sure we were alone, I replied, "Guess not."

Approaching the grain elevator, I used hand signals to get Trixie to slow down and walk quietly. This was a tactic we used in the backcountry when trying to photograph a wild animal.

I pointed at a large tree and mouthed "You and Annie stay here."

She nodded in agreement. Quietly, I approached the old grain elevator sales office. Normally, the front door was reached by climbing a small stairway. A deck walkway leads to the door. I wasn't sure that the building was empty, so I kept low along the side of the building until I reached a back corner of the deck. I slid under the railing and crawled upon my hands and knees until I reached a window. As I slowly stood up, I noticed that the original clapboard siding and wooden window frames were holding up nicely.

I peered into a corner of the window into the darkness within the building. It was very difficult to see anything except the outline of some stacks of grain bags. I cupped my hands round my eyes and peered as deeply as possible into the building. Nothing moved. It was deserted.

I looked back at Trix, who was intently watching my progress, and gave her the sign to come forward with me.

"It looks empty," I whispered as she and Annie joined me on the deck.

We tip-toed forward to the front door. I was confronted by a large glass and aluminum door that looked as if it had been salvaged from a more modern retail store.

I gave the door a push and was shocked to find it unlocked. I looked at Trix and whispered, "That was a surprise!"

We entered the dark room and stood for a moment to let our eyes adjust to the darkness.

"It's going to be hard to find anything in here," she whispered.

"We have matches," I replied. "But I don't know if the building is safe yet. Let's leave the door open and see if we can get some other doors or windows open.

Various bags of seeds and feeds lined the walls of the cold and dusty room. Hand-made signs hung on the walls above the bags. "50 LBS. BIRD SEED - $25." "DEER FEED -25 LBS. - $20."

20 to 30 piles of a variety of feeds, corn and wood stove pellets lined the walls.

Near the back of the building was a room that was full of junk – mostly boxes of left over farm-related tools, seed bags, lighting fixtures, and old grain grinding equipment.

Trix bent over to look into a box. "If there are any vegetable seeds here, this is the sort of place we'll find them."

"Right. Can you see anything?"

"Barely!" She pawed through a box of old magazines and instruction guides. "Nothing in this one."

She moved on to another box. This one had some pamphlets from Michigan State University on how to get rid of ground moles. "We could have used these last summer."

Another box contained old sales receipts. Still another was packed with state maps and travel brochures.

Trix looked up at me and said, "I don't think we'll find anything in here."

"Let's move on then."

We found another store room, but all it contained was small pieces of lumber, probably used for building fix-up jobs.

Here and there dim light filtered through the dirty windows. We walked down a downward-sloping corridor until we reached a door.

"Let me go first," I whispered.

With a loud creak, the door opened into another large area. High windows, some with broken panes of glass, filtered dusty light upon an old Ford tractor and GMC pick-up truck. Boxes and bags of stuff littered the walls. Tools and other farm-related hardware were scattered around the huge room.

"Great," Trix muttered. "We'll never find what we are looking for in here."

"At least the broken windows would allow the gas to escape," I replied.

We picked up the pace as we looked through the boxes of junk. The light was better here.

At least a half-hour passed, then Trix said "Eureka!"

"Did you find seeds?"

"No – but I found candles!"

"Good. They will be useful later."

We continued searching, and all we had to show for our efforts were candles, a piece of canvas tarp, and some rope. At least we could rig a rain shelter now.

We took a break and found a couple of chairs and sat to rest. I pulled a couple of Clif Bars and one bottle of apple juice from the backpack. I threw a handful of kibble at Annie, who was stretched out on a piece of cardboard.

"Phew," Trix said, as she chomped on her lunch. "I'm tired of looking for seeds."

"Me too." I took a drink of juice. "Maybe we should move on."

I handed her the juice.

"Where are we going to sleep tonight?" she asked.

"I imagine we'll find a barn or empty house. It's too damn cold out to camp."

"I don't like the idea of sleeping in someone else's house. Uninvited."

"Me neither. But there really isn't another option."

Without further discussion, she stood and said, "I have to pee."

I sat quietly and munched on my Clif Bar. Chocolate. It wasn't exactly delicious, but it was real food. I pulled off my hat and ran my hands through my filthy hair – it had been days since either of us had taken a shower. My skin was itchy, but at least for the moment, I wasn't cold. This part of the building had cement block walls, which kept out the wind. I stood to look out of a dust-covered window. I reached out to wipe off the dust with my glove and nearly screamed as I saw a face staring back at me from the other side.

*****

Trix re-entered the room and looked up at me with excitement. "You'll never guess what I just found!"

I stood, trembling, my back against the wall. I held Annie by her collar – a low growl warned us that we were no longer alone. "Shhhh...there is someone out there."

We stood quietly and listened, waiting to see if the visitor was going to make himself known.

She handed me a small package. In the dim light I read, *Seed Vault Survival Garden. Heirloom Seeds. Over 30 varieties.*

The package, which was made from some sort of foil, was unopened.

"Awesome," I whispered. "This will definitely help."

As we stood waiting, the sound of footsteps alerted us that someone else had entered the room.

Annie let out a loud "BARK!" I held her collar tightly.

Hoping to avoid a violent confrontation I said in a loud but friendly voice, "We don't want trouble. Is there something we can do to help you?"

The low sun shone against the back of the intruder's head as he stood in the entrance to the room.

I could tell that the person was tall, but I had no idea if he was young, old, strong, or frail.

Trying again, "I said, we don't want trouble."

The voice was weary. "Neither do I."

I stepped forward, still keeping plenty of space between us. "We were just seeing what we could salvage here."

"Makes sense," was the reply. "I had the same idea."

Hoping a little friendliness would go a long way, I said, "I'm Greg." I reached out and offered my hand. "This is my wife Trixie." Annie relaxed immediately and sat beside me on the floor.

His hand was bare and cold, but I could feel a lot of strength. He stood well over six feet and carried what looked like 200 pounds on a large frame.

He held my hand and looked me in the eyes. "Bruce. Bruce Penn."

"Hello, Bruce. I wish the circumstances were better."

I took a step back as our hands released. It was one of those moments where you found yourself wondering if this new acquaintance was safe or dangerous. Like us, he was dressed in natural fibers, but he didn't wear shoes – just a pair of dirty wool socks. He had a soft face, and if I had to guess, I'd put him at 40 to 45 years old.

He looked warily at Annie and said, "You didn't happen to find any boots or shoes in here, did you?"

"No." I looked at Trix and she shook her head in agreement.

"Damn. My feet are freezing."

It was a good thing he was a much larger man, because he had no reason to try and take my boots. "We got lucky," I answered.

"I guess." He looked me over. "Seems like you have made out okay."

"Like I said, we got lucky. We were home when things started to get..." I thought for a moment to find the right phrase, "Weird."

"Weird. That's a good word for it."

We stood for a moment in a state of indecision. This was new territory for each of us – it just wasn't normal for people in our town to be wary of one another. People were friendly. We helped each other out in times of stress. But the plastic meltdown had created a completely new experience for everyone, and the protocol for human interaction had yet to be established. I figured it would only take a week and people would seek each other's help and camaraderie – unless their baser instincts were revealed, and we all went to war. Things could go either way.

Trix broke the ice by asking, "Have you had anything to eat, Bruce?"

He shifted his weight from leg to leg and replied, "Not much."

Trix shuffled through the backpack and found another energy bar and bottle of juice. Handing it to Bruce she said, "We can afford to share what little we have."

Actually, we couldn't, but what the hell, the man was hungry and we wanted to be rid of him as soon as possible.

He sat upon a wooden crate and devoured his food. The juice disappeared in one long swig.

"Damn, that was good! Didn't mean to be such a pig, but damn, I was fuckin' hungry!"

We all laughed. The tension in the room, which had been palatable, was now gone.

I really wanted to get moving, because we only had a few more hours of daylight.

"We're heading out of town to find our daughter and grandkids," I explained.

"How far do you have to go?"

"Lansing."

"Crap. That's a haul."

"Yes. We hope they are there when we get there. But there is no way of knowing."

"I was halfway home from work when my car stopped running," he replied. "Had to walk half the day to get home. Then there were explosions – and fires were burning everywhere. I finally got here, only to find out everything is messed up."

"There are a lot of burned out cars out on the highway," I replied, "You were lucky."

"I guess. My feet are raw. The walk was miserable – I didn't have any clothes, but I made it home. I thought everything would be okay here, but shit, it's no better. No better at all."

"Do you have family in town?"

He looked up at the window, lost in a moment's thought. "No. My wife and kids live in Flint."

"Oh." I didn't need more information – he was obviously divorced or separated and knowing the details wouldn't make a difference either way.

"Do you think that this..." He struggled with words. "Do you think this is the end times?"

Actually, I hadn't considered that the plastic meltdown was anything but a catastrophe caused by human beings. Super-smart people who screwed up.

I shrugged. "Who knows? All we know is that anything made of plastic or synthetics is just... disappearing."

Trix interjected, "Greg calls it the 'plastipocalypse.'"

"Plastipocalypse?!?" He chuckled. "If it wasn't so fucked up, it would be funny."

Chapter 6

Trix and I said our goodbyes to Bruce and headed west out of town. Annie, who was not used to long, cold walks, trudged along beside us. I hoped the old girl would make it. Her companionship was a comfort.

As soon as we were away and out of earshot, I asked, "Where did you hide the seeds?"

She patted the front of her sweater and answered, "Right here."

There weren't enough seeds to share with our farmer friend, but we could plant a garden.

We managed to walk another six miles before the day's grey light faded to black. Rural houses clustered together on the edges of former farmland – their dark windows revealing little to us as we walked past. Every third house was burned to the ground. The houses that weren't consumed by flames – did they contain dead bodies of folks that fell asleep and never awakened?

Trix looked up at the dark sky. "I'm cold. And tired."

"Me too. We'll find shelter soon."

We turned a corner where we recognized a farm that we'd passed many times on our bicycle rides.

Stopping, I whispered, "Let's see if the barn is open."

We cut across the farm property, staying close to a row of trees that separated the yard from a stubbly corn field. The barn was set-back about 75 yards from the house. In the darkness, we had to be careful not to trip over a deadfall or step in a hole.

The barn was one of those nice old storage buildings. Even in the darkness the front of the barn was visible to the house, so I led Trix to the side, hoping to find another entry door or window. Without warning, I stumbled down into what seemed like a small ditch and banged my shin against some stone.

"Sonofabitch!" I muttered.

Trix came up behind me, "Are you OK?"

"Yeah, it's just a flesh wound. Nothing structural."

We stepped over the stone and realized that we had discovered a lower-level doorway, bordered by two stone walls that were elevated a couple of feet above the opening.

"Good thing those walls were there or I would have dropped quite a bit."

We continued down the slope and dropped the last few feet over the wall, pulling Annie behind us.

The barn door hung was the type that slid on a horizontal track that was mounted at the top. I carefully slid it to the left, cringing as the metal wheels squeaked loudly. I opened the door just a foot or so, making just enough room for the three of us to squeeze through. Trix and Annie led the way into the gloom as I closed the door behind us.

"Do you think it's safe enough to light a candle?" Trix asked. "It's impossible to see anything in here."

"Just a sec. Let's give our eyes a chance to adjust."

We stood in the cold basement of the barn, surrounded by masonry, stone, and wood. Gradually, I was able to make out bags of seed lining the entry way, heading up a slope to what must be the main floor of the structure. Feeling my way along the wall I discovered a hallway that lead to another area in the lower level.

I had just about had it with the cold. My legs ached and I needed to rest.

"Stand back!"

I lit a match and threw it as far as I could.

Nothing.

"That was bold," she muttered.

We went inside. "OK, light a candle here," I replied. "No one will be able to see it from the house."

Candlelight revealed a storage area which in the past might have been where cows were milked. The cows would have walked from the pasture into the building and then walked right into this room. The walls were stone. A few dirty windows faced the direction of the house.

I looked at Trix and said, "Keep the candle low. The windows are filthy – I doubt much light could get through, but you never know."

We dragged a few seed bags over to the corner of the room and made ourselves a reasonably comfortable place to lay down. Trix found a bunch of empty burlap bags, which she used to further soften the surface.

I laid down on the bags first. "Not exactly the lap of luxury, but it will do in a pinch."

Trixie took a long swig of water from the canteen and passed it to me. The water was delicious – I hadn't been drinking enough and knew that I was close to being dehydrated.

She pulled a metal bowl and filled it half-way with water and set it on the floor for Annie. The old girl responded immediately, and drank it all up enthusiastically.

"That's all you get for tonight, girl," she explained. "But here's some food for you."

While Annie crunched her dry dog food, I found the package of Foster's venison jerky and popped a piece into my mouth.

"Delicious!" The salty meat was tender and had just a hint of a jalapeño flavor.

Trix gnawed off a hunk of meat. Her face, lit by the candle, revealed the sort of smile of someone who is eating something that is very, very tasty.

"That hits the spot," she exclaimed as she chewed the meat.

We each ate another Clif Bar (peanut butter and blueberry) and shared a bottle of apple juice, then walked out of our immediate area to find a place to take care of bathroom needs.

I came back to find Trixie scrubbing her mouth with a washcloth. A box of baking soda rested on the floor next to our bed.

I gave her a pat on the back and said, "You think of everything!"

With clean teeth we crawled onto our seed bag bed and covered ourselves with our wool blanket. We both left on our coats, hats, and gloves – which surprisingly, was how we'd spent many nights camping in the backcountry.

"I miss my sleeping bag," Trix muttered as she snuggled next to me, trying to extract what little warmth I had to share.

"Me too," I answered. "I would love to have our inflatable sleeping pads, but they have plastic valves."

Annie climbed onto the bag bed and after her ceremonial 360 degree spin, lay down beside me, where we all fell fast asleep.

*****

Ice pellets rattled against the side of the barn, waking me in the darkness. I lay there for a while, cold, needing to pee, yet unwilling to get up from our makeshift bed.

Finally, the pain in my bladder would not relent so I slipped into my boots and found a dark corner to pee in. I hoped that we wouldn't need to spend much time here, because otherwise we'd have to do a better job of managing our bathroom habits.

I crawled back into the covers and listened to Trix and Annie, both still asleep. Gradually, the ice pellets slowed their frequency. My mind wanted to worry about the future – about the details of our survival – and if I dwelled upon our upcoming struggles I would never fall back asleep. So instead I thought about warm days in the park, playing with my grandson, little three-year-old Declan. I thought about swing sets, plastic slides, ice cream, and swimming. I thought about train rides and apple cider. I thought about Thanksgiving dinner, where the table was spread with enough food to feed a small army. I thought about warm houses, favorite TV shows, and playing my guitar on the front porch.

*****

I awoke as Trix climbed out from under the blanket. I lay there for a moment while my two girls took care of business. They returned to the room as I was lacing my boots.

The wind outside was howling. Rain smacked the side of the barn, raising in intensity for several moments, and then suddenly abating.

I looked at Trix and said, "It sounds nasty outside."

"Uh-huh," she agreed. "Let's hunker down here for a bit and see if it lets up."

We shared some more of our water with Annie, and when her bowl was empty I took the bowl outside where I found a stream of water pouring from the barn roof. I filled the bowl and took it back inside.

"Here's some rainwater for you girl."

As she lapped up the water, I said, "We should probably take advantage of the situation and refill the canteen."

Trix watched me as I stood in the barn doorway and carefully directed the canteen under a stream of water that fell from the barn roof.

"Yuck," she complained. "This water won't be very clean."

"There's nothing we can do about it. How about we have a cup of coffee?"

I hated to use our limited supply of iso-butane, but it was the sort of dreary morning that could only be improved by a hot caffeinated beverage. Trix removed our backpacking mess kit from my backpack and handed me the pan. I put a couple of cups of water in the pan, lit the stove, and waited for the water to boil.

The rain continued to fall and we took turns looking through the basement windows, trying to see if we could detect any activity at the farmhouse.

"Here you go." Trix handed me a metal cup full of steaming instant Folgers. "Careful, it's hot." My gloves protected my hands as I sipped the delicious coffee.

Once or twice I thought I saw someone walk by one of the farm house's windows – but I wasn't certain. It could have just been a reflection from a tree.

The house was in good condition. It still had clapboard siding and wood windows. The barn, where we hid, was located back near the rear of the property. We were surrounded by fields, which were divided by fence rows that gave refuge to wild ash, oak, and maple trees. We had a clear line of sight on two sides of our shelter – we could see the back third of the house and we could see the fields behind us.

The driveway was empty. If the owner of this farm had a car, it was either stored in one of the outbuildings or it was gone, probably abandoned on a road somewhere.

I was getting restless and wanted to get moving.

"How about we check upstairs first," Trix suggested. "Maybe there is something we can use."

Using caution, we walked up the ramp and entered the main room of the barn. In the dull light we could see the sort of stuff you'd expect to find in a barn: Lawn mower, old small tractor, newer large tractor, ladders, rakes and shovels, bundles of twine, wire, and lots of tools.

"It's your lucky day, Annie!" Trixie smiled at the dog as she revealed a large bag of Purina dog food.

"At least the pooch gets to eat," I replied.

I spotted an old motorcycle in the corner. As a fan of vintage bikes, I was intrigued, so I walked over to inspect the machine. It was an old Yamaha SR400 – exactly the sort of bike I had lusted over for nearly a decade.

"Look! It's an SR400!"

Humoring me, Trix joined me alongside the bike. The vinyl seat was surprisingly intact. But the plastic light lenses and motor covers had disintegrated. This bike was a quick, light machine. Its single-cylinder 400CC motor was a beast – it put out a ton of torque and was certainly a fun ride.

I smiled and thought about sharing some of my bike knowledge with Trix, then thought better of it. I doubted that we'd ever live to see a time when we'd have the luxury of owning motorcycles.

We continued our examination of the barn but didn't find much of immediate use. Trix stuffed as much dog food as she could into a paper sack that she'd brought.

"That's got to be enough for now, Annie," she said to the dog. "That's all I can carry."

We walked back downstairs, where I opened the sliding door so we could see what the weather looked like. Fortunately, the clouds were breaking up and patches of blue sky were revealed.

Gathering our gear, we said goodbye to the barn and quietly left the property, heading out on the road again for another day of walking.

*****

"Will plastic ever be stable again?"

"Huh?" I was lost in my own thoughts, just trudging along a quiet country road. We chewed up the miles. Our walk to Lansing was about half done.

"Plastic," she repeated. "Given enough time, whatever is dissolving it might weaken."

"Oh, I hadn't really thought of that." Maybe it was possible that in the months or years to come, chemists might figure out another way to make plastic stable again. We walked up a hill and reached a freeway overpass. The wind, blowing stiff at our backs, was the only sound we could hear. Where there was normally a loud rumble of tractor-trailer rigs and other vehicle traffic, now there was just wind. The Interstate was littered with semi-disintegrated vehicles, many resting in the lane where their engines stopped. Others were on the shoulder, looking as if they expected a tow truck to arrive any minute. There were no people visible – they had all cleared off to somewhere else.

"Look," I pointed. "The cement is intact. The highway didn't burn." Only a few vehicles had burned, probably due to cigarette smoking.

We stopped and rested a moment, sharing a drink of water and some hard candies that Trix had wrapped in a bit of brown paper.

Trix led the way off the bridge. In another half-mile, we reached a main road that would take us pretty much to the north side of Lansing. This road would take us through a mixture of residential and commercial neighborhoods.

"I wonder where all of the people are."

Trix scanned the horizon and nodded. "I think they are all still in a state of shock."

"Probably. But you'd think there would be at least a few people out, heading somewhere, just like we are."

"Just wait a few days," I replied. "Maybe they'll come to their senses and begin preparing for the future."

We walked well into the early evening, reaching the outskirts of Lansing just as the sun was setting. Our feet hurt like hell, but so far neither of us had developed any blisters. Annie was, if you can excuse the pun, dog tired.

"I guess we ought to find a place to rest for the night."

"Ok," she replied. "I sure was hoping we'd get to Em's tonight."

"I think the two of us could make it, but poor old Annie Girl is tuckered out."

Trix bent and gave the yellow Lab a nice rub on the head. "Let's stop somewhere. Annie is worth keeping around."

*****

Neither of us could get used to the idea of sleeping in someone's home, uninvited. We anxiously looked for a quiet out-building, something similar to the barn that we'd used the night before. Cold rain sputtered off and on as we dragged our tired bodies down a quiet stretch of gravel road. Houses were sparse in this deeply wooded area just east of Lansing.

In our tired and hungry condition, I had trouble recognizing exactly where we were. This wasn't our local bicycling or walking area, so it all looked unfamiliar. Then I realized that we were on the edge of some protected state hunting land.

"I know where we are. This is the road that goes behind the Rose Lake State Game Area."

"Oh, good! Is there any place around here to camp?"

"There are a couple of spots back in the woods," I replied. But as the rain began to intensify, I added, "It would be better to sleep indoors."

After another quarter of a mile or so, we rounded a corner. In the darkness we were able to make out a dark commercial building. We wandered onto the property and as the rain and wind swept around us, found a sign in the front yard that proclaimed that this was the local Department of Natural Resources headquarters.

Looking up at the building, Trix said, "This looks safe enough."

"I hope we can find a way to get inside."

The main entrance was locked up tight.

"We could shatter a window," Trix suggested.

"Let's look around back and see if we can find a better way in."

We worked our way around the brick and glass building and found the rear entrance. The employee parking lot was empty. A dumpster sat near the rear of the lot. The entire building was surrounded by dense forest on three sides. It was a quiet setting, but without lights it was undeniably creepy.

Even though I fully expected the door to be locked, it opened easily as I pulled on the handle. I gave Trix a look of surprise, but we pressed forward and found ourselves in a dark hallway.

I stepped inside so I could assess the air situation. This building was built in the last 10 years, so it would be fairly air-tight. At first I thought that the air was still, but as I walked a few steps further down the hallway I felt a faint breeze on my face.

"It should be safe," I told Trix. "I feel air moving."

Trix fished a candle and matches from her bag and soon we had enough light to keep from tripping over stuff. On our left was an employee break room.

"Jackpot!" I exclaimed.

The room contained a snack and pop machine. Trix held the candle so we could see what sort of salty or sugary treats were waiting for us.

"Damn! It's empty!"

"Oh well," Trix replied. "At least we have a dry place to sleep." Trix laid the bow and her bag on the floor as I shrugged off the backpack. It felt really, really good to be free of the weight on my shoulders.

Just then, Annie turned suddenly and began to growl at a dark shape that stood in the doorway.

Chapter 7

Trix grabbed Annie's collar to keep her from pouncing on the intruder. Slowly, I moved my arm and put my hand on the hilt of my knife. My pulse quickened and my throat was suddenly very, very dry.

A tall, elderly man entered the room. In his right hand was a medium-sized handgun, which was pointed directly at the center of my chest.

As a man who had spent his entire lifetime seeking peace and rejecting violence, I found myself facing death. A coppery taste filled my mouth and I quickly realized that I was biting the inside of my cheek. Just in time, I was able to keep myself from pissing my pants.

"Hold on to the dog," the man commanded. "Hold the candle so I can see your faces."

With a shaky hand, Trix lifted the candle higher.

"Please," I begged. "We are only seeking shelter for the evening."

He stood there in silence, just looking at us. I could see that he was a grizzled old guy. Dressed in full brown and green colored camo, he looked like he was ready to go hunting. He wore a dark stocking cap, and even though the light was dim, I could make out a "Colt" logo on the front of the hat.

"This is my place," he grumbled in a low voice.

I didn't know if there was any good way to reason with him, but I tried. "We can leave."

"Then what?" he asked.

I thought to myself, "Then what?!?!" That's a strange thing to say. I gave Trix, who was doing her best to subdue Annie, a side long glance and rolled my eyes a little bit, trying to urge her to be calm.

"We head west."

"West. What's west?"

"Family."

"What else?"

"There is nothing else. Just family."

"Are you sure that's all there is?"

Using my calmest, most authoritative voice, I replied, "Yes. That is all there is."

He seemed to consider my answer, then said, "Sit down." He pointed the gun at the back wall. "Over there. Put the candle on the table."

Since the plastic chairs had lost all molecular cohesiveness, we were forced to sit on the cold, dusty cement floor.

We leaned against the wall and sat down on the floor. He turned slightly and lifted my backpack and dumped its contents on the table. He did the same with Trixie's bag.

"Quite a stash you've got here."

I didn't seem like explaining ourselves anymore to this weirdo. At best, he was going to hold us for a while and take our meager possessions. At worst... well I knew that I wouldn't let the worst thing happen.

As he pawed through our provisions, Trixie decided to open up a dialog.

"Where are you from?" she asked.

After a few more seconds of looking through our stuff, he replied, "Close enough. Why do you want to know?"

Moving quickly he moved over to us and pointed his gun right at Trixie's forehead. Never in my life had I ever been so scared... and angry. This was my wife he was messing with!

"You want to find my house and take my stuff, bitch?!?"

There was no way I was going to just stand by and let him assault Trixie. Even though this guy was trying to come off as one of those bad-ass survivalist guys, he hadn't bothered to check to see if I was armed.

In a moment of sublimely perfect timing, Annie lunged at the man's arm and chomped her teeth around his wrist. I swept up with my knife and embedded it deep under the man's left armpit.

The handgun fell harmlessly to the floor. Annie kept her mouth tightly on his wrist, and I guess she wouldn't ever let go unless I gave the command. I didn't know that the dog had it in her, but somewhere in her breeding she had learned to be wary of creepy guys in camo. Trixie picked up the gun and held it straight out, pointing directly at the middle of his chest.

"Fuckers!" He yelled. "You fucking stabbed me!"

"Shut up!" I replied. "You deserved it. We weren't going to do anything here but rest for the evening."

"Fucking uppity city people."

"What did you say?" I still held the bloody knife in my right hand, so I pushed him against the table and put the tip of the knife against his throat. Annie still had her jaws tightly clamped on his wrist.

His eyes showed no fear, just anger. It was clear to me now that he had no intention of ever letting us go.

"Trix, grab the rope so we can tie up this asshole."

I tapped Annie on the head, and told her, "Good job, Annie! Let go now." Reluctantly, the dog relaxed her jaws.

Trix held the gun at his chest as I walked around him, where I yanked his arms behind his back and began tying his wrists together, not giving a damn if the rope rubbed where Annie bit him. He was a tough SOB, because he never complained, even with a 3-inch stab wound in his chest.

After I was sure his wrists were tied tightly, I yanked off his boots and tied his feet together. Taking it one more step, I looped some rope around the door handle so if he tried to move, we'd hear it.

"That should do it. Now hold still!"

Using my knife, I tore through four layers of clothing to check out his stab wound.

He looked me square in the eyes and stated, "You will regret this."

I ignored his prophesy and looked at his wound. It was bleeding a little, but was less severe than I would have expected. He was nothing but bone and gristle. It would take more than a stabbing to take this dude down.

"You'll live."

I stood and found another candle in our stockpile. "Watch him for a bit, Trix. I'm going to see what else I can find around here."

I walked out of the room, holding the candle in my left hand, the knife in my right. There was a chance that Mr. Camo had some buddies lurking in the building – but I had a hunch that he was more of a lone wolf.

The building was fairly typical of most office buildings. There was a maze of cubicles, a front reception area, and a main conference room. One of the large windows at the rear of the building had been smashed. Either Mr. Camo used the window to gain entry or he broke it to ventilate the building.

I found Mr. Camo's stash in the conference room. He had all of the snacks from the machine dumped out on the conference room table. Anything that was in plastic packaging lay exposed, drying out and getting stale. I ignored the food but found his pack on the floor. I lifted it and was surprised at how heavy it was. I picked it up and hauled it back to our break-room hideout.

"Look what I found!" I entered the room and threw the pack on the table.

"Hey, that's my stuff!" He had trouble seeing on the table from his reclining position on the floor.

I emptied the contents of the pack, careful to keep it separate from our stuff.

He had another handgun, a sharp looking Sig Sauer with an extended clip. He also had a metal bottle containing water, and a glass bottle of alcohol, probably vodka. Assorted energy foods were wrapped in foil. He had two cans of corn and five cans of Dinty Moore stew. Four large boxes of ammunition completed the stash.

"For a guy who looks like a survival expert, your stuff is pretty shitty," I taunted.

He just glared at me, not caring if I knew how much he hated me.

"So what's the plan now?" Trix asked.

"I'll watch him for a while so you can get some rest."

She left the room to take care of her bathroom duties, and then returned a while later with an armload of cloth.

"Curtains," she explained. "I can make us a bed."

Mr. Camo lay on the floor, breathing heavy but not even moaning. I had to give him credit, because I'd whine like a baby if I'd been stabbed in the armpit.

I sat on the floor, looking at both handguns. The original gun was a smallish Colt. This I knew from reading the writing engraved on the gun – since I am certainly not a gun expert. I easily found the safety, which had been off during this entire affair. I actually could have killed the guy – it would have only taken a momentary loss of self-control and BANG, he would have a bullet in him.

I had no idea what caliber of bullet the gun used, but I could match the stockpile on the table with what was in the gun to make sure I had replacement ammunition. At this point I had already decided that I wasn't going to kill the guy, but he wasn't getting his firearms back. Trix and I didn't need them or want them, but I didn't want an asshole like Mr. Camo using them either.

The other gun, the Sig Sauer, was, I had to admit, very cool looking. An amazing amount of technology and development went into a quality firearm like this one.

"You don't even know what you are looking at."

I looked over at Mr. Camo. "It's a gun. It's used to shoot stuff."

"No shit, Sherlock. I bet you don't shoot."

"What gives you that idea?" I replied, casually holding the Sig Sauer as if I had one in my hand all of the time. The truth was, I'd never ever shot a handgun. I had done some hunting, but that was always with a shotgun. Still, I had seen plenty of television shows and movies that ranged from professional target shooting to pure escapist violence – so I was no stranger to the weapon's capabilities and operation.

"You strike me as the sort of liberal douchebag that I absolutely fucking hate. You are probably responsible for whatever caused the plastic to evaporate."

"Yeah, sure. You have found the one guy on the planet that single-handedly made plastic disintegrate. I wish I had that kind of knowledge – but I'm sorry to report that I'm just not that smart."

"Fucking Prius driving liberals. You people fucked up this country."

"Yup!" I replied. "It was always on our agenda to turn the USA into Sweden." I had to admit, it was fun getting his goat, especially since I had the upper hand.

"You wanted to take our guns and make us all marry fags. Fucking fag lovers."

I just sat there and laughed at the stupidity of his comments. Yet there was something here to fear as well – because it was clear that at this point in history, the country was completely divided politically and socially. Half of the country railed against Planned Parenthood, universal health care, global warming... and then bought guns and hated anyone who wasn't white. The other half.... well I guess that's were Trix and I belonged. We always believed that the USA was formed around the concept of creating a level playing ground for everyone, not just rich white people with guns. Maybe the act of surviving in the modern world would bring us together, or maybe we'd end up in tribes, each fighting to keep territory.

I was about to reply with another snarky comment, when POW!!!, Trix bashed Mr. Camo on the side of his head with the vodka bottle. The dude was out cold.

She looked down at him and then at me. "Shut up! I am trying to sleep."

*****

Anxious to see our daughter and grandchildren, we ate a cold breakfast and headed back out on the road. I left Mr. Camo tied up to the door, figuring he'd eventually free himself from his bondage. He must have had one hell of a headache from the bang on the head Trix had delivered, for he didn't mutter a sound as we packed up and left the building.

The early morning sky revealed soft, white clouds and patches of blue. We stepped around patches of ice, moving as quickly as possible to reach Emily's house.

Every now and then we felt a gust of warm air blow past our faces, indicating a welcome change in the weather. As we reached the

Lansing city limits, we pulled off our hats and gloves and enjoyed the warmth of the late-winter sunshine. Here and there we spotted people – some clung to bags of loot, others simply stared at us from a distance.

I reached into my pocket and felt the Sig, finding comfort in its cold metal exterior.

"Keep the Colt accessible," I suggested to Trix.

We passed a large Meijer department store. This store hadn't survived the fires. Smoke still poured from the remains of brick and metal that lay smoldering on the ground.

It didn't take long before the commercial district evolved into a residential area. We walked past several burned-out homes before we reached a neighborhood where the houses were unscathed.

"How come these houses didn't burn?" Trixie asked.

"I have no idea." The road had burned but the houses never caught fire.

Just before noon, we intersected the north-south highway, US-127. Looking south we could see smoke pouring from the city center. Evidently, the Capitol had burned. Emily's house was about two miles east of where we were, but if we walked the straightest line, we'd have to go through some rough neighborhoods.

Pausing, I looked at Trix and said, "Let's head north on the highway for a bit. Then we can cut west on a main road that will take us just two blocks from Em's house."

Useless derelict automobiles, pickup trucks, and tractor trailers littered the highway. We carefully walked around the biggest vehicles, looking out for anyone who might be lurking. In one place, we found a pile of intertwined vehicles, over 20 in all, all jammed together in what looked like a chain-reaction accident.

Fire had consumed many of the vehicles. There was a group of cars and SUV's near the middle of the accident that still held the remains of people.

I glanced at Trix. Her eyes were opened wide, aghast at the scene before us. "I guess the first responders didn't make it here in time."

Near the front of the pile-up was a group of vehicles that looked as if they'd been knocked sideways by a large gravel hauling rig.

Simultaneously, our jaws dropped and we broke into a sprint towards a small blue Ford Focus. It was the car that belonged to our daughter.

*****

"There's no one in it," I said, relieved.

"Thank God!"

"Hopefully they got out okay and hoofed it home."

Feeling a renewed sense of urgency, we broke into a jog and quickly covered the last half-mile of highway. We jogged up the exit ramp and crossed the highway and entered a mixed industrial and residential neighborhood. For some reason the fires had not reached this area either. Since most of the fires started on Sunday – when the people who worked in these buildings were all at home – there was no one around to create a spark. But I had no doubt that dangerous gasses still inhabited the structures.

We ran through an intact residential neighborhood. The houses here were old and placed very closely together. An old man sat on the porch of a well-kept two-story house, watching us carefully as we walked past his home. A substantial-looking rifle lay across his lap.

I nodded at him in a sort of "hello," and we walked by without incident.

"Almost there!" I encouraged. We continued jogging, dodging cars, sometimes using the road and sometimes using the sidewalk, whichever was easier.

Suddenly, in a moment that would forever haunt my dreams, a young man darted out from behind a tree and knocked me to the ground. Another youth ran to Trix, swinging a baseball bat. Trix managed to dodge the brunt of the impact, but the blow still had enough force to knock her to the ground. Just as Annie lunged at the attacker, I heard a gun fire and my dog, my dear Annie, fell to the pavement. One of the attackers grabbed me from behind as I struggled to my feet and held a knife to my throat.

"Hold still, old man!" I could smell his rancid breath, which had the aroma of warm beer and stale Doritos.

Trix had dropped the bow, but still had Annie's leash tied around her left hand. She crawled to the dog, and laid her hands upon the shaking animal.

"You shot her!" she yelled as a third assailant approached.

"Shut the fuck up, bitch! Or do you want to die today too!"

This group of thugs was a motley bunch. The guy with the gun, who I assumed was the leader, wore leather boots, jeans, and a dark leather jacket.

Neither of the other two men wore shoes. One had on short pants and a sweater that looked like he'd stolen it from a child – it barely came to his midriff and the sleeves were comically short. The other guy wore old woolen trousers and an unbuttoned cotton shirt. The buttons were gone, as they were most likely made of plastic.

Rifling through Trixie's bag, the thug in shorts said, "They have some good shit, DeAndre'!"

The leader, DeAndre', came up to me and put muzzle of his large handgun in the center of my chest. I did not know if he had more bullets or not, but I couldn't risk finding out. All I wanted now was to get out of this situation alive – even if it meant losing our hard-fought possessions.

DeAndre' looked me straight in the eyes. I saw a young dark-skinned man who was wise to the ways of the street. He was a survivor – and also a leader. The calmness that he displayed as he stared at me indicated that he was also a killer.

"What kind of shit you got in the backpack?" he asked, pressing the gun harder into my sternum.

His shoeless assistant, who still held me from behind, laughed in a hysterical, maniacal way that scared me worse than the man I was facing. "Dibbs on the white guy's boots!"

"You want his boots, Marshall?" DeAndre' asked. "They are yours!"

He pulled his face close to mine and whispered, "Sit your ass on the ground. Hand Marshall your pack and take your fuckin' boots off."

As I began to sit I wondered for a moment if I'd be able to use the Sig to somehow even the score with these guys. I knew I had a full clip of bullets. How many did DeAndre' have? Still, it would only take one bullet to end our quest for survival. My main objective at this moment was to get away alive.

Marshall took my pack and immediately began plowing through the contents. "These motherfuckers have a lot of good shit! Energy bars, Snapple...."

"Just wait a goddamned minute, idiot! Put the fuckin' bag down."

DeAndre' took a step back and commanded me to remove my boots.

I looked at Marshall's feet and knew that the boots were too small. "They'll never fit him."

The gun muzzle swung hard at my head. The impact caused my glasses to fly off and land hard on the ground.

"Shut. The. Fuck. Up." He screamed, "Take off your boots!"

Carefully, I removed first my left boot, then the right boot and tossed them towards Marshall.

"What are we gonna do with the bitch?"

DeAndre' looked at Trix for the first time and smiled. "You ever have dark meat, bitch? Anthony wants to give you the best fuck you've ever had. Way better than this limp-dick white dude."

Trix and I'd lived our entire lives without ever being in a similar situation. We'd seen it happen over and over in movies and on TV, but until it happens to you it's impossible to really come to terms to how terrifying it all was. Time stood still, yet everything happened at hyper-speed too.

Anthony removed his pants and revealed his huge black cock. He pressed his knife at Trix's throat, and whispered, "Take off your pants, cunt."

Trix, who must have been scared beyond belief, looked as cool as a cucumber. As her left hand reached towards her pants, her right slid into her jacket pocket.

All three thugs must have been fascinated by Trixie's potential undressing, because no one had considered that she might have a hidden handgun. The Colt in Trixies pocket fired and blew a hole in the center of Anthony's chest. I was just as stunned as the remaining two assailants, yet I managed to roll and remove the Sig from my pocket. But before I could bring the gun to firing position, a bullet entered the back of DeAndre's head and exited the front, ejecting brain matter and skull all over Marshall and me.

Marshall, who held my pack and boots, suddenly bolted and ran for cover. Another shot rang out, hitting him in the back of the right thigh. He dropped my belongings and continued half running, half limping and disappeared between two houses.

Shaking terribly, I crawled over to Trix and held her. "Are you OK?!"

"No," she cried, "I am not. But it could have been worse."

Before I could ask if she knew where the other shooter was, a shadow covered us and blotted out the sun.

"This must be your lucky day,"

Chapter 8

The elderly black man introduced himself.

"Name's Smitty. I was sitting on my sister's porch a few blocks away and saw you walk by. I thought to myself, 'Shit, they gonna run into DeAndre' and his buddies.' You guys were hard to keep up with! Looks like I got here just in time."

I helped Trix stand and put my arm around her for comfort. "You sure did! Damn, that all happened so fast."

Smitty walked over to where DeAndre' lay on street and nudged the body with the toe of his boot. "He never was any good. Always givin' people trouble. I knew he'd end up in a bad way someday, just didn't think I'd be the one to end it for him."

I looked at Trixie and saw that she was mostly over the shock of the assault. She still held the Colt in her right hand. I looked at the gun and said, "You can put it away now."

She pocketed the gun and reclaimed her scattered belongings as I retrieved my pack and boots. I also retrieved my eyeglasses, which were bent but not broken. Smitty watched as I sat on the curb and laced my boots.

"Too bad about your dog."

I looked at Annie, who lay on her side. She gave us nine good years of comfort and protection. Now she was gone forever.

"Do you have a shovel so I can bury her?"

"Sure." He pointed back towards the neighborhood we'd just walked through. "I just live over there block or two."

Trix and I picked up Annie and set her down carefully on the grass.

"What about those two?" I asked, pointing at DeAndre' and Anthony.

"I suppose they need to be taken care of too. There's a vacant lot behind my house where we can bury them."

"Mr. Smith," Trixie asked, "We are only a couple of blocks from our daughter's house. We've been on the road for three days..."

"Oh? Well hell, the burying can wait for these guys."

"I'll tell you what," I said. "We'll go get our daughter's family and then come back here to help."

"That will work," he replied.

"We should be back in a few hours," I told Smitty as I shrugged on my pack. The Sig rested uncomfortable yet close in the waistband of my pants.

"I'll be here," he replied,

It wouldn't take long for us to get Jory and Emily and the kids outfitted for the return trip to our home... assuming they were okay... and away from the potential lawlessness of the city.

We stayed in the middle of the street as we jogged towards Em's. Our nerves were on edge now, and as we ran through a small community park I was especially alert. Weeks ago we had encountered a group of nasty-mouthed youngsters hanging out here as we played with our grandson Declan. I couldn't help but notice that the mostly plastic playscape was now an unrecognizable mess.

We cut across the parking lot of a plumbing and heating business that looked intact. There probably wasn't anything there worth looting in a post-plastic world.

Entering the home stretch, we sprinted across a deserted five-lane road that was formerly the location of many of the Lansing's north side businesses. Fast food restaurants, gas stations – all had been thoroughly looted. Even without pausing to look we could tell that there would be nothing of value found here.

Finally, we reached Em's street. I ran at full speed, wanting this part of our ordeal to be over, before remembering that Trixie was not keeping up. I stopped and turned around to see her slowing to a walk several yards behind.

"We're almost there!" I encouraged.

We held hands and walked the last few hundred yards together.

Trixie prayed aloud, "God, please let them be okay."

Em's house was all right!

"Look," I said. There was smoke pouring from the chimney. Somehow Emily realized that the disintegrating plastic caused explosive gas – and she was able to remove the plastics and ventilate the house over the last several days.

Trixie reached the front door first and gave the knob a twist.

"Locked!" She exclaimed. She knocked loudly and yelled, "Emily! It's mom and dad!"

I suddenly realized that I had broken into a cold sweat. At no point in my life had I ever been this afraid or concerned for the safety of my family. Before the plastipocalypse, I certainly always thought about my children and what they might be up to as they went about their lives in another city 40 miles away. Yet we never *really* think about their well-being on a moment-to-moment basis. There was no point, because the concern would be overwhelming if you thought about it too much. But now, as I stood at Emily's doorway, I was consumed with the deepest love and worry I'd ever felt for my daughter, her husband, and my grandchildren.

Finally, after what seemed like an eternity, the door opened. Knox, a terrier-mix, and Coco, a beagle mutt, greeted us, barking loudly.

"Mom! Dad! Oh, thank God that you are here!"

Emily, dressed in sturdy cotton overalls and a flannel shirt, held the baby Cora in her arms. Declan, just 3 years old, stood next to his mama. We all stood, stunned at the joyfulness of the moment.

Just as tears began to streak my cheeks, little Declan said, "Coppa! Comma! You made it! You made it!"

*****

Anxious to sit for a few minutes and rest, Trix and I threw off our bags and carefully put our weapons high on a shelf. As Trix leaned the bow against the wall, Declan asked, "What is that, Comma?"

"This is called a bow. It's used for hunting. You shoot arrows at animals so you can have meat."

She showed him one of the arrows. "See, the tip is very sharp."

He poked his finger on the arrowhead and let out an exaggerated yelp.

"Did you shoot an animal, Comma?"

Trix laughed, "Not yet honey. But if we get hungry we might have to shoot a deer."

She picked him up and carried him into the nearly bare living room and asked, "Where is the furniture?"

Em gave a laugh and replied, "After it all started to fall apart I pitched it into the back yard. I think that's what saved the house. I got the largest stuff outside and the house must have ventilated while the doors were open. I finally had enough nerve to start a fire last night."

"Where you here when the roads burned?" I asked.

"No, but I saw it happen when I was downtown. Most of the houses west of here are gone. But the houses on my street are okay."

I sat on the floor holding Cora, my infant granddaughter. She had a confused look on her little face.

"I don't think she likes my glasses or my beard."

"Those are some funky glasses, dad," Emily replied.

Trix interrupted, "We were lucky to have them. Otherwise it would have been a very blurry hike."

Both dogs jumped on my lap and begged for attention. For a moment, everything felt almost normal.

We all sat on the floor. After a few minutes of relaxing and enjoying the warm wood-heated room, I let out a deep sigh and began to tell a condensed version of our story, leaving out the worst details so I wouldn't scare Declan.

I stood and retrieved the canteen and a couple of energy bars. "Tell us what you've been doing for the last few days,"

We shared the bars with Declan and Emily as Emily began to tell her story.

Chapter 9

"Sunday – just two days ago, I decided to take the kids to the pet store to pick up some dog food. At first the morning was very normal. Jory was at work, I had the kids all day. We left for the store around 11 am. On the way to the store I wondered how the steering wheel got sticky but with two kids, anything can happen. We got to the store all right and got the food, but as I was putting the big bag of dog food in the trunk of my car, the bottom of the bag gave way and all of the food spilled out over the parking lot and into my trunk. What a mess!"

Trix and I looked at each other and nodded, clearly understanding what had happened.

"The bag was plastic," she continued. "But since I didn't have any idea that there was something wrong with plastic, I went back into the store, carrying the broken bag, which I showed to the clerk. I told her, 'Look, the bottom just blew out of the bag!' and she replied, 'That is the second time today that's happened. Go ahead and grab another bag of food.' So I walked back to the dog food aisle and looked at the food in plastic bags –it all seemed to be okay, but just to be safe I grabbed a brand food that came in a paper bag."

"Good thinking," Trix replied.

"I got the food and kids back into the car, but for some reason Declan's car seat was a mess! It was sticky all over. I really didn't have any options so I strapped him in. Cora's seat wasn't nearly as bad, so I got her in the car and headed home. For some reason, I don't know why, I decided to take the highway home instead of local streets."

"When did you call me?" Trixie asked.

"Just after we got on the highway. I was talking to you and then the phone just quit working all of a sudden. It went completely dead."

She continued. "The traffic was very weird. Some cars were going eighty miles per hour; others were sputtering and lurching along at fifty. Suddenly my car began to sputter and I nursed it along for another mile or so. Just as the car was dying I managed to pull over to the shoulder, thinking to myself, 'Dang what am I going to do now? I have two kids in the car and a fifty pound bag of dogfood!' Then, BANG, I looked in the rearview mirror and saw a pile of cars being pushed towards me by an out-of-control semi-truck. I shouted at Declan, 'Hold on!' and braced for the impact. The pile of cars slid into my car, but only pushed us up the road ten or fifteen feet."

"My God," I exclaimed.

"After I quit shaking I turned and looked in the back seat at the kids. Their eyes were huge with fear, but they were all right. So I got out of the car and unbuckled both kids and stood on the side of the highway and looked at the damage. Other people, some of them unhurt - one guy had a huge gash on his forehead - staggered along the side of the road in shock. A woman came up to me and asked if we were okay. She told me she was headed north another hour and didn't know how she'd get there now. I told her I lived just a mile or two away, and she said, 'Honey, you get those two babies home. Something strange is happening today.' So I told Declan that we were going to walk home and come back for the car later. We didn't even get a half mile before I realized that my clothes were beginning to fall off my body. Luckily Declan had on jeans and a flannel shirt, but his shoes were disintegrating. Cora's jacket was okay, but her fleece sleeper was coming apart. We crossed the highway and I urged Declan to keep up with mommy – he really did a great job – and we did fine until we got to the main commercial strip.

There were cars stopped everywhere and people walked around in a daze. People were running out of the corner party store with armfuls of stuff – they had begun looting already! A man ran up to me and yelled 'Grab what you can, because there will never be any more where this came from.' I just stared at him. I was freaked out and amazed at the same time.

I hurried the kids across the main road and down our street and we got to our house. Then I remembered that I left my keys in the car! I was just about to have a complete meltdown when I remembered the time that Declan locked Jory out of the house while I was at work – and Jory said he hid a key under the deck but never showed me exactly where. I sat Cora on the cold ground said to Declan, 'Watch her while mommy looks for the key.'

So there I was, almost completely naked, crawling around under the deck looking for the key. Of course it turned out to be pretty easy to find, but I guess I was just too stressed out to think straight.

After we got inside the house I threw on a bathrobe and found another intact onesie for Cora. The power was out but we had heat from the wood stove, which meant we wouldn't freeze to death! Plus we could cook on the stove too.

I sat on the couch with Cora and began to ball my eyes out. Where was Jory? Would he be okay? What should I do now? Declan climbed up on couch and asked, 'What's wrong mama? Why is the power out?'

How do you look at a three-year-old and tell him that all of the stuff you've always had – electricity, running water, toys, a refrigerator full of food – are now all gone? Right then I had an urgent idea. I jumped up and ran over to the sink and turned on the cold water. There must have still been pressure in the pipes because we had running water! I grabbed my biggest pan and was able to fill it up, thinking, come on water! Don't stop now!

I was able to fill up the pan but that's about it. We had enough water in the pan to last about two days if we used it carefully. I looked at the dog dishes, which were plastic and seemed to be holding up. Fortunately, I had filled them with water before we left to go to the store.

I looked in the refrigerator and was surprised to find that it was still cold and that the plastic packaging on our food was still intact. I guess it had something to do with air. That's why the stuff inside our house hadn't begun to destabilize – it hadn't been exposed to the air. I quickly closed the refrigerator door, hoping that I hadn't sped-up the destabilization process.

But I knew that it would only take a day or two and the inside of the house would start to fall apart too.

The crazy morning must have tuckered out the kids, because when I went back to the living room they were both asleep on the couch, which by now was beginning to show signs of deterioration. Thank

God I hadn't started a fire in the stove yet! I moved the children to another room, then I opened the doors and windows and dragged everything that was made from plastic outdoors.

Then I decided that I had to see what I could do to survive until Jory got home. First was food. Cora was still nursing, so she would be okay. But Declan and Jory and I would have to eat. I emptied the cupboards looking for food that was packaged in plastic. I took all of the cookies and crackers from their packaging and wrapped them in aluminum foil. I was surprised that we didn't have a ton of dry food that was packaged in plastic. Most of the plastic stuff was in the refrigerator. We had quite a supply of canned soup, refried beans, and stuff like black olives and mushrooms. So we wouldn't starve... right away.

My biggest concern was water. We just didn't have enough in that pan to last more than a day or two.

I paced around the house and said to myself, where can I find water? Then I remembered that the hot water heater was full of water! I opened the door to the utility room and there it was, 30 gallons of drinking water. But how to get it out? The light in the utility room wasn't great, but I felt around the bottom of the tank and found a drain spigot – but it was missing a handle! I cursed at Jory for leaving it like this, and left the room to find a pair of pliers so I could turn the spigot.

I have a few tools in the house and I tried a pair of pliers but I couldn't make them work. I saw that the spigot had a square thingy that should turn as long as I could get a wrench on it. But all of the wrenches were out in Jory's shed!

I managed to leave the house without waking the kids and walked out to the shed. Then I heard the first explosion. It was loud, but I couldn't see any fires so I figured something blew up just west of here – probably near the airport. I heard more explosions from the south – which might have come from downtown. The sky turned orange as the flames shot up into the sky. I crouched on the grass and prayed that the flames wouldn't head our way.

Thinking I might not have much time remaining to get the water out of the water heater, I got back to opening the shed. I should have known that Jory would have it locked up tighter than Fort Knox! A huge padlock kept me from opening the door – and the shed has no windows so I couldn't climb in that way. I needed a crowbar or lever so I could break the lock or the door hinges.

I walked around our back yard for a bit, trying to find anything that would work for leverage – and eventually got around to looking in Jory's dad's old pickup truck. That old beater has been parked way back on our property line for two years, so I guess I forgot about it. The interior was a mess of semi-dissolved plastic, but I found a hydraulic jack and jack-handle behind the seat.

I didn't know exactly how I could use the jack, but I thought the handle might give me enough leverage to break into the door somehow. At first I tried to break the door hinges – but the handle wasn't big enough. The same went for the lock – I couldn't get enough leverage to make it budge.

Heavy, black smoke drifted across our back yard. I sat on the picnic table and started to have a breakdown, but stopped short when I remembered my babies inside the house. 'Come on 'Em,' I said to myself. 'Think!'

I stood and looked at the door again. There was just enough room to get the jack under the bottom of the door. Maybe I could use the jack to lift one side of the door and break it loose? I put the jack in place and pumped the handle and the door began to lift! But the ground was too soft and the jack began to sink into the muck. I walked around the house again, looking for something I could put under the jack. It turns out I was standing on what I needed – a small piece of flat stone that was part of a sidewalk that was put here by the previous owners.

I used the jack handle to pry the stone from the ground and lugged the stone over to the shed. It was perfect! I put the jack on the stone and began cranking the handle. The door lifted several inches, and the screws that hold in the lock thing..."

"Hasp," I interjected.

90

"Hasp," she continued. "The screws were pulling out of the door frame! I only needed a little more lift from the jack and I'd be inside the shed. But the jack was at its fullest extension. Well, it turns out that it took only a little bit of effort to use the jack handle to pry the screws out the rest of the way.

The hasp popped off along with a bit of door frame that is sure to make Jory mad, but the door was open! And you know what? Lined up against the wall were ten gallons of water - unfortunately in plastic bottles - that Jory had stored out there! He never told me that he was storing water! But I was so happy! We had a couple of weeks of drinking water if I could find a way to store it. Plus there was water in the hot water heater! I was so excited that I almost forgot what I went out there for – a crescent wrench! I grabbed the wrench, a couple of gallons of water, and went back into the house.

"How's the water holding out?" Trixie asked.

"Not as well as I'd hoped. I noticed that the bottles that were stored in the dark corner of the shed where still holding water, so I kept them there and used pans to carry the water inside. We used two gallons yesterday - heating soup, drinking, and for cleaning up the dirty dishes. When I went out this morning to get more water, it was gone! Someone, a neighbor most likely, must have stolen it!"

"It's not going to matter," I said. "You guys are coming to our house and we can't carry that much water anyway."

*****

Time slipped away from us and we all dozed for a while in the warm house. It was late afternoon before I remembered my promise to Smitty that we'd be back to help the kind old man bury DeAndre' and his pals. Oh well, I thought, that will have to wait until tomorrow.

Emily and Trixie got to work making an inventory of our food. I occupied the children, playing with a wooden Thomas the Tank Engine train set that Declan absolutely loved. Unfortunately, the plastic wheels had disintegrated.

"What happened to Thomas's wheels, Coppa?"

"Well, Declan, they are broken. Coppa can't fix them."

"We will have to find another Thomas train then," he announced in his matter-of-fact three-year-old manner.

The afternoon passed into evening. Emily heated a couple of cans of chicken and barley soup on the stove, and we also had a side of pickles and olives. I would have loved some crackers with my soup, but the packaging had dissolved and they had gone stale. Plus, no one really wanted to eat crackers that were covered in dissolved plastic.

"Is my daddy going to be home to eat with us?" Declan asked.

"I am sure daddy is walking home right now," Emily replied.

The truth was we had no idea if Jory was going to make it home or not. His walk home from Marshall to Lansing was about 50 miles – just a bit longer that the trek Trixie and I had taken to get to Emily's house. But Jory was much younger and in phenomenal physical condition. He was an infantryman in the National Guard – which knowing Jory as I did – meant he might have decided to help the citizens of Marshall before returning home. Or, he might have run into some sort of trouble on the way home. We had no way of knowing his situation.

There was enough food and water for the five of us to stay at Emily's house for another day and night. Hopefully, Jory would turn up and we could all hoof it back to the safety of our rural home. I wasn't looking forward to spending the night at Emily's – there could be desperate people out there that would try to take our food and water by force. Someone had already taken the water stored in the shed, and they might come back for more.

I stood and looked out the front window. I could see about 100 yards in both directions and the street was quiet. As darkness fell, rain drops began to splatter against the windows. It was a good thing we weren't outside walking home in the miserable weather.

Trixie sat and read Dr. Seuss books to Declan while Emily nursed Cora. The house was quiet and we were all lulled into a feeling of comfort and safety.

*****

I awoke with a start sometime in the middle of the night. Where was I? Oh yeah, I had fallen asleep on the floor next to the wood stove. Trixie was lying on the floor in the guest room. The kids and Em were all asleep in the master bedroom.

I wondered what had awakened me. The two dogs were no help – they both snoozed quietly on the floor. I walked around the dark house and looked out the windows but could see nothing in the darkness. There was no moon. Small snow and ice pellets pinged against the windows. I walked to the back of the house and looked out the bathroom window towards the shed. It was just possible for me to make out the building, but I could see very little of anything else. Suddenly, a dark shape emerged from the shed and lumbered towards the house.

I scrambled quietly towards the living room and looked for something I could use to deter an invader. My gun was up high on the shelf, and just as I began to reach for it the front door burst open and a large body entered the room.

I backed quietly towards the wood stove and said, "Jory, is that you?" Both dogs sprang to action. Coco barked loudly and the Knox, the Terrier, growled in a surprisingly menacing way for such a small animal.

The large person stood quietly and looked at me, crouching next to the stove. I reached around and found the wood poker and quietly picked it up, hoping that the intruder didn't see it.

"Go away," I demanded. "There's nothing here for you."

Just then Trixie emerged from the guest bedroom. "What's going on?"

Suddenly, the big person backed up and left the house. I sprung up and slammed the door shut and locked the deadbolt.

"Phew! That was scary and strange," I said. "Whoever it was just waltzed in as if they owned the place."

"Looks like our vicious animals kept us safe," she replied as she squatted and rubbed Knox behind the ears.

Emily emerged from the back of the house. "Is everything all right?"

"Nothing to worry about," I answered. "Go back to bed."

As Emily disappeared back into her bedroom, I told Trixie, "Get some sleep. I'll stay up and stand watch for a while."

I made myself a comfortable place on the floor and for an hour or so, the adrenaline that coursed through my veins kept me awake. But sometime in the early hours of the morning I dozed off. I didn't awaken until well after sunrise.

*****

An inch of snow covered the ground outside. I looked in the shed and couldn't tell if last night's intruder took anything or not. I grabbed an armful of wood and took it inside.

"What's for breakfast?" I asked as I stoked the fire.

Both women replied in unison, "Eggs!"

"Do you think they are still okay to eat?" I asked.

"Sure. They've been in the refrigerator," Emily replied. "It's still fairly cool inside."

Trixie held a gallon jug of milk over the sink. She carefully opened the jug and smelled the contents

"Not bad," she said. "I am surprised that the container is still intact."

I walked over and gave the milk jug a poke. It still felt like plastic.

"I suppose that some plastic will last quite a while, as long as it's not exposed to air."

There were eight eggs in the carton, and Trixie broke them all into a metal mixing bowl. She added a splash of milk and stirred up the mixture.

Emily placed a metal frying pan on the wood stove. In a few minutes we were all enjoying hot scrambled eggs, relishing in the comfort of a warm house and good meal.

After filling my hungry stomach I said, "As long as we can find a way to keep producing things like eggs we should be able to survive this catastrophe."

"I wonder if people will remember how to do things the old way," Emily replied.

"Our grandparents largely lived without plastic," Trix stated. "At least for the first part of their lives. Too bad the old people are mostly gone. They could teach us a lot."

Emily ate the last of her eggs and asked, "What is the game plan for today?"

I thought for a moment and carefully prepared what I needed to say: "Do you know there was an intruder last night?"

"Yes. Mom told me."

"It isn't safe to remain here. We will be much safer at our house. I have worked out a deal with our neighbor and we are going to form a survival team. They have heat and shelter; we have food and survival skills. Plus, due to our remoteness, it's unlikely that anyone will make the effort to harass us."

"What about Jory?"

I hesitated … this would be a very difficult decision for Emily and I wanted to phrase my words carefully. "We will leave him a note. Hopefully he is just delayed somewhere and will soon be here. The same goes for your brother. Graham is a long, long way away. It took us about 12 hours to drive to Sioux Falls when we moved him out there last year. That's something like 900 miles. He might decide to stay there, at least until summer. I hope both men are all right, but first and foremost, we need to look after ourselves."

Emily stood and looked around her home. She might never see this place again. Her first home. Where she and Jory started their lives. Where she raised her two children.

With tears streaming down her cheeks, she answered, "Okay. Let's pack up and go."

*****

We put all of Em's stable food in a pile. There was no way that three adults could carry it all, plus manage a baby and a three-year-old. Plus, there was the issue of the dogs. We really couldn't leave them here to starve, or worse, to eventually end up as someone's dinner.

I needed to find a wagon. An old Radio-Flyer would be perfect. We could easily pull both children and still manage to carry our food and other provisions.

"There's an antique store just a mile or so up the highway," Em said. "That would be a good place to look for a wagon."

So I grabbed my Sig and headed out into the world, alone. The streets were quiet. Scary quiet. I always thought that the apocalypse would be a noisier affair: Space invaders blasting humans with heat rays. Fire and brimstone falling from a rogue asteroid. Fire and rescue vehicles screaming by, hauling victims of some worse-than-Ebola virus to the hospital.

Yet the world I now inhabited seemed to be tiptoeing into oblivion. Where were the *Road Warrior* bad guys? Don't get me wrong —I was happy to walk towards the antique store unmolested by violence, but I *did* wonder where everyone was. Probably most people lacked warm clothing so they were hunkered down indoors. They wouldn't venture out until the air was warmer or their food ran out, whichever came first.

I walked north, staying out of sight as much as possible as I followed the state highway. Oh, I did see people here and there, but they were not at all interested in me. One woman, who seemed to be wearing nothing more than a poncho made out of a wool blanket, scampered from one building to another. Maybe she *was* afraid of me?

The day was cold but calm. The sky was full of dark clouds that seemed to be going nowhere. I longed to look at my smartphone to check the weather map. Life was so much easier when I could check the ten-day outlook!

It wasn't long before I reached the parking lot of the "Antique Mall." I'd driven by this place a zillion times but hadn't ever shopped there. The sign above the front façade proudly proclaimed "Over 35 Antiques Vendors!"

Trix said that there was an awesome tamale vendor inside, but the days of eating cheap tamales are long gone. The immensity of our situation was finally beginning to hit me. For the last few days I was in full survival mode – only worried about my immediate needs. Now, walking alone through this deserted, ugly as sin commercial district, I missed tamales and smartphones. I'd be lying if I said I wasn't looking forward to the challenge before me. Survival and self-reliance had always been part of my psyche. But it's one thing to dream of a grand "last man on earth" adventure; it's quite another thing to live through it.

Like most buildings I've seen, this one has already been looted. The front doors were locked, but I was able to cautiously crawl through broken glass and gain entry. Feeble light shined through the front window, and I wished I'd brought candles. I did have matches, and the odds were good that I'd find a candle here.

Moving as quietly as possible, I moved from the front hall and entered a dark labyrinth. Striking a match, I could see that I was in a large space that was divided by second and third hand cubicle dividers. I had a chuckle at the idea of cubicles. No one would ever again have to have to sit in a soul-sucking office cubicle, trading hours of life for a crummy paycheck. Cubicle dwellers and shitty bosses are now a thing of the past.

Striking another match, I searched for a candle. Ah, there's one! I picked up a glass container that proudly proclaimed "Harley-Davidson." Inside was a brand-new white candle. Now I had light and could actually see that there was still a lot of stuff in this place that might be useful. My only problem was that we really didn't have any way to transport anything.

I saw collections of knives, antique spoons, glassware, knick-knacks, sports memorabilia, and bins of record albums. I picked up the jacket to the Beach Boys "Pet Sounds" and pulled out the sleeve. The album was still intact, but at the time I didn't know why. Something to do with light?

I bent over to look at a bin of military medals – thinking that there might be something here of trade value – when I heard someone talking quietly in another room. With my Sig in my right hand and the candle in my left, I quietly walked around a rack of paperback books (which I reminded myself to look at later!) and went to see who was in the building with me. Shielding the candle with my hand, I peered around the corner and saw two people, who like me, were searching through the antiques. They didn't look dangerous, so I cautiously cleared my throat to get their attention.

They quickly spun around to face me, and I found myself staring at a shotgun.

To demonstrate that I wasn't threatening, I lowered the Sig and pointed it towards the ground.

"Easy," I said. "I'm not here to hurt anyone."

A man, dressed in jeans, boots, and heavy wool coat, looked me over and probably thought it would be wise to take me out right then and there. Fortunately, his companion, a young boy, probably 12 or 13 years old, put his hand on the shotgun and said, "Dad, lower the gun."

I took a deep breath as the gun was pointed away from me. "What do you want?"

"I'm looking for a wagon. I have two very small children that I need to haul about 35 miles."

The boy replied, "Hey, I saw a wagon when we were here the other day. Maybe it's still here."

I pocketed the Sig and the man relaxed. I reached out to shake the man's hand, "My name is Greg."

His grip was firm. From his build and demeanor, I figured he must work with his hands. This wasn't one of those cubicle dwellers I'd been thinking about just a few minutes ago.

"I'm John and this is Jack."

"Hi there, Jack." I smiled at the boy. "Do you live near here?"

John looked at me with suspicion. I realized that under the current situation, it wouldn't be wise to tell someone where you live. Where you stash your stuff.

The man didn't answer, but just then, Jack said, "Come this way. Let's see if the wagon is still here."

We followed the boy through a maze of antiques and collectibles. There were stacks of magazines, piles of books, collections of metal signs, stamps, lamps, tools, and everything else people sold in these places.

"It's still here!"

Jack stood before a slightly rusty red wagon. He held his candle so I could see it. Painted on the side was "Western Auto," which I remembered was a hardware store chain popular in my youth.

The wagon was full of magazines. I picked up the two stacks of Life and Redbook and set them on the floor. The wagon was in very good shape. I could see that a price tag was attached: $175.00.

"I wonder if the vendor will take an I.O.U.?" I joked."

I started to pull the wagon into the aisle, but Jack grabbed it and said, "Let me help."

He led the way while John and I followed. "That's quite a boy you've got there."

"Yes," John replied. "He's all I have left."

"Do you have a safe place to stay?"

"We're working on that. My old lady left us when he was a baby, so I thought we'd try to make it to my brother's place out in the country."

"Good. The country will be safer. Get yourself set up with a garden and a few animals and try to make it through next winter."

"Do you think that the whole world is this bad?" he asked.

"Actually," I replied, "I do. Think about it. We started having problems with plastic on Sunday. Today is only Wednesday and look at what remains."

"Shit. I was hoping that this would just be isolated to Michigan."

"There may still be places... islands? The South Pole? Where plastic is still intact. But it's my guess that this was caused by some sort of airborne plastic-eating virus."

"Virus?" He cringed. "Are we next?"

Trying to relive his concern, I replied, "I don't think so. What I believe happened is that some sort of lab experiment got out into the wild. Scientists have been working on ways to use biology to clean up oil spills. I think they made something that worked... worked too well. It got out and this is what we are left with."

We walked back past the rack full of paperbacks. "Hold on."

It was packed with science fiction. I saw *The Andromeda Strain, Lucifer's Hammer, War of the Worlds, I am Legend, The Stand, World War Z*. All books that I'd loved and had read many, many times.

"Ugh," I grunted. "I think I'll pass on these."

I left the Antiques Mall a half hour later, my pockets stuffed with things I thought I could use for trade: Military medals, old coins, wooden buttons, and a sewing kit. The Western Flyer rolled along behind me, carrying a selection of John Grisham legal thrillers and Bernard Cornwell historical novels. I also had a paper bag full of wool and cotton children's clothes ("Your grandkids will need these," Jack said as he handed me the bag).

Jack and John were now behind me, on their way to somewhere. Hopefully somewhere safe. Somewhere with a future.

Chapter 10

We pulled out of Em's place before noon. Declan and Cora sat upon a wool blanket as Trixie pulled them in the Western Auto wagon. Declan laughed and exclaimed, "We're going for a ride! This will be fun!"

We had one stop to make before leaving town.

I banged on Smitty's front door, but there was no response. I looked around the back of the house and found the old man tinkering with what I could only imagine was a homemade alarm system. He had strung a wire around wood stakes and hung metal cans from the wire.

"Smitty!" I called. "What are you doing?"

He looked up and immediately recognized me. "I thought you was gone!"

My family was standing behind me now, looking curiously at Smitty and his contraption. "We had some stuff to do before we could return," I explained. "This is my daughter, Emily, and her two children."

Both dogs yapped and pulled at their leather leashes, "Oh, and our vicious attack animals, Knox and Coco."

Smitty nodded, "Howdy. Glad to see you are okay."

"Uh," I asked with a bit of hesitation, "Did you manage to bury those guys?"

He nodded in the affirmative. "They are all taken care of. And your dog is buried over here."

He led us over to the side of his house, where a mound of fresh dirt covered our beloved Annie.

Trixie and I paused for a moment to reflect upon our love of this incredibly loyal and lovable yellow lab.

"Thank you. Have you had any other incidents since the other day?"

"Nope. It's been quiet. It's like everyone has given up. Either that or they expect help from the government."

"That's not going to happen."

"Agree. We've gotta take care of ourselves."

I pointed at his wire and can system. "What are you working on here?"

"Alarm. I'm gonna plant a garden. I imagine folks might get hungry eventually and try to steal my food. This should give me some warning."

I gave a can a slight kick with my boot and it rattled quite loud.

"Filled each can with pennies and nickels," he explained. "Don't need money for anything else."

"Good idea," I answered. "You know," I continued, "You should come with us."

He smiled and looked at the sky. "No, this is where I belong. I figure I've got a few good years left in this old body. I believe I'll stay put and see what happens here."

Trixie interjected, "You should reconsider. We will be safe at our place. We are out in the country where people won't be bothering us."

"Ma'am, I do appreciate the offer. I really do. But I've still got my 12 gage and enough shells to deter just about anyone."

"Do you have seeds for your garden?" I asked.

"Yes. I had quite a bit of carrot, lettuce, and string bean seeds left from last year's garden. I've got some spuds in the cellar that I can plant."

I stood quietly and looked at the ground. With nothing further to offer I reached out and shook the old man's hand. "Well then, this is goodbye."

Trixie reached out and handed him a piece of paper. "Here's our address if you decide you need to get away from here."

He nodded and I think I saw the hint of a tear in his eye. "Thank you, Ma'am. You are good people. I wish you the best."

We turned and walked away, leaving a good man alone in the north side of Lansing, Michigan.

I don't pray much, but I whispered a prayer for Smitty. "God, let this nice old man live the rest of his life in peace."

*****

At first the walk towards home was fun. The kids were content in their wagon and we were all happy to be together, working towards our collective survival. But remember when I said I wished that I could check the weather on my smartphone? What we didn't know was that Michigan was smack-dab in the middle of one of the biggest winter storms to hit our state in decades.

It started with sleet and freezing rain. At first it was no big deal. We were pelted by ice for a few minutes before huge, wet snowflakes began to fall. The temperature was still in the mid 30's, so we really weren't cold at all. Every now and then a gust of wind ripped at our clothes, but we pressed on, hoping to get at least half-way home before camping for the night.

We avoided the back roads on this return trip to our home, instead hiking right down the middle of the interstate. We continually dodged and walked around stranded, broken down vehicles, but otherwise made very good time. The snow began to fall harder, and before we'd walked another half mile there was almost two inches on the pavement.

"We need to find a place to shelter," I told everyone.

We crossed a bridge and looked at a commercial building that sat next to the highway.

"Let's go down there," Trix suggested.

I lifted the children and wagon over the guard rail and pulled the wagon over the bumpy ground between the federal highway and county road. The kids thought this was great fun, but the heavy falling snow didn't make it easy for me. When we were all safely on the service road we walked towards the building. It looked like it had been a gas station in a former life. Now it was an office for used car sales. I pulled the children to the side of the building, stopping next to the service bay-garage part of the operation.

This was not an ideal overnight spot for us — even if we could get in the building, there were houses nearby. It was possible that the car lot owner lived in one of those houses and wouldn't appreciate us breaking into his business. I looked at my grandchildren and sighed.

"Trix," I explained, "Stay here with Em and the kids while I check it out."

I found the back door. Heavy steel, locked.

Walking around to the other side of the building, I found a small window. Since the front of the building was mostly glass, any attempt to break in would be easily seen. This small window was my only hope. Unfortunately, it was up about a foot higher than my reach, so I had to find something to stand on. Looking around the car lot, I spotted a 30 gallon drum sitting near the rear of the garage. The heavy snow muffled the sound of the barrel as I rolled it across the parking lot.

I righted the barrel and climbed up on it. I could break the window easy enough and drop into the building. Then I hoped I'd be able to unlock a door and let everyone inside.

I pulled my knife, and just as I was about to strike the hilt against the glass I was startled by a strange voice.

"Now don't be breaking my window!"

I turned and looked down at an old woman, a hunting rifle resting in her arms. Trix, Em, and the kids were all standing behind her.

"You can stay at my place instead."

*****

Martha led us to her brick ranch and said, "Go on in and get those babies warmed up."

The snow was coming down now with unusual intensity for the month of March. In just a few minutes, another couple of inches had fallen. Everything was white and clean again, but this storm didn't promise renewal. Instead it promised that survival would be difficult and dangerous. It promised that food would be hard to find. It promised that those without fortitude and creativity would not survive until spring.

Fortunately, Martha's home was for now, a cozy sanctuary.

"I put in the wood stove about three years ago," she explained. "Propane was costing me an arm and a leg."

She was referring to two winters ago – when Michigan was hit by a massive Christmas ice storm that left many in the state without power for more than a week. Heavy use of generators pushed gasoline prices over $4.00 per gallon. Then, just after the ice storm, a polar vortex descended over the Great Lakes and the temperature stayed below 15 degrees for the month of January and part of February. Propane was rationed and in some cases, the price rose to over $5.00 per gallon.

"I still have a couple of cords of wood in the garage." She looked at me and smiled, "And you can help me split it!"

"No problem," I replied.

I introduced my family and asked her, "Are you here alone?"

She went over to the kitchen table and sat on an old wood chair. "Yes, my husband Fred passed last year."

"Sorry to hear that."

"I keep busy. The used car business was Fred's life work, but since his passing I've kept it running mostly by myself. Most days I don't seem to have enough time to get everything done. I work from 6 AM to 6 PM at the shop, I cut wood, and I belong to the ladies auxiliary at the hospital. Plus, I have two sons and five grandchildren."

"Oh, where are they?" I asked.

"One lives in Southfield, the other is in Kalamazoo. My youngest grandchild is 10."

"You are fortunate that your place didn't go up in flames a couple of days ago."

"Yes, I am! I heard explosions from across the highway, and one of my neighbors places went up in flames. It didn't take me long to figure out that the dissolving plastic was turning into gas and blowing everything to smithereens. I got the house opened up and stayed out in the dealership workshop for a couple of days until I thought it was safe to come back inside."

I looked at my two grandchildren and smiled. Declan and Cora sat on the floor in front of the wood stove and played with the dogs.

"So where are you headed in this awful storm?" she asked.

Trixie and I each found a chair and sat with her at the table. It felt good to be off our feet.

"We live just 20 miles west of here," Trixie answered. "Out in the country, between Owosso and Flint. Greg and I hiked over to Lansing and found Em and the kids. Em's husband, Jory, did not make it home from work. We hope he's on his way, and we left him a note telling him to come to our house."

Martha sighed, "I hope he makes it. Those kids need their daddy."

"He's in the Guard," I replied. "Just went through his basic training last year. But Jory is the sort of guy who will run head first into any emergency, so we think he's still down in Marshall helping the people there."

Martha stood and walked over to the pantry and brought out a couple of quart jars. "Are you hungry? How about homemade chicken-vegetable soup?"

*****

The storm lasted all night and well into the next day. Huge drifts of heavy, dense snow covered the driveways and roads. Warm and safe in Martha's home, we relaxed and passed the time playing checkers, dominoes, and cards. I taught Declan how to build a skyscraper with cards and dominoes. Trixie showed him how to set up the dominoes so that they could all be knocked down in sequence.

I chopped wood in the garage. It felt good to use my body and work my arm muscles. Normally I'd be out shoveling snow, clearing my driveway so we could get to work. Sometimes we'd wait for days for the plow to come down our road. Snowstorms are a way of life in Michigan.

While Martha had plenty of food in her pantry now, with the additional mouths to feed the food wouldn't last forever. I was anxious to get back out on the road, but until the snow melted, we weren't going anywhere.

Finally, after three days of waiting, the temperature warmed and the big meltdown started. It's not uncommon for snow to virtually disappear overnight around here, and by mid-afternoon, pavement began to appear from beneath the melting drifts.

"I think we will be able to hit the road tomorrow," I told the group as we played the thousandth game of "Go Fish."

"There's no need to rush out of here," Martha replied. "I've enjoyed your company."

"We are grateful for your kindness, Martha," Trixie added. "But we need to get back to our place so we can prepare for next winter."

"You are welcome to come with us," I offered.

"Thank you," she responded. "But I doubt these old legs could walk that far. I'll manage here on my own."

Just before darkness, I stood out in the backyard and marveled at the beautiful sunset. The sun slowly fell into a bank of clouds, setting off a brilliant array of orange and red color. As I watched darkness descend, three white-tailed deer crossed the field behind Martha's home. For a moment I considered getting the bow and arrows, for Martha could surely use the venison. But before I could turn and return into the house, the deer were gone, disappearing completely into the night.

*****

We were back on the road. Em pulled the children, Trixie carried the bow and I had a pack full of heavy, homemade canned food. Before leaving, Martha insisted on loading us up with as much soup as we could carry.

"But you need to eat too," I urged as she stuffed quart jars into my pack.

"Pfftttt," she replied. "Those babies need it more than I do. There will be hard times ahead. Take this food and eat it. But make damn sure that you do everything possible to prepare enough food to get you through next winter."

She followed us out onto the road and we said our goodbyes.

"You mind your mama," she told Declan. "Help out too as much as possible."

Declan looked up from the wagon and said, "Will you come with us Comma Martha?"

"No honey, I will stay at my house. But you can come back when it's warmer and visit me."

Fighting back tears, we each gave the sweet old girl a hug and turned silently and walked away.

We headed east, back towards our home. I couldn't help but wonder if we would be just as safe at Martha's house as we'd be at our home. She had heat, and there hadn't been any sign of unfriendly neighbors.

Still, we had a home and that's where I intended to make my stand. I turned and waved one last time as we crested a small hill and out of sight.

Chapter 11

The snow was mostly gone from the roads. We trudged on the wet surface, which was an odd dirt and rock amalgamation – what was left of the former pavement. The going was easy where the road was frozen, but in a few spots we struggled through a mucky mess. I lead my family towards the interstate, which was made from concrete. There the walking was much easier. We had about 15 miles to cover before we'd be home, which would take about seven hours, give or take.

It was hard to believe that there was no one else out on the road, trekking somewhere to find family or friends.

"What day is it?" I asked Trix.

"Gosh, let me think… we left for Lansing two days after the plastic melted… Sunday… and it took us two days to get there. We stayed there for two more days, but got stuck in the storm at Martha's house for three days. So what does that make today? Sunday?"

I shrugged. "I can't figure out why more people aren't traveling."

"I've wondered about that too. But every now and then I see someone walking around outdoors."

"Is it possible that the vast majority doesn't own any natural fiber clothing? Or are they just afraid?"

"Fear is probably a big part of it," she answered. "I bet most are expecting the government to get things running again."

"That's not likely," I replied. "It's been a week. Most people are going to run out of food, if they haven't already. I bet things will begin to turn ugly any day now."

We pressed onward, more vigilant now that we thought we had an idea about what our fellow man might be up to.

Rather than stopping for a long break, we each ate a Clif Bar while walking. Finally, we reached the last off-ramp before the one that lead towards our home.

"My feet are killing me," Emily announced. Her shoes were not optimum. She wore a pair of Jory's work boots, which were at least three sizes too large. Two pair of wool socks took up some of the space, but the fit was still very sloppy.

"Another mile and then we get off this highway," I replied, offering encouragement. "Then five more miles – which should take about 3 hours, and we'll be home."

Just ahead I spotted a Little Debbie delivery truck, stranded on the interstate.

"Well, will you look at that," I announced.

"Nutty Bars!" Trixie yelled. "Oatmeal Cream Pies!"

The truck sat near some other derelict vehicles. It appeared unmolested. Hopefully there were still some edible snack foods on board.

I approached the rear and found the door to be unlocked. I gave the heavy door a push and it slid open on rollers.

Stacked inside were Swiss Rolls, Zebra Cakes, Cloud Cakes (which are sorta like Twinkees), and Banana Pudding Rolls.

"Look," I exclaimed. "The four major food groups!"

Trixie grabbed a box of cakes and ripped open the top.

"Hey!" She exclaimed. "Still looks delicious!"

Without thinking we all grabbed our favorite snack cakes and crammed them into our mouths, laughing as we enjoyed the deliciously sweet carbohydrates.

"How about we just grab as many boxes as possible and get out of here," I suggested.

Suddenly, a loud BANG rattled my ears and something struck the side of the truck.

Without taking time to think, I grabbed Declan and ran. "Follow me," I yelled. We dodged between some cars and found a place to hide behind a massive tractor-trailer tire. Em, who had Cora in the wagon, crouched down behind a pickup truck. The dogs, which were not at all used to gunshots, cowered and shook with fear.

"Where's your mom?" I whispered.

"I thought she was behind me!"

I scrambled over towards Emily, dragging Declan behind. "You stay with your mom, Declan. I'm going to find Comma."

So far I had only heard the one shot. That meant that unless Trixie was hit by a ricochet, she must be unharmed.

Using as much stealth as possible, I worked my way around the deserted vehicles until I could see the rear of the Little Debbie truck.

Standing by the truck was Trixie. A hand gun was held to the back of her head by our forgotten adversary, Mr. Camo.

*****

"Well, well," Mr. Camo said loud enough for everyone to hear. "If it isn't the douchebag and his lovely wife."

So this was it: the consequences of leaving the asshole alive, when I could have easily killed him just a week ago. Because of my passiveness, Trixie was just one twitchy trigger finger away from death. I could not allow this to happen, but I did not expect Mr. Camo to cut us any slack. He would not be happy until he got his pound of flesh from me or Trixie.

I crawled back to where Em was hiding with Cora. "Mom and I ran into this guy on our second night out. He has a bone to pick with us."

"Why?" she asked.

"Because I stabbed him."

"Wow."

"And your mother knocked him out with a vodka bottle."

"Seriously?"

"Well, you can tell he's an asshole."

"So what do we do now?"

"I've gotta get where I can get a clean shot at him."

"But you could hit mom!"

I grimaced at the thought. "I'll try my hardest not to do that. I'll work my way to the right," I said, pointing towards a cluster of vehicles. "When I get in position I'll give you a whistle. You try to make some noise, but for God's sake, don't expose yourself!"

"Be careful, Dad!"

I nodded solemnly and crawled my way through the vehicles. I found a decent vantage point behind a Chevy Equinox SUV and carefully aligned my body so I'd have a decent shooting angle. All I needed was one lucky shot.

Mr. Camo stood about 30 feet away, still holding the gun to Trixie's head. If Trixie could just lean back a bit, or maybe crouch, I'd have a clean shot at his upper body.

"Hey douchebag! You still there?"

My mouth was very dry. I whistled as loudly as I could and waited for Emily to create a distraction. Instead, she emerged from behind a late-model Dodge Dart and yelled, "Over here!"

BANG! Mr. Camo's gun fired just once. I will always remember the moment. Everything really does happen in slow motion, just like in the movies. The only thing missing was an intense soundtrack.

Emily collapsed to the pavement. Trixie, suddenly pushed into Mama Bear mode, lunged at Mr. Camo and drove her fist into the very area where I'd stabbed him.

He screamed and brought the pistol up to Trixie's chest, and I don't know if he pulled the trigger or not but the gun never fired. Trixie instinctively dove to the ground, and with as much calmness as possible, I squeezed the trigger of the Sig and put a hunk of hot lead in middle of the motherfucker's chest.

"I should've done that a week ago," I said to myself, as I ran forward to check on Trixie.

"Kick his gun away!" I yelled.

A pool of blood was quickly forming around his body.

"No worries," she answered. "He's dead."

She picked up his pistol and looked in Emily's direction. "Oh nooooo!"

Emily sat with her back against the tire of a pickup truck. Her head was down and she was in tears as she looked directly into the face of Cora. Declan emerged from behind the truck and saw his mama and began to howl, "Mama! Mama! Mama!"

Trixie and I reached Emily at the same moment. "Emily! What's wrong?"

I thought for a moment that Cora had been struck by Mr. Camo's bullet. But it's more likely that Emily's motherly instinct took over and she took the bullet herself.

"I'll be okay," she whispered. "I think the bullet only grazed me."

"Greg," Trixie commanded, "Take the children away. I'll see what I can do here."

My body was shaking from fear, and I was probably in shock. But I shook off the terror and grabbed Cora and took Declan by the hand and led the children away.

I didn't want Declan to see the dead man on the ground, so I walked a few yards down the highway and sat down on the cold cement. "Come on Declan, let's rest for a little while."

With Cora in my arms, Declan sat and leaned his small body against me. "Is Comma going to fix Mama?"

I looked at the little guy and with all of the faith I'd ever possessed, replied, "Yes she is. Comma is a nurse. She will make your Mama all better."

We sat. My life with Emily ran through my head, and I replayed our best and worst times together. Summer softball, bicycle rides, swimming lessons, National Honor Society, driving, dating, college, and marriage. She had been a good daughter – not perfect – but she was certainly a better daughter to Trixie and me than we deserved. Most importantly, she had given us two delightful grandchildren. I did not expect grandchildren to be such a gift, but I found playing with Declan to be one of the joys of my life. Cora, who was still just an infant, would certainly grow to be my favorite. What Grandfather could resist the charms of his granddaughter?

"Greg?" I guess I had fallen into a trance and hadn't noticed that Trixie had walked over to where we were sitting.

"Emily is hurt pretty bad. I think we can get her on her feet. If she can make it to someplace warm and clean, she might have a chance."

"Where was she struck?"

"The bullet is lodged in her chest. It might have punctured her right lung. I do know that the lung is collapsed – but I've stopped the bleeding for now."

I wanted to bury my head and bawl my eyes out. But, using all of my remaining strength, I stood. I took Declan's hand and walked over to where his mother was resting.

The two dogs, leashed to the wagon, were strangely subdued. I don't know why they never barked during the entire ordeal. Or maybe they had, but I just didn't hear them.

I put the children in the wagon as Trixie helped Emily stand. "Come on, you can do it. We have to get you someplace where we can get you fixed up."

Grasping for breath, Emily said, "I just want to go home."

We loaded as much of our gear in the wagon with the kids and each put our arms around Emily. She walked very slowly, but this was one strong young woman. She fought against the pain and made herself move. The going was tough for all of us, as I also had to pull the children and dogs with my free arm.

Since we had returned home via the highway instead of back roads, we were about 8 miles south of our house. Finally, after about 30 minutes, we reached the off-ramp that would lead us towards home. We trudged up the ramp and stopped at the deserted intersection. To the right was Durand, a small city that had a satellite office for the county hospital.

"If we go right," I explained "In about a mile we'll reach the medical office."

"Can you make it, Emily?" Trixie asked.

Without enough breath to speak, Em nodded, "Yes."

Chapter 12

I banged loudly upon the front door of the medical office. "Help!" I yelled, "We need help!"

Emily lay upon the cement sidewalk, covered in the wool blanket that the kids had been sitting upon in their wagon. Trixie held Cora and one of Em's hands, Declan held the other.

I banged again, but received no response. I looked at Trixie. "I was hoping there might still be someone with medical training hanging out here."

"Can you get us inside the building?" Trixie asked. "Maybe there is something I can do."

Trixie was skilled in natural childbirth, basic life support, and first aid. As a midwife, she knew how to suture. But did she know how to re-inflate a lung?

I went back to the door and before I could yell again, a slight body appeared on the other side of the glass. Through the reflection I could see a very tired looking middle aged woman. She wore jeans and sweatshirt that looked three sizes too large.

"What do you need?" she yelled through the glass.

"Are you a doctor? My daughter has been shot in the chest!"

After a brief hesitation, the woman unlocked the door and emerged from the safety of the building.

She went over to Emily, where she took her pulse and looked at the patch-up job that Trixie had performed.

"When did this happen?"

"About two hours ago," I answered.

"She's in shock. But she's alive and that's saying something. Help me get her inside."

Trixie ushered the children inside the lobby first and sat them on the floor. Then the three of us carried an unconscious Emily into the building.

"Hold her here for a moment while I get a room ready."

After several minutes the woman came out and directed us to a procedure room. We put Emily on a table and watched our savior prepare to save our daughter.

"My name is Greg," I explained. "This is my wife, Trixie, who is a midwife."

She nodded and answered, "I am Miranda. I am a general practitioner."

"This is our daughter, Emily. Have you ever treated a gunshot wound?"

"Can't say that I have," she replied. "This will be the first time."

I looked at Trixie and sighed. It would take a miracle for Emily to survive.

"I think I'll go out and occupy the children while you two look after Emily."

Thanks to large windows, the lobby was well-lit. Declan was looking at "Go Dogs Go." Cora lay upon our wool blanket, asleep.

I sat next to Cora and leaned back against the cold wall. The last two hours had been pure adrenalin and now I was completely exhausted. I closed my eyes and allowed myself to sleep.

*****

Trixie shook me awake.

"How's Emily?" I asked as I rubbed my eyes.

Trixie picked up Cora and held her granddaughter close. "She's resting. Miranda is cleaning up. We need to find a way to get these kids fed."

"What's Cora going to eat? She can't nurse now, can she?"

"Not for a while. It may take a few days for Emily go be able to nurse."

I found my backpack and pulled out our cook stove and one of the jars of Martha's homemade soup. "How about a hot dinner?"

*****

"The good news was that the bullet did not puncture Emily's lung," Miranda explained. "But the lung collapsed and we had to find a way to get the air out from between the lung and chest cavity."

I grimaced. I'd never been overly interested in medical procedures.

"Fortunately, while I was living here over the last week, I took an inventory of medical supplies and found an assortment of glass syringes. I found a spot between Emily's ribs and inserted a hollow 20-gauge needle, which allowed the trapped air to escape."

"And her lung began to inflate?" I asked.

"Yes," she answered, "The air pressure equalized and her lung filled with air. Then I had to remove the bullet – which was fortunately lodged in rib cartilage. I don't know why the slug didn't go in deeper, but we can only thank God for that."

"What did you use for antiseptic?" I asked as I gave the jar of soup a stir.

"Since most of our alcohol is stored plastic bottles, I managed to save some in a few jars we had stored."

Trixie handed me four coffee mugs and I shared the soup equally among us. We were lucky to have metal spoons too, and we all dug into the first hot meal we'd had all day.

"Good soup, Coppa!"

"Thanks, Declan."

Miranda continued. "Fortunately, Emily did not lose a lot of blood. The bullet did not hit an artery. But we still have to worry about infection, so I administered broad-spectrum antibiotics."

I nodded in understanding, but then asked, "Aren't pills coated in some sort of plastic?"

"Yes. The pharmaceutical industry uses what are called 'Enteric' coatings. These coatings, which are polymers, are designed to dissolve in the stomach over a period of time. But I have Ampicillin, which aren't coated."

She added, "I have the medications stored in paper envelopes."

We all sat on the floor of the cold room and finished eating without further conversation. Trixie left Cora with me and went to check on Em, and then came back out into the lobby and exclaimed, "She's awake and wants to see the children."

I handed Cora to Trixie and took Declan's hand. "Come on little buddy, your mama wants to see you."

Emily looked exhausted, but her face looked up as Trixie carefully lay Cora on the side of her chest that was not injured. I pulled over a chair for Declan to stand upon.

"Hi Mama! Are you going to be okay now?"

With a gentle laugh, she reached her son and rubbed him on the back of his head. "Yes baby, I am going to be okay."

*****

Emily fell back asleep so we all went back to the waiting room.

"Miranda," I began. "Thanks so much for your help."

She looked me in the eyes and nodded. "You're welcome."

"Now I wonder what to do next. We're going to have to stay here until Emily regains her strength."

"I don't have enough food for all of us," she replied.

"We don't expect you to feed us," I responded. "We will share what we have with you. I will have to go out and forage for more food. It's going to be difficult."

Trixie held Cora, who was fussy. "I've got to find a way to feed this baby. But maybe you can get us some meat. There should be rabbit or deer around here."

"I'll try. But we will also need plenty of water."

"I have something that might help," Miranda said. "Follow me."

She led us down a hallway and opened a store room. Stacked upon the floor were several cases of Enfamil baby formula.

I opened a box and pulled out a can of formula. "No plastic!"

"I've also got glass bottles and rubber nipples," Miranda added. "We use them for our new mama training."

Miranda led us to the building's small kitchen, where we found a can opener and prepared a bottle of formula for Cora. Since this was the first time the infant had had anything other than breast milk, it took Trixie quite a long time to get the baby to suck on the nipple and swallow the formula.

"There she goes," Trixie sighed with relief. "Drink, little one. You need this!"

"I am nearly out of water here," Miranda said, pointing at several glass mugs that still contained drinking water. "I started with two full water coolers. I was working late last Sunday, working on updating my patient notes on my computer when I noticed that something weird was happening to plastic. Early in the afternoon, one of the water coolers sprung a leak, but I didn't notice it until it was almost too late. I managed to save a few gallons from that tank, but fortunately, there was another full five-gallon tank in the kitchen that was still intact. I dumped as much of it as I could in the sink and in every glass container I could find in the building. I found a metal trash can – it was not too disgusting – and dumped the remainder of the water in there. Fortunately, the can doesn't leak but I'm not going to drink that water until it's my last resort. Just when I thought things couldn't get worse, we lost power."

I asked, "What have you been eating?"

"Whatever I could scrounge up. For the first few days I ate leftovers from the fridge. We also had a few boxes of granola bars in the cupboard. I really didn't expect to stay here, all alone, for this long. I thought about walking home, which is about 35 miles away, but without warm clothes I decided I was better off here for a little while."

"Don't you have anyone at home that will be worried about you?" I asked.

"Not anymore." She looked down at the floor, failing to hide her sadness. "Divorced."

"Well," I responded, "From our perspective, we are glad you stayed. And we are happy to share our food with you."

"Thanks. Your soup was the first hot meal I've had since last Sunday."

As we talked, the room dimmed as darkness began to descend. Trixie handed the baby to Miranda, then lit candles and left the room to check on Emily.

Returning to the room, she said, "Em's doing okay. She's still asleep and her breathing sounds good."

I stood and gave Trixie a hug. "We need to make ourselves a place to sleep. Tomorrow I will go out and get us water and whatever food I can find."

*****

True to form, the Michigan weather took a 180 degree swing. A thunderstorm passed overhead during the night. I ran outside to see if I could collect rainwater, but unfortunately, all we got was wind and lightning. But the temperature had climbed up into the sixties, which was a pleasant respite for the colder weather we'd been enduring.

I told the women that I was going to go find us some water. I had our canteen, some quart jars, and a couple of metal water bottles (bearing the logo "Fifth Third Bank") that I'd found in one of the Doctor's offices.

I walked towards the center of town, where there was a huge water tower. Certainly someone had figured out a way to tap it.

For the first time in a week I saw a few people milling about. One man sat on the sidewalk, his head between his knees, apparently sleeping. A pair of teenage girls sat upon the wooden steps of their porch and watched me walk past.

I stopped and asked the girls, "How are you getting along?"

They both had the look of hunger in their eyes. I guessed they were sisters, because they both had similar dirty-blond hair and blue eyes.

The one on the right, who looked a year or two older than the other girl, replied, "We want this to be over."

"What have you been doing for food and water?"

"My dad rationed what food we had. But we ran out yesterday. He's out somewhere now, seeing if he can find more food."

I nodded. "I hope your dad can find you something." The truth was, there would probably be very little food left in stores. Going forward for the next few weeks, the only real choice was to hunt.

"What about water?" I asked.

"We brought snow inside and waited for it to melt. You might be able to get some at the tower. They've set up a system where everyone can fill their bottles once per day."

If I'd had any food to share with the girls, I would have given it to them. But I nodded my thanks and walked on towards the tower. I passed a block of burned homes, and then another block of intact commercial buildings. The city streets were nothing but burned-out rubble.

At the water tower, there was a queue of about 50 people waiting to fill an assortment of non-plastic vessels. Some carried pans, others large glass jars. One man had a wooden cask, like the sort you make wine or beer in.

The folks here were eerily quiet. They were starving.

As I moved up in the queue, I could see that someone had used a ladder to reach a relief valve on the side of the tank. This valve, which was at least 30 feet above the ground, poured water through an improvised sluice made from an aluminum rain gutter. A man on the ladder controlled the valve, turning it off and on so that there would be very little water wasted.

Another man stood nearby. He carried a shotgun, and I suppose he was there for security should anyone try to take more water than they were allowed.

I had to give credit to the people of this town. It seemed like they were working together peacefully. Someone had solved the water problem and they were all sharing equally.

The man with the shotgun approached. "You there, with the canteen. I don't recognize you."

It was clear that he was speaking to me, and I hoped that being an outsider wouldn't get me excluded from the water – or worse.

"I live just a few miles north. I did a lot of business here. Before..."

The man, who appeared to be in his late 40's, wore jeans and a cotton t-shirt that had a faded logo from the band "Kiss" on the front. He wore his hair long, but it was tied back in a ponytail.

"You been out in the world? What's it like between here and your house?"

"Actually," I replied, "I've been to Lansing and back during the last week."

"Do you think there is any food between here and Lansing? Is anyone working to get some sort of authority up and running?"

At that moment I realized that people would be craving information what was happening in neighboring cities and towns. For now, all they had to go on was news from travelers like me. Eventually, someone would set up some sort of pony express system or maybe even get some wire communications working. A week ago we all had broadband Internet. Tomorrow we'll be lucky to have a telegraph system.

"I imagine that all of the stores have been looted by now," I answered. "But the looting only lasted a few days. We saw very few people on our hike back from Lansing."

"That snow storm was insane," he replied. "I'll bet it made things real difficult for a lot of folks."

The woman standing in front of me, who had until now had been silent, began to cry.

"I have family in Battle Creek," she blubbered. "Do you think they are okay?"

"They should be fine," I said, hoping to reassure her. "There is plenty of water, and everyone should be able to make their food last a couple of weeks."

Ponytail Man nodded. "Then things will get tough."

Eventually I worked my way to the front of the line. I filled my odd variety of water vessels, and walked back to Ponytail Man. "Thanks for the water."

"Take care now," he replied. "Good luck."

As I walked back to the medical clinic, I reflected on what I was witnessing. Here was a small working-class town. People here never had much, even in good times. But they had found a way to survive without resorting to brutality. There were no police keeping order.

The National Guard wasn't arresting people and putting them in cages. Post-apocalyptic anarchy hadn't broken across Middle America.

I knew that with starvation things would change. In just another week, hunger would force people to do unspeakable things.

*****

Our food was beginning to run out. Trixie and I were each eating less than 1000 calories daily, when we should be eating 2500. It was time to move out, whether Emily was ready or not. We still had food stashed at our house, which would require us to hike about five miles north of our present location.

Trixie and Miranda had encouraged Emily to walk just one day after the lung-reinflation. By day three she was moving around without too much difficulty.

It was evening, and everyone was resting on the floor of the waiting room. "I think we should strike for home tomorrow," I announced.

Trixie and Emily nodded in agreement.

"Miranda," I continued. "We would like you to come with us."

She took a deep breath and sighed. "I really don't see that I have a choice. There's nothing left here to eat and there's no one at home to worry about."

The next morning we all stood outside with our hands in our pockets, trying to stay warm on a brisk, clear morning. The children were back in the wagon, but sharing the space was a bundle of medical supplies. Miranda scrounged every sort of thing she could find that was stable in a post-plastic world. Bandages, syringes, needles, antibiotics, pain killers, scissors, tweezers, cotton balls, a stethoscope, and an assortment of prescription samples. She had separated all of the various pills into piles and wrapped them in paper, which she labeled with a pencil.

The only thing Miranda lacked was a decent pair of shoes, so I had awoken early and went into the village to see what I could scrounge. Fortunately, I was able to liberate a pair of boy's leather dress shoes, sans laces, that should fit her smallish feet ("A size five or six in woman's or four or five in boys will work!") from a Goodwill resale store. I found the shoes in the back in a pile of inbound donations – they hadn't made it to the inside of the retail area yet, where nearly everything useful had already been pilfered.

I looked at Em and announced, "You set the pace."

Without fanfare, Emily led our small group of survivors towards home.

Chapter 13

Our feet crunched on the stones that remained on the road surface. Emily trudged onward, with Miranda at her side for support if it was needed. Trixie and I took turns pulling the wagon, where Declan did a good job keeping our medical supplies and his little sister from falling out of the wagon. The little guy clearly did not understand the gravity of our situation. For him this was a grand adventure.

We walked past the smoldering remains of a farm. Everything here was gone. All that remained were the metal skeletons of various grain storage systems. Smoke drifted skyward, indicating a slight breeze from the northeast.

"Wow," Trixie said quietly, not wanting to scare the children. "There's nothing left."

We walked by and didn't stop to look around. There was no point. Most farms in the region produced soybeans, seed-corn, and wheat. There would be precious little livestock for us to salvage.

We plodded onward, and after a few moments, reached the final crossroad before reaching our own road.

"Two more miles!" I exclaimed.

We passed a cluster of intact ranch homes, each built on one or two acre lots. An old farmhouse on the right had burned to the ground. There were still no people outside. The snow had melted from the fields, revealing acres and acres of wet ground that might never be farmed again.

Even though the day had begun with bright sunshine, a gray overcast sky loomed in the west.

Finally, we reached our road.

"The home stretch!" Trixie announced.

Emily, excited to be finally done with this long walk, picked up the pace. We passed two more houses, but neither revealed any human or animal activity. Just ahead was the Foster's, and finally, our old farmhouse.

We stopped in the road in front of the Fosters. "Hello!" I yelled. "It's Greg!"

A curtain moved in the front window. My small party of travelers waited patiently for Connie or one of her two children to recognize us.

Eventually a small, person cautiously emerged from the house. With eyes were surrounded by dark circles and hair that looked as if it hadn't been combed in a month, Connie looked us over one by one.

"Greg? Trixie? Is that you?"

She left the house and ran out to us. Trixie and I covered her in an embrace, tears streaming down each of our dirty, tired faces.

"We're here," Trixie said. "We made it back."

Connie stepped back and looked at our group, one-by-one.

"You've got some new people with you!"

As Trixie made the introductions, Hailey and Josh emerged from the house and joined our impromptu celebration.

Just then we were shaken from our revelry as lightning struck nearby, quickly followed by a massive boom of thunder.

"Let's get everyone inside," Connie shouted, "Before we get soaked!"

*****

"Where's your dog?" I asked.

"No idea! We haven't seen her for a few days."

"That sucks," I replied. "We lost our Annie too."

Connie directed everyone to her basement. We followed her down into the finished recreation room.

I took Connie aside and gave her a very brief retelling of our ordeal to find Emily and the kids, leaving out the bit about DeAndre' and his gang. I did explain that Emily had been hit by a "random bullet." The woman was showing considerable signs of stress and I didn't want to pile more fear upon her.

She led us around a corner, where blankets, books, and odd non-plastic toys were scattered. "It's been comfortable down here," she explained, so this is where we've been living." She pointed at a fireplace, which held a pile of hot coals. "We had plenty of wood stored. Mike uses it..."

She stopped mid-sentence and choked back her emotions. "Mike still isn't back."

"It's good that you stayed warm," I replied. "That was one hell of a winter storm we endured a few days ago."

"We got walloped! The kids and I rode it out down here. Other than going outside for wood and, uh, the call of nature, we've just been hunkering down inside this basement. God, I could use a bath! I must look a mess!"

She ran her fingers through her dark hair, cringed, and announced to everyone in the room, "This is the longest I've EVER gone without washing my hair!"

All of the women laughed, and Trixie looked at me and said, "Greg will figure out a way for us to get cleaned up."

"I will?"

Another loud crash of thunder shook the house.

"You can wait until after the storm passes," was her reply.

*****

I am not a meteorologist. But I *have* lived in Michigan for my entire life, and the storm that hit us was like nothing we'd ever experienced. The first flashes of lightning and rumbles of thunder were just a minor opening act. They were the band you'd never remember that opened for U2 or The Stones.

No, the real storm was epic in a way that left each of us utterly terrified. I don't think any of us had ever been really scared before — even with everything that had happened and all that we'd lost over the last week or so. This storm ripped trees from the ground, leveled homes, and demolished what little shelter people still possessed.

We felt reasonably safe in Connie's basement. The crack of lightning was subdued by the 8 feet of earth which surrounded our underground shelter. There was very little to see out the small basement windows – just torrents of raging rain, branches, and other flying debris.

"The wind must be blowing over 100 miles-per-hour," I said quietly to the adults, hoping that the children, who were playing with old wooden dominoes in the far corner, would not be able to hear us. Suddenly, a massive CRACK! BANG! SMASH! Something fell against the house. "I think a tree or branch just landed on the roof."

The storm raged and we called all of the children over to the west wall, where they would have the most protection. Connie passed out blankets, and I sat on the cement floor with Declan snug between my legs. Emily held Cora. Trixie sat quietly beside me, but next to her was Miranda, with her face buried in her hands, sobbing.

"I can't take this!" she cried. "I just can't take this!"

Trixie put her arm around the frightened woman, held her tight and looked me in the eyes and shook her head, as if trying to tell me that there was nothing she could do.

I understood. There was nothing any of us could do except hope that we wouldn't be killed by the fury of nature.

The storm raged for hours, and despite the noise, everyone but Trixie and I eventually slept. I watched the corner of the basement where a sump-pump would keep out water. Without power, I fully expected the underground crock to overflow and spill over the basement floor.

Even I must have dozed at some point, because I shook myself awake sometime in the middle of the night. As I'd suspected, the floor was wet. Water was creeping towards us at a fairly fast rate. A candle burned quietly upon a distant table. I stood and walked over to the basement stairs. I climbed the stairs and pushed against the door that led to the kitchen.

It was jammed. Something that fell upon the house must have fallen through the roof and was now blocking the door. I gave another push, but the door did not budge.

From the top of the stairway, I reluctantly made an announcement to my gathering of sleeping survivors: "Guys, we've got a problem!"

Emily was the first to rise. "What's wrong, Dad?"

"Water is coming into the basement from somewhere."

"Uh oh."'

"That's not all. The door is jammed. We are sort of stuck down here."

By now the entire crew had awoken. Strike that. Miranda was either ignoring me or she was really deep asleep.

Connie pointed at a window. "We might be able to climb out."

I looked at the window and nodded my head in agreement. "Maybe. It will be a tight fit."

"Greg," Trixie said with an urgent tone. "The water is coming in faster."

Sure enough, where there had only been ¼ inch of water in the corner, an inch or so of water had reached the center of the room.

I told the group, "Just to be safe, everyone, please go stand on the stairway."

I turned to the window and looked it over carefully. It was the type of basement window that hinged at the top and pushed out from the bottom.

"Good thing we've all been dieting," I muttered as I unlatched the window and gave the bottom a push. The old wood, paint, and moisture all colluded to resist my effort. I gave the frame a couple of really hard knocks with my fist and then shoved with all of my strength. Whoosh! It opened and I immediately felt the wet, cool morning air against my arms and face. I could also hear the heavy rain pouring from the sky. I pushed a metal folding chair over so I could attempt to climb out.

"Let me try!" It was Josh. "I can go out and see what's blocking the basement door."

I nodded in agreement. I would need to trust this boy if we had a chance for survival. After all, he and I were the only "men" in a room full of women and children.

I gave him a boost. "See if you can move whatever is in front of the door. If that doesn't work, report back to me."

"Sure thing!"

He disappeared from sight in a flash. I sloshed across the floor – water was now up to my ankles – and squeezed past everyone as I walked up the basement stairs. I put my ear to the door and listened. I heard a CRASH and a BANG or two, and then silence.

"Josh!" I called through the door. "Are you all right?"

There was more silence. I listened carefully, and then heard a loud grunt, followed by another CRASH.

The door knob turned and the door opened just enough for Josh to poke his head in.

"There is a huge tree branch in the way. I pulled it away as much as I could."

"Do you think you could cut it with a saw?"

"Well," he replied. "I could, except that the garage is gone."

"What do you mean, 'gone'?"

"It must have blew away in the storm. You should see it out here. It's a mess!"

I heard a woman's voice speak from the bottom of the stairs. "I'll help."

I hadn't noticed that Miranda had joined everyone on the stairs. "My blanket was getting wet anyway," she explained.

She sloshed through the water, which was now knee deep, and climbed onto the chair and squeezed through the narrow window opening.

"I'll see what I can do to help Josh," she said as she disappeared.

"Hurry, it's getting wet in here!"

I went back to the top of the stairs to listen.

There was more banging, some scraping sounds, and finally, a large CRASH.

The door opened another foot, and I squeezed out between the door frame and some large tree limbs.

"We used leverage." She held a good sized 2 x 4, which she'd used to pry the branches away from the door.

I looked out into a clearing morning sky at a barren landscape. Nearly all of the trees were uprooted. As far as I could see, nearly every tree was down. It was a sight that I will never forget.

The roof and three walls were completely gone from the house. Oddly, the kitchen appliances all remained intact and in place where they belonged.

Trixie emerged next to me. "What about our house? Is it gone too?"

*****

The landscape had been utterly destroyed by the winds. Trees had toppled from their roots. Other trees had lost their tops, sheared by the wind. Unplanted fields had turned into lakes. Every low spot contained massive puddles. Thankfully, the rain had stopped before causing a full-blown flood.

Debris from houses also littered the property. Trixie and I ran quickly towards our house, using the road since it had remained relatively clear. We couldn't see our house at all – there was a huge pile of downed trees completely blocking our view.

"Do you see anything?" Trixie frantically asked.

I squinted and tried to peer through the branches. "Maybe..."

I grabbed her arm and we ran around to the far side of our property. A row of white pine trees still stood – bent and surely damaged, but they hadn't been unrooted. A large empty place remained where our garage used to stand. The grainery, where Trix and I had spent the evening waiting for methane to clear from our house, was also gone. A massive catalpa tree lay against the side of our house, branches poking through the roof and into our second-floor master bedroom. Had we been up there sleeping, we might have been killed.

We stood, hand-in-hand, our jaws open.

Call it a testimony to the strength of 110-year-old lumber and forgotten building techniques, but our house was still standing. Windows were shattered, part of roof was missing, and it would take hours to remove the debris from the yard. But we would have shelter, at least for the short term. We could make it work.

*****

Emily and Declan joined us and assisted with the clean-up. Miranda, who had found an old cloth camp chair, sat with little Cora.

We recovered my bicycle from under a pile of shingles. It was banged up but still rideable. We tromped through the saturated yard and piled up all of the salvageable lumber so it could be re-used where possible. Trixie recovered our stash of food, which had been hidden inside the house, and for the first time in two days we had full stomachs.

We sat upon large tree branch and ate. Between mouthfuls of blueberry Clif bar, Trixie pointed up at our bedroom and asked, "Where are we going to sleep?"

I'd been wondering the same thing myself. "Downstairs, I guess. We need to be someplace safe in case we get another epic storm."

"We can all sleep in the dining room."

"Okay. Let's hope that the rain doesn't leak through down there. The roof is a mess."

Emily, who had been listening, asked, "What about heat? What about cooking?"

I had an idea. I rose and continued chewing my Clif bar as I sloshed through a puddle and walked towards our propane tank, which we used for heating fuel for our furnace and hot water heater. I lifted the cover from the regulator and found that the tank was about 65% full. All I had to do was find our propane grill in the wreckage, cobble together some fittings, and then we could cook, boil water, and even heat a small room.

By noon it was getting hot outside. Correction: hot *and* steamy. At first I just thought it was typically variable weather for March in Michigan, but as I worked to move broken branches and tree limbs, I began to wonder if something else was going on.

I had no reason to believe that the plastipocalypse was just a local phenomenon. If it were just confined to Michigan or even the Great Lakes region, there would be some sort of rescue and recovery staged by the federal government. We hadn't seen a single airplane or helicopter. Not one. We had to be experiencing a global catastrophe. I hypothesized that the atmosphere was now full of vaporized polymers – in the form of methane. What happens to the climate when billions of cubic tons of methane is released into the sky over just a few days? My best guess was that we would experience unprecedented global warming. Methane, which is a greenhouse gas, would trap heat in the atmosphere. We had seen evidence that warming had created "superstorms" in our recent past. Was the storm we endured last night a "superstorm?" It was certainly unlike anything I'd ever experienced. What was odd was that it was a straight-line wind. As far as I could tell, there had not been tornados. Yet.

As I worked, I also wondered about nuclear power plant meltdowns. I did not know exactly where the nuclear power plants were in Michigan, but I was pretty sure there was one on the south side of Detroit. Surely, the plants would fail eventually, and then what? Were we in danger of nuclear fallout?

I shook my head and decided that I already had enough to worry about. I'd fix what I could and worry about the other stuff later.

I returned to the Foster home (basement now!) and found Connie and the kids hard at work clearing debris from what used to be the kitchen.

"Connie," I said. "You should give up and come over to our place."

She looked over the mess with teary eyes. I could tell she was just about to let loose with a good cry. Hell, I was close to losing it myself.

"Seriously, we still have part of a house left. We can make it work, at least until we come up with something better."

With a look of resignation, she yelled across the yard at Josh and Hailey, who were standing in the middle of a huge puddle, splashing each other.

"Josh! Hailey! Let's see what we can salvage. Then we'll take it next door to Mr. and Mrs. Bowman's. We will be sleeping there tonight."

She sniffed and dried her eyes. "Thanks. We'll be over shortly."

My first priority though was to find our propane grill. I walked the border of our property, staying on dry ground as much as possible. God I was tired. Yet I had to press on.

"That's the ol' pioneer spirit," I said to myself, as I stepped over and around pieces of aluminum garage door. I flipped over the door and found what I was looking for – the grill. It was lying on its side, and the small propane canister was still attached to the hose. I pulled the grill from the pile of rubble and gave it a quick once-over.

"Looks good to me," I muttered.

I wheeled the grill over to the corner of the house and looked at the main gas line connection. Underground copper tubing was connected to some sort of regulator, which entered the house via a ½" diameter galvanized pipe. The pipe ran into the basement, and was connected directly to our furnace. I needed to find enough plumbing parts to connect the propane tank to our grill – which I hoped to place inside the dining room. We'd need to keep a window cracked; otherwise we could suffocate from carbon monoxide poisoning. Sure, the house was now drafty as hell, but I planned on getting it buttoned up tight again as soon as possible.

After rummaging through more rubble, I found a roll of metal-reinforced flexible rubber hose that would work perfectly. I looked it over closely – it was intact and did not appear to be affected by the plastipocalypse. I didn't recall ever buying the hose – it might have blown onto our property from a neighbor's house.

"Finders keepers," I said to no one in particular.

Hailey and Josh approached with a bucket full of salvaged items.

Both kids, bursting with excitement, tried to speak at the same time, but Hailey, who was the elder of the two, overpowered her brother. "Mr. Bowman, I mean, Uncle Greg! We found some good stuff!"

She held up the old metal bucket, which contained an old wooden hammer, a small "C" clamp, a hacksaw (missing a handle, which must have evaporated), a box of assorted nails, a metal carpenter's square, and a chisel (also missing a handle).

Josh stepped forward and showed me his treasure. "I found an axe!"

What I needed wasn't in the bucket.

"Guys," I explained. "I need a pair of pliers or an adjustable wrench. Do you think you can find me either of those?"

They looked at each other and shook their heads in agreement. "We'll keep looking, Uncle Greg!"

They took off again, so I went inside the house to see what I could do about our living arrangements.

The windows on the west side of the house were broken. I would have to find a way to cover these with wood or cardboard, anything to keep out the wind, bugs, and birds. Our old house still had working pocket doors that separated the living room and a small office from the dining room. We could open or close those doors as needed.

We had very little usable furniture. Our couch was nothing but a wooden frame and springs. We had some nice wooden tables that would be useful, and a leather recliner and another wood and leather rocking chair.

Trixie entered the room. "Oh, you had the same idea as me. I wanted to see where we would put everyone."

I looked at our large dining room table and the four oak chairs that we'd purchased together as a set when we first moved into the house, more than 30 years earlier.

I said, "I think we should keep the table as is."

"I agree," she replied. "We can move the other two chairs in here as well. We'll have to sleep on blankets."

"Let me guess. All of our mattresses were made from synthetic materials?"

"Yes. But thank God, we have enough down-filled pillows for everyone."

"I haven't had a comfortable night's sleep since this whole thing began."

She nodded in agreement and grimaced. "Me neither. My shoulders and hips are killing me from sleeping on the floor."

I told Trix about my propane stove idea. "I'm still looking for parts, but what I need most is a good set of wrenches. Or even a decent pair of pliers.

"I'll keep my eyes open," she replied, and then she headed outside to resume the clean-up.

At this point I was feeling that things had really spiraled out of control. It wasn't bad enough that we'd lost the use of almost all 20th and 21st century technology, but because of the storm we had to deal with the loss of what few comforts that still existed.

I decided to check out our basement, just to see if there was anything down there we could use.

I walked down the creaky steps and looked into the darkness. I had never liked it down there. The ceilings were low and I was always banging my head on plumbing. A gazillion spiders lived in the stone foundation and under the floor beams. I don't mind spiders, but I don't enjoy crawling through spider webs. We had thoroughly cleaned out the space a few years back, so I didn't expect to find much of value.

Cautiously, I descended the stairway. Somewhere near the bottom I stepped into cold water. I went down two more steps and reached the cement floor. I was standing in water up to my knees.

"Great. This is just great." I ran my hand against the wall as I moved forward in the darkness. As my eyes adjusted, I realized that there was faint light entering through the small, filthy windows. The basement was separated by stone walls into three areas. The first area held the hot water heater and our canned tomato soup and fruit, which we had already eaten. I entered the larger middle room, which housed our furnace. I ran my hand against the cold gas supply pipe. It was firmly connected to the furnace, but if I could find a wrench I could redirect the pipe towards our dining room. Then I could connect one end of the hose I'd found to the pipe and the other end to the grill, assuming I could find a hole in the floor large enough for the hose to fit through. I continued into the rear of the basement. The water was deepest here, well over my knees. I knew from past experience that water in this old home ran out through a tile that went all of the way to the other side of the road, where the water would dump into the ditch. Unlike modern homes, ours had no sump pump.

In the past, the basement only flooded when the culvert under the road was frozen solid. I figured that it was possible that there was still ice in the culvert, or more likely, there was just too much water in the ditch. A dry spell would be welcome, but if it did rain more over the next few days, the water would eventually pour out of our basement windows.

I ran my hand across an old work table, and to my delight I felt the cool metal of a pipe wrench. "Bingo!" I yelled in joy.

With the wrench in my left hand, I continued feeling along the table to see if there was anything else I could salvage. To my utter surprise, I felt the familiar shape of a screwdriver. A screwdriver with a *plastic* handle! How could that be? Unable to come up with an answer, I continued feeling my way across the table. I felt a strange shape – it turned out to be a discarded container for cross-country ski wax. Also made from plastic! I put the screwdriver and plastic container in my pocket.

Excited, I worked my way back across the basement and headed back upstairs. I walked outside and found Trix and Emily, who were putting broken tree branches in a pile.

"Hey guys, look what I found."

I pulled out the plastic box and held it flat on the palm of my hand.

Both women looked at it in confusion.

"Isn't that plastic?" Emily asked.

"Yup." I turned the box over in my hands and inspected it carefully. It looked perfectly normal. "Maybe it's a special kind of plastic?"

Trixie added her opinion. "Maybe whatever was dissolving plastic ran its course."

"But why did this plastic survive?" I asked. "Oh, and I found this!"

I pulled out the screwdriver and showed it to them.

"It has a plastic handle!" They said, almost in unison.

For the first time in over a week something positive had happened. We all felt much happier. For a moment we thought that the worse was over.

I gave the plastic box a squeeze and to my utter disappointment, the sides flexed and my thumb pressed right through the side.

"Shit!" I exclaimed. "It's failing."

Absentmindedly, I put the screwdriver back in my pocket and sat down on a downed tree so I could think. Fact: The plastic from the basement was in fine shape until I brought it outside. Did the problem have something to do with air? Another fact: the plastic stuff in the house had also failed. It took a little longer, but it did fail. So what was different about the basement?

I could feel the answer forming in my head. I put my hand in my pocket and felt the screwdriver handle. It still felt solid.

I looked up at the women. "The answer is light."

Chapter 14

It turned out that the problem was *visible* light. Any plastic, polycarbonate, or synthetic polymer that was exposed to light would eventually evaporate. But there was some good news in this discovery. It would be possible for us to recover items that had been stored in warehouses, basements, and other dark buildings. As an experiment, I wrapped the screwdriver handle in a rag and set it in the hot sun. An hour later it was still perfect.

As darkness fell we all gathered together in the dining room to discuss the events of the day. Declan sat upon the floor playing with a wooden Thomas the Tank Engine train. Emily nursed Cora.

Our food supply was running out – we each had an energy bar and a can of warm diet Coke. I told everyone about my discovery – that light was responsible for dissolving plastic.

"We will be scavenging dark places for the next few days, seeing what we can find."

"We need more food," Trixie added. "What you have in front of you is all we have left."

Emily spoke up. "What about wild game? Surely there are still deer and rabbits in the area."

I nodded in agreement. "There should be. But with all of the flooding, even if we do manage to shoot something, it might be difficult to get it home."

Connie asked, "What's the status of your stove project?"

"I have most of what I need. Hopefully tomorrow I'll be able to get everything connected."

Trixie turned to Connie and asked, "Do you know how to process wild game?"

"Not really. That was always Mike's thing. But I did watch him a few times, so maybe I can figure it out."

We decided to form teams. Josh and I would be on the scavenger/hunting team. Emily and Trixie would work on local cleanup and restoration of the house. Connie and Hailey were in charge of food preparation. Miranda would provide medical services and watch over the two children, Declan and Cora.

"One more thing," I added. "Trixie and I have a cache of vegetable seeds. We will all work towards getting a garden planted as soon as the ground is ready. Our survival depends on this."

Darkness fell inside the dining room. Trixie lit a candle and we all laid down to rest, with no padding on the hard floor other than a few wool blankets.

"What we really need," Trixie said as she lay upon her back on the floor, "Is to figure out how to make comfortable bedding!"

*****

I doubt that the temperature dropped much lower than 80 degrees Fahrenheit that night. And the wind! I went outside once during the night for a call of nature and was hit by what felt like a blast-furnace. I looked up and saw stars poking through breaks in the clouds. Looking southwest, I was temporarily blinded by the most brilliant flash I'd ever witnessed. The entire sky lit up. I listened for a moment for the sound, and sure enough, a low rumble reached my ears about 30 seconds later.

"That was weird," I said to myself.

The rumble did not sound like thunder. And the flash didn't look like lightning.

*****

We all sweltered in the excessive heat that night. Everyone was exceedingly cranky the next morning. I asked Trixie to suggest a list of what we needed most, because I was planning on heading out on a scavenger hunt with Josh.

Her response had a tired, angry edge. "Go find whatever you think we need!"

Josh and I left the house with empty stomachs. Just in case we saw some game, I had him carry the bow and arrows. I wore some cut-off

140

blue jeans and a cotton t-shirt that I'd purchased a few years back at a Springsteen concert. Josh had on jeans and a Detroit Tigers t-shirt. I carried the same cotton bag that Trix and I'd had from the start, and inside the bag was the Sig. I could feel the weight of the pipe wrench, which I'd brought just-in-case. I also carried a glass bottle of Snapple. We'd have to share it and make it last until we found more.

"Were are we going, Uncle Greg?"

"I don't exactly know, Josh. I guess we'll recognize it when we find it."

We headed east towards the small town of Lennon, which was about five miles from my house. There were several businesses there, and they might have food or other things we so desperately needed.

That is *if* the village was still standing. We passed five homes – three had burned in the first firestorm, the remaining two had been demolished by the storm. There wasn't a soul stirring around any of them. The next house we encountered was made from brick – and just like in the story of the Three Pigs, it was still standing.

"Let's see if anyone is home," I said to my young friend.

Cautiously, we walked up the driveway, moving around several trees that tried to block our approach.

Not wanting to appear threatening, I kept my hands visible and the gun in the bag. We reached the front porch – a simple cement riser – and I knocked on the door.

"Hello," I yelled. "Anyone here?"

The house was silent. I opened the outer storm door and tried the front door knob.

Locked.

I lead Josh around to the back of the house. Sticks and branches lay everywhere, but the house was completely intact. It was a modest brick home that would make a good place for us to relocate to if the need should arise. Josh and I reached the back of the house and found that the storm had destroyed the back deck. Lumber lay everywhere, most of it broken and useless.

I cautioned Josh to stay behind while I attempted to look in a sliding-glass door. The bottom of the door was about at my chest level. I cupped my hands around my eyes so I could see inside. I couldn't see much. I could make out a refrigerator, stove, and dining room set. I was looking into the kitchen.

Just to be sure, I gave the sliding door a tug to see if it would open. Strangely enough, it moved easily.

I looked at Josh and shrugged. "That was easy."

He smiled and walked over to where I was standing.

I yelled inside the house. "Hello! Is anyone here? We aren't going to hurt you. We only want to see if you are all right!"

After waiting a minute without a response, I said to Josh, "Let me give you a lift up and then I'll follow you."

In a moment we both stood in the kitchen. "We need to see what sort of food we can find, Josh. But if it is in plastic packaging or a plastic container, we need to keep it from the light."

I reached inside my bag and brought out a cotton pillowcase and handed it to the boy.

"This should do the trick. Put whatever you find in the bag, but try to keep the bag out of the light as much as possible. It's likely that light can still shine through the cloth. So let's both see if we can find something better to put our stuff in."

We made out pretty good in the kitchen. By the look of things, the house had been unoccupied since the beginning of the plastipocalypse. There were Oreo cookies – and we couldn't resist breaking into the package immediately.

"An army marches on its stomach, Josh. You ever heard that before?"

After he'd finished swallowing his fourth cookie, he replied, "No, I have not heard that. But it makes sense."

We found two boxes of brown-sugar/cinnamon Pop Tarts. We found a huge unopened bag of Cheetos. We found four massive jars of dill pickles.

"Not much nutrition here, is there Josh?"

"No, Uncle Greg. These people eat junk food."

I opened a cupboard and immediately found something we could all really use.

142

"Josh, look at this!" I pointed at a huge plastic container of vanilla protein powder.

He looked at it, but clearly did not understand its significance.

"It's protein powder. Normally you mix it with milk and it makes a very nutritious milkshake. It's for people that need to gain weight or build muscles."

"Oh," he said with a smile. "People like us!"

"Yup!" I closed the cupboard. "Let's keep it in the dark until we find a good way to get it home."

Josh continued looking through the kitchen. I walked through the dark house, being careful not to bang a shin in the unfamiliar surroundings. I left what must be the living room and entered a hallway. The first two doors led to bedrooms. We needed more clothing, so I opened the first bedroom door on my right. The room looked like a converted office. The metal parts of a desk and chair lay upon the floor with the metal and glass guts of a computer. I found the closet and cautiously slid the door open, doing my best to keep light from striking the contents. There were several women's garments hanging on metal hangers. The clothes all looked as if they were from the 1970's. The women in my care would all look like frumpy senior citizens in these clothes, that is if any of this clothing were made from natural fibers.

I moved on and decided to look in the other bedroom. As I approached the room I noticed an absolutely disgusting smell. Steeling my nerves, I cautiously opened the door to the bedroom. I quickly turned away and slammed the door shut.

I didn't get a chance to look, but I could tell that there was something dead in that room. Probably the home's owner. It felt crass to just leave the body in that room, but I had my own people to worry about.

"Thank you," I said out loud. "We are grateful for then things you have provided."

The last door on the left was the one I was looking for: the bathroom.

There was dim light shining through the opaque window.

"Rats!" I exclaimed. I looked into the shower and found what I was looking for, except that now it was a congealed mess stuck to the bottom of the tub.

"Maybe there's another bottle of shampoo somewhere else."

I cracked open the medicine cabinet and could see that it was full of stuff, which I threw into my cotton bag. Next, I looked under the bathroom sink and found all sorts of useful items – toilet paper, tampons, several bars of soap, and two jars of Scope mouthwash. I put everything that would fit into my bag.

"Eureka!" An economy-size bottle of Prell shampoo lurked near the back of the cupboard. "This will make the ladies happy."

I found Josh in the living room. "Don't go down that hallway," I cautioned. "There is a horrible smell. I think someone died in their bedroom."

He cringed. "Oh, okay."

Josh and I continued our search through the house. The basement turned out to be a disappointment, since it had been flooded with at least four feet of water. But Josh found a heavy green canvas military-style duffle bag in the garage.

"Will this keep the light off our stuff, Uncle Greg?"

"It will do perfectly. Good job!"

Using as much caution as possible, we quickly moved all of the food, bath supplies, protein powder, and medicines we'd found into the heavy green bag.

As I was pulling unopened boxes of cereal from a cupboard I found a case of bottled water. Our duffle bag was quite full, but we managed to cram a few bottles inside. We each drank a bottle as quickly as possible and left the remaining bottles in the back of the cupboard.

We exited the house, this time using the front door. The green duffle bag was heavy. "Grab an end, Josh. This thing is heavy."

We lumbered down the driveway, reached the road and headed for home.

"We'll probably come back here, Josh. We will need to get the remaining bottles of water. Plus, the place looks sturdy enough to withstand another superstorm."

"What about the dead person in the bedroom?"

I looked straight ahead as we walked down the road. "We'll cross that bridge when we come to it."

*****

Just as we were nearing our house, a sound rumbled loud enough to shake the ground we walked on.

"What was that?" Josh asked with a look of concern upon his face.

I scanned the sky. We were under a heavy gray overcast. "I have no idea. It doesn't look like a storm is approaching."

I thought back to the other night, when I'd awoke and went outside to go to the bathroom. The rumble we had just heard sounded like the one I'd heard then. But that rumble was preceded by a bright flash. This one wasn't.

Unless it was obscured by clouds. The flash definitely happened the other night. I figured we couldn't see it this time because of the clouds and because it was daytime.

Everyone was happy to see the two of us return safely, especially since we brought back so much food.

I explained the necessity of keeping everything in the dark as much as possible. "In the light, the packaging will begin to deteriorate in just seconds. I suggest we wait until night falls, then blow out the candles and have a feast in the darkness."

A couple of hours later we all had a modest meal of Pop Tarts, Cheetos, and Protein Powder mixed in water. In between bites, Josh and I related our day's experience.

"There isn't much food left in that house, but there is still some bottled water. Josh and I need to go back and see if we can scavenge any parts for our propane stove connection. Then we'll work our way east house by house and see what we can find."

"I had a thought while you were gone," Trixie said. "You should check out the National Guard Armory in Corunna. I'll bet there's food there."

145

I could have kicked myself for not thinking of this earlier. "Great idea! Unless..."

"Yeah, I know," she continued my line of thought. "Unless someone got there before us."

After eating I went outside to look at the sky. There was no flash, no rumble. All was quiet.

*****

Figuring the plumbing project could wait, I struck out on my own the next day to reconnoiter the National Guard Armory. My bicycle would be the fastest way to get there and back, but I'd be unable to lug very much loot on a bike. So I hoofed it.

The day was steamy. The cloud cover was still thick and heavy yet brief showers of rain fell all morning. It took me just over two hours to reach town, and as I entered the remains of the city I was forced to move much slower due to the large number of downed trees and other rubble. I felt as if I were walking through the remnants of a biblical flood.

Once or twice I spotted people, who like me, were probably scavenging. I had hoped to find some sort of organization here. Surely there was someone left alive that could lead the remaining survivors?

I thought I'd save myself several blocks of walking by cutting across the city park, but due to all of the deadfalls, I had to turn back and walk through the center of town. Even after everything I'd already witnessed, I was shocked to see that more than half of the city center was gone. What hadn't burned was blown apart in the storm. I was tempted to explore the remnants of an attorney's office, but decided it probably wasn't worth my time.

I continued towards the armory. Would there be anyone there? It seemed like the armory would be a good place to hunker down for a while. The building was fairly new and made from heavy cement blocks.

Sure enough, as I approached the large front yard of the armory, I could see people milling about. Two men wore military uniforms; a third was dressed as a civilian.

It was obvious that I wouldn't be looting this building. But since I'd already come this far, I decided to speak to the survivors and see if there was any information we could share.

Using the cover that the downed trees provided, I got as close to the building as possible. My goal was to just watch for a while and see if I could tell if the people here were friendly or not.

One of the two military men spoke loudly to the civilian. I couldn't tell what was said, but the tone was harsh and demanding. The civilian, who was a moderately overweight man in his 60's, retrieved two metal buckets from inside the building and carried them in my direction.

Just as he reached my hiding spot, I decided to take a chance.

"Pssst!!" I whispered. "Over here."

He was so startled that he dropped one of the buckets, which was full of human waste. He looked back at the armory and then at me. "Good thing they didn't hear that, or they'd grab you for questioning."

"Are they the authority in this area?

He picked up the bucket and walked over to where I was crouched.

"You could say that. I think they are a couple of ex-military guys. They like to boss me around and I think one of them treats me like I'm his personal slave. But I haven't seen them do anything really bad."

"Are they feeding you?"

He looked me over carefully. He could see that I was thin and hungry. "Yes. MRE's. They taste like crap, but they're filling."

I recalled receiving a Meal Ready to Eat once from a friend who thought I'd like it as a backpacking meal. We never ate it, because even the packaging was unattractive. But now? I'd be happy to have a case or two of the pre-prepared meals.

"Aren't the MRE's stored in plastic packaging?" I asked.

"Yes. But we keep them in the bomb shelter. As you can imagine, it's dark down there."

"So you also know that light is what causes the plastic to evaporate."

"You mean *sublimate*."

"Huh?"

A voice boomed from the front of the building. "Burnsy! Get your ass back here!"

He looked in the direction of the yelling and rolled his eyes. "My master beckons."

"Look, stick around here for another hour and I'll come back."

Before I could respond, he walked a couple of yards away, dumped the contents of the buckets in a nearby hole, and headed back to the armory.

*****

I made myself as comfortable as possible and waited. The rain had finally stopped, so at least I was dry.

My canteen was nearly empty. I'd forgotten to fill it in the river on my way into town. Which could be a good thing, because who knows what's in river water? I could be bent over, retching. Hopefully I'd find some water elsewhere before heading home.

I must have dozed for a bit, but was awoken by someone kicking gently at my foot.

"It's me. I'm back." He placed a large box on the ground next to us.

I stood and extended my hand to this kind stranger. "My name's Greg Bowman."

"John Burns. Call me Burnsy."

"Glad to meet you, Burnsy."

Looking towards the box, Burnsy said, "I was able to liberate a case of MRE's for you. There should be 12 meals in the box."

"Wow, thanks!"

"Don't thank me until you've eaten one. You might not be so grateful."

"My people are getting pretty hungry," I replied. "We've consumed everything we've found."

"I understand. I consider myself fortunate that I am getting fed by the sergeant and corporal."

"Is that their actual ranks?"

"Probably not, but it's what I call them."

"Do they let you come and go as you please?" I asked.

"Not usually. But yesterday one of them discovered a cache of Miller Light. Right now they are both in the officer's lounge getting loaded, bragging about all of the women they'd had before."

"You don't have any women in the building?"

"No. We haven't seen a woman in over a week. There were two, but they were accompanied by four pretty solid looking guys, so the sergeant and corporal left them alone.

He asked me to share my survival story with him. I told him about most of our ordeal, but I purposely held back information about where we were living. You never know – even though he seemed like a nice man, he could actually be a spy. And if the "sergeant" and "corporal " discovered that I was taking care of women, they might have unsavory ideas.

I explained to him how we had also figured out that plastic only evaporated when exposed to light.

"Not evaporated. Sublimated."

"You used that word earlier. What does it mean?"

"In simple terms, it means that the plastic turned into something else."

"Are you a chemist?"

"Actually, yes. I am... I mean was... a professor at Michigan State University."

"Oh. Please go on. Tell me what you think caused the plastipocalypse."

*****

"The plastic changed from solid to gas," he explained. "Sublimation."

"But what caused it? Did something escape from a laboratory?"

149

"I've been wondering the same thing," he replied. "But then again, it could be a natural phenomenon."

"Seriously? After 100 years, plastic suddenly decides to turn into methane?"

"If I could get to a working lab, I'm certain I could find the answer."

I sighed. "Not likely to happen, is it?"

He shook his head. "No, I think we'll always wonder if it is a man-made or natural phenomenon."

I had another question. "What about the weather? Is all of the methane causing the extreme heat and storms?"

"Most certainly. Sunlight is penetrating the methane, but the same sunlight is getting trapped between the earth and the upper atmosphere. The result? Extreme heat and crazy storms."

"What about the flashes and loud rumbles I've been hearing?"

"Methane again. Lightning ignites the gas."

"Do you think this firestorm can reach us, or will they stay at high-altitude?"

He thought for a moment before replying. "I think we are safe here. But I wouldn't go climbing any mountains."

He reached into a bag he was carrying and handed me a can of beer. "I almost forgot about this."

We sat quietly for a moment and enjoyed our beers. Even though I was never much of a beer drinker, I had to admit, it tasted very, very good.

"What are your plans, Greg?"

"I've been so focused upon our daily survival. I haven't been able to think about next week."

"I understand. But you said you have 'people.' I think you might have noticed that there are very few survivors. You need to keep your 'people' alive so we can begin to rebuild our planet."

I nodded in agreement. "We do have some seeds. I located a solid building yesterday. It has a dead body occupying a bedroom, but otherwise it's all right. It should be able to handle a storm."

"I wouldn't wait too long to get yourself situated. The storms..."

"You think they are going to get worse?"

He looked me straight in the eyes and said, "Absolutely."

*****

We said our goodbyes. I lugged the heavy box of MRE's and walked back towards town. It was beginning to get late, and the western sky was rolling with heavy, dark clouds. But I had to make one stop before heading home.

I reached the Community Library without incident. The building, which used to be the county jail, was a fairly modern looking one-story affair. It was still standing and looked to be in decent condition. The doors were locked – which meant that the place might not have been raided yet. I walked to the back and found a window above an air-conditioning unit that would allow entry once I'd shattered the glass.

I hid my box of MRE's in the shrubbery and climbed up on the a/c unit. With reluctance I knocked a good sized brick on the glass, which cracked without difficulty. I carefully removed the remaining glass. A couple of seconds later I was in the building. Just as I landed upon the floor, I heard the rumble of thunder from outside.

"Great," I said to the empty room. "Another storm."

I trusted that Trixie would keep everyone safe at my house, but for good measure I said a quick prayer for them. I've never been an overly religious person, but I have always been willing to pray when I needed help.

I found the main library room and was astonished to find that it had never been looted. You'd think that survivors would want what I was after – books about survival! There was a particular series of books I was interested in. I found the non-fiction section and looked carefully at the shelves of books.

A massive roar of thunder rattled the building. Sheets of rain poured from the sky, and darkness consumed me. Thankfully, I'd thrown a candle into my bag. Soon I had light, and I continued my search. I had no idea who the author was, and I had to carefully look all of the way through the alphabet before I found what I was after.

"There you are." I reached out and pulled *Foxfire Volume 1* by Eliot Wigginton from the shelf. I chuckled when I saw the full title: *The Foxfire Book: Hog Dressing, Log Cabin Building, Mountain Crafts and Foods, Planting by the Signs, Snake Lore, Hunting Tales, Faith Healing, Moonshining, and Other Affairs of Plain Living.* Hog dressing and log cabin building are useful things to know. But I doubted we'd ever try faith healing.

There was an entire set of *Foxfire* books on the shelf. I carefully carried them over to a table and found a sturdy wooden chair to sit upon. The storm slammed the library, but looking west, I could see that the sky was already clearing.

"Huh," I said to the empty room. "This is just a puny *regular* thunderstorm."

*****

I wandered through the shelves of books, thinking that if the plastipocalypse were a global event, it might takes decades for books and other media to be printed again. So much would need to be reinvented. Were there people alive that would know how to make ink? Paper? Binding glue?

I eventually made my way into the research section. There they were – the encyclopedias. I personally hadn't looked at an encyclopedia for years, not since Google and Wikipedia became so ubiquitous. Oh, how I longed for the instant gratification of whipping out my Android smartphone and looking up the collective knowledge of humanity!

I grabbed the "N" from the bookshelf and shuffled through the pages. I found articles on Nazis, Napoleon, NASA, Norway, Noam Chomsky, Nuremburg Trials, and so much more that I could have read for hours and hours. Eventually I found what I was searching for: nuclear energy – specifically a map of nuclear energy reactors in the Great Lakes region.

In 2011 an earthquake resulted in a tsunami striking the coast of Japan, causing the Fukushima reactor disaster. While I was no expert on Fukushima, the evening news had made me aware of the scope of this tragic event. As far as I knew, it would be centuries before human beings could occupy the area.

After skimming several pages of detailed information I found a map showing the general locations of all nuclear power plants in the United States. The map didn't have a ton of detail, but it showed three reactors in Michigan, all in the southwest side of the Lower Peninsula. My guess was that the plants were using water from Lake Michigan for cooling.

I was fairly certain that these nuclear power plants were no longer operational. But were we in danger from nuclear fallout? The plants were all more than 200 miles away. Would prevailing winds blow fallout to mid-Michigan?

Pulling the "F" encyclopedia from the shelf, I looked up Fukushima. Fortunately the encyclopedia was up-to-date, and I found the article about the Japanese reactor disaster. I was fascinated to discover that the reactor disaster occurred mostly because of a failure to cool the spent fuel rods. As a result of the earthquake and subsequent tsunami, the electricity-producing reactors were unable to provide enough energy to power the cooling pumps. Two backup diesel generators also failed.

Even though the entire Fukushima region was evacuated as quickly as possible, it was estimated that 36% of all children who lived in the area at the time had abnormal growths in their thyroid glands.

During the days and weeks following the disaster, the Japanese government established a three kilometer "prohibited area," an "on-alert" area of 3 to 20 kilometers, and an "evacuation prepared" area of 20 to 30 kilometers.

I was relieved that my family was well outside the evacuation zone. Hopefully, the technicians at the plants were able to contain inevitable meltdowns. I doubted that the backup generators would have worked more than a few days at most – but I had no choice but to remain optimistic.

There was no point in sharing this information with my people, for it would only scare them. The best course of action would be to do nothing and stay the hell away from the western side of the state.

I packed up the Foxfire books, plus a few other "how-to" guides I'd found and left the building the same way I'd entered. My MRE's sat under the shrub in a damp cardboard box. I quickly removed the plastic-wrapped MRE's from the wet box and threw them in my bag.

As I trekked towards home, I reflected upon how quickly the world had ground to a halt. Just 10 days ago everything was fine. But now a town that currently held 1,500 people was down to just 10 or 20 survivors. Is everyone really dead? Or did they just march off to some other community? I did some math in my head as I walked. Let's see, half of the city went up in the initial methane explosions. That would leave 700 or 800 people. I third of these survivors were elderly, and the elderly already have their own health problems. So for a week or so, another 400 people died in their homes, unable to gain access to healthcare. The superstorm could have taken another 100 or so, so there should still be 3 or 4 hundred people left. Of those 3 or 4 hundred folks, many more might have asphyxiated in their homes, killed by odorless methane gas as they slept.

Maybe there are more folks out there than I thought. They could be hunkered down somewhere, afraid to leave whatever safe place they had found. I supposed that without food they wouldn't want to be moving around much anyway.

One more thought – very unpleasant – entered my thoughts. What if the survivors were turning cannibal? I shuddered and picked up the pace, knowing that I also had a hungry group of people who were waiting to be fed.

Chapter 15

It was well after dark when I finally reached home. I quietly lay down on my blanket next to Trix, so I wouldn't wake anyone. It felt good to rest after such a long and tiring day.

"I was getting worried about you," Trix whispered. "Is everything all right?"

"I'm okay. I brought back some food."

"Oh, thank God. We are getting down to our last rations."

"Is everyone here all right?"

"Emily had a headache all day, but otherwise, we are fine."

Even though the room was hot I reached over to Trix and held her hand. "Good. Tomorrow's another day. We'll get through this."

She replied something, but I was so tired I dozed off and quickly fell into a deep sleep.

*****

The next morning I took the MRE's into the damp-but-drying basement and opened the packaging in the darkness. I had twelve meals, and each meal contained an entrée, an energy bar, side dish, cheese and crackers, candy, freeze-dried coffee, powdered drink mix, and a flameless ration heater. Working in near darkness, I discarded the plastic packaging and dumped all of the crackers and candy into one bowl, the main dishes into another bowl, the side dishes into another, and so on. I left the plastic-wrapped ration heaters alone, figuring we might find a way to use them later. They worked by chemical reaction, but I didn't need them. Yet.

I set the energy bars and instant coffee aside for later consumption.

I carried everything upstairs and went outdoors. I fired up my gas grill, which was burning the propane that remained in the small container that was attached to the stove.

I filled a large metal pan with water that we'd salvaged in the metal milking machine tanks I'd placed under the gutters way back on day one. The garage and gutters had blown away in the storm, but the tanks, which had quickly filled with water during the storm, were full to the top.

I put the water on the grill, dumped in half of the main dishes and side dishes, and stirred the entire concoction together with a metal spoon. Mac and cheese was mixed with spaghetti, green beans, and peas. It was a mess to look at but I doubted anyone would complain.

Gradually my crew began to emerge from the house. I handed each a hot bowl of food as they approached, and said "Breakfast is ready! Eat up!"

Even little Declan, the fussiest eater I'd ever known gobbled his bowl of United States of America military slop.

Emily nursed Cora and simultaneously devoured her ration. Everyone quietly sat upon the wooden deck and emptied their bowls.

"Burp!"

"Josh," his mother exclaimed. "Mind your manners."

"Excuse me!"

We all laughed for what seemed like the first time in days.

I was just about to stand up and begin assigning jobs to everyone for the day, when I looked towards the north. A figure, who was wearing a backpack and carrying a rifle, was accompanied by a dark dog.

Trix looked at me from her perch and asked, "Do you see something?"

"We have company."

*****

I dashed into the house and retrieved my Sig from the top of the refrigerator, where I'd been stashing it so the kids wouldn't play with the weapon. I shoved the pistol into the back of my trousers and ran back outside. The man and dog were now getting close enough to make out their faces.

"It's Mike!" Connie yelled. She and the kids sprinted across the yard, eager to embrace their husband and father.

Trix and I looked at each other and smiled. "It will be good to have another man around here," I said.

"Looks like Radar found her master!" Trixie replied.

We all watched the joyous homecoming. For a group that had gone through so much over the last week and a half, this was the first really good thing that had happened. We all knew that Mike was a trapper and hunter of repute. His skills would certainly help us survive the difficult times that lay before us.

The Fosters, reunited as a family, all beamed with happiness as they joined Trixie, Miranda, my children, and me. Mike dropped his pack and rifle as I reached out and gave him a handshake and a "bro-hug."

"Ouch! Easy on the ribs!" he exclaimed.

I cringed. "Sorry! What's wrong?"

"Broken ribs. But otherwise I'm all right. I'll tell you the rest later."

"It's great to have you back, buddy!"

"It's great to be back, Greg." He surveyed the damage to my property and sighed in dismay. "It looks like you've had it rough."

"We've done better than most," I replied.

He shook his head in agreement, his face indicating that he'd certainly seen his share of trouble. "Let me visit with my family a bit and then we'll catch up with each other."

The four Fosters and their pooch walked towards what used to be their home. I understood that he needed to see if anything was left and that he would be back soon. Mike wasn't the type to desert someone who had helped his family.

*****

We moved into the shade, swatting at mosquitos in the oddly hot early April afternoon. Mike grimaced in pain as he sat against a tree. I'd broken a rib once mountain biking and I knew from first-hand experience that it hurt like hell.

157

"I can't remember ever having mosquitos in April," I said.

"No, me neither. But with all of the water, and the heat…"

"I talked to a scientist fellow the other day. He said it will get worse."

I explained our story from the beginning, culminating with the events the day before at the National Guard Armory.

"So if I get you right," he asked, "We are going to be hit by some hellacious storms."

"The odds are against us, Mike. But this being Michigan, things could end up being much better. Or much worse."

We both understood that the Great Lakes that surrounded our state had a huge impact upon our weather. In the winter, cold air moving across the lakes created localized snow storms across much of the state. We call this "lake effect" snow. In the summer, the lakes tend to reduce the severity of the storms that move across the Great Plains and the rest of the Midwest.

"I wouldn't want to be a survivor in Iowa or Indiana," I continued. "The storms there were probably way worse than the one we experienced. We'll just have to wait and see what happens. Now, enough of my jabbering. Tell me what happened to you."

*****

Mike told me his story.

"I have a trap line north of Clare. On land that belongs to my friend Jim."

"So you were more than 100 miles away?"

"Farther. I was out in the boonies. I went up early on shit-storm Sunday. The day this all started. I got to my first traps without any problems and found I had a couple of raccoons and a coyote. I walked about three miles deep into the woods and loaded my bag with a couple more 'coons and a gray fox. I started having problems on my hike back to my truck. My shoelaces! They just gave out! The zipper on my coat quit working, and my hat shredded to smithereens. I was

158

lucky that I had on cotton pants and a warm wool shirt, because otherwise I'd have ended up stark naked.

"I lugged everything back to my truck, but sonofabitch, it wouldn't start! The inside of the truck was really weird, too. It was... soft. I had plastic residue all over my hands from touching stuff like the steering wheel and upholstery. Let me tell you, I was pissed! Here I was in the middle-of-nowhere with no transportation.

"So I tried to use my phone to call my buddy for help. The fuckin' thing would not work. In fact, it fell apart in my hand. So I left all of my crap in the truck, which turned out to be a bad idea, and hiked it to Jim's house. I figured I'd get Jim to give me a ride back to my truck.

"I walked down a dirt road for a bit and reached the main highway. By now my shoes were just flopping around, since the laces were completely gone. But the soles were holding up, and I had on nice wool socks. I sorta trudged along for a spell. Eventually I came across a couple of other vehicles that must have been left by people who were in the same boat as me, only then I didn't know that this was happening everywhere.

"I had to pass through Clare to get to Jim's place. The power was off but it wasn't like there was anyone out looting or rioting. I think people just didn't know *what* to do. Who expects their clothes to just rot off their body? Who expects their car to melt in front of them? I imagine most folks where hunkered down inside, waiting to see what was going to happen.

"So I get to Jim's, and he's like everyone else. Doesn't have a clue what's going on. But he and his wife, Kelly, tell me that I can stay with them until this all blows over.

"Jim was sort of a survivalist. Hell, a lot of folks up that way are. He had a cellar stocked with tons of canned food and survival rations. Plus, we were both hunters and trappers so we'd be able to get plenty of game to eat. Jim found me some rawhide bootlaces and a wool coat and hat, so I was pretty comfortable outside. I wish I could say the same for other people I saw. That afternoon, I decided to hike three miles to Dick's Sporting Goods to see if I could find some supplies for my long walk home. I saw people walking – and it was cold out –

nearly naked. I wish I could have helped them but I had my own family to get home to. I figured it would take me four or five days to get back here.

"Anyway, I am on my way to the sporting goods store when Whoosh! A Kentucky Fried Chicken just explodes. Shit is falling from the sky and I ran like crazy, looking for someplace safe to hide. I ran behind a dumpster. Suddenly the ground beneath me began to tremble, and then KAWAM!!! The road, the parking lots, everything around me exploded in a wall of flames.

"I must have been thrown clear, because much later – it was beginning to get dark, I woke up. I was lying in a pile of melting snow. I stood and my ribs hurt like hell. I was more than 30 feet from the dumpster! I couldn't believe that I'd been thrown that far and was still alive.

"Even though it was getting dark, I could see a bright halo of light from the city. It was on fire. At the time I didn't know what was happening, but eventually I worked it all out. The plastic evaporated and turned into explosive gas. Most folks in northern Michigan burn wood for their heat. I imagine they all felt fairly safe in their cozy houses, even with the plastic disappearing around them. They had heat. But eventually the gases built up inside the houses and they went up in flames. I imagine that the folks that didn't die from the explosions died from asphyxiation.

"The fires spread into the city. I was on the outskirts when all of this happened. It turns out that the only survivors were people like me that were outside scavenging. That meant that in a city of over 5,000 there were probably just 20 or 30 people left alive.

"I really wanted to go back and check on Jim and his wife Kelly, but since I was close to the sporting goods store, I decided to finish what I'd set out to do. I had to walk through fields and woods because the burned-up roads were still too hot to use.

"It turned out that I needn't have bothered. The place hadn't exploded, but there was nothing left inside the store that I could use. It was like locusts had been through the place – what hadn't evaporated had been looted earlier that day.

160

"Let me tell you, Greg, I was getting pretty despondent. I had nothing. No food, no water, and no transportation. I was more than 120 miles from home. My ribs hurt like hell. But I thought of Connie and the kids and knew that I had to keep going. For their sake.

"But first I had to check in on Jim and Kelly. I owed them. But when got back to their house I knew right away that they hadn't survived the firestorm. The place was still burning. Huge flames shot into the sky. I sat against a tree and bawled my eyes out until I dozed off. I woke up sometime the next morning, stiff from the cold. The fire was out but the foundation was smoldering.

"My first thought was to find something to carry water and food in. Jim's underground storage cellar was covered by the cement floor of the garage. I found a large crowbar in the ashes. I picked it up without thinking and nearly burned my fingers right off! So I used a tree branch and pushed the crowbar into the snow so it would cool. Then I used the crowbar to push stuff out of my way so I could get to the hidden cellar door. This was one of those metal doors that lays flat. It had a latch and a lock, but Jim had left it unlocked. I used the crowbar to open the door without burning myself again. I lowered myself into the dark cellar and groped around for food. I didn't have any matches – and it's probably a good thing I didn't or I might have been involved in another explosion! Jim had a supply of hunting gear stashed in a cabinet, so I was able to find a hunting rifle, some shells, a couple of metal water bottles, and an old metal-framed backpack. I stuffed the pack with as much food as I could and high-tailed it out of there. I expected the cellar to go up in flames at any moment.

"I headed south right away. Since the roads were unusable, I went cross country, unless I found a dirt road to walk on."

"Did you encounter anyone at all on your way home?" I asked.

"Oh yeah." He hesitated and looked at his feet for a very long time before continuing. "I was skirting the suburbs of Mt. Pleasant and ran into a group of dubious looking dudes, all riding horses! I stumbled into them as I crossed a grassy hill, otherwise I'd have stayed well away.

"There were five in the gang. They circled me. Each had a rifle, but they weren't pointing them at me. They asked where I was headed, and I told them that I'd been out trapping but was now trying to get to Corunna to see if my family was okay. Right away I realized that I should have lied about where I was going, because now they could come find us. But the damage was done. They made me show them what I had in my backpack, and one of them, probably their leader, laughed and said I'd be lucky to make it twenty miles. Then they all turned and left.

"I was shaking in terror and I have no idea why they let me be."

"You didn't have anything they needed," I replied.

"Probably. But from that point on I made sure to stay out of open spaces as much as possible."

I scratched my head, thinking about something. "You said they were on horses? Did they have saddles too?"

"Sure. Saddles don't use plastic."

"Hmmm. Good thing. Still, I wonder if at some point the horses might be end up being served for supper."

He shrugged. "I doubt it. If a man has a horse, he can hunt a long way from home."

I nodded in agreement. Up to now I hadn't considered using a horse for transportation. I had no idea how we'd feed a horse, other than grazing.

"Should we have a horse?" I asked.

"We should keep our eyes open. There aren't a lot of horses around here, but we might find one that got loose."

"Tell me," I said. "Did you have any more problems getting back here?"

"Well, there *was* the storm. I was holed up in a high school locker room that night, so I was safe. But I had one hell of a time getting anywhere the next day. Trees, powerlines, wires... everything is down and it was all in my way. It took me almost two days longer to get here than I thought it would."

"We are very, very glad you made it."

He put his hand on my shoulder and said, "I am thankful for what you did for my family. I will not forget it."

We sat for a bit and contemplated our situation. I explained sublimation, methane, superstorms, and firestorms to him.

After taking a few moments to digest all of this, he stood up. "It looks like we have been sent back to the 19th century. No power. No plastic. No government."

As I stood, I added, "And no experience. Who remaining has any idea how to rebuild society? How do you make gunpowder? Steel? Glass? There's so much we don't know how to do."

I told him about Burnsy.

"We need to recruit him. He needs to come live with us."

"His 'military' pals might have other ideas. But I agree, he would be an asset."

I led Mike into the house and dumped my collection of *Foxfire* books onto the dining room table. "At least we have these!"

He looked them over and smiled. "Good thinking! These books might give us a fighting chance."

"Let's not forget that we all have useful skills. Trix is an expert at canning. She is an OB-GYN nurse practitioner. Miranda is also a doctor. A general practitioner. We have health-care covered! You have hunting and trapping skills. I have outdoor survival skills. Plus, I was a mechanical designer and engineer in a previous life. Emily is a certified teacher! The children *will* continue their educations."

"Connie and my kids will help. They can garden and forage."

"We have the beginnings of a community right here. Let's all work together and take one day at a time, but also create a strategy to survive for the long haul."

"Agreed!" he said with conviction. "First, I want to see about getting that scientist dude to come live with us. He might be the key to getting a working civilization back up and running."

*****

The ground was drying. Using a shovel I'd recovered from the storm wreckage, I dug a couple of short furrows. Trix wandered over to watch.

"Are you thinking about planting a garden?" She asked.

"Yes. I think the ground is ready. But it's still early April! Most years we don't plant a garden until early June."

She walked around on the yard. "The grass is beginning to turn green in a few spots. But I think we should wait a week or two before planting, just to be safe."

I nodded in agreement. "Mike and I had a chat. We think you should be in charge of gardening."

"Good. But I wasn't going to ask for permission from you two men."

I laughed. "You are right. Since Mother Nature has essentially hit a giant reset button, this is our chance to get things right. We two men shouldn't assume that we are the leaders."

"Gregg Bowman, there's hope for you yet!"

I had a sudden thought. "Remember that farmer we ran into when we were recovering our food stash? The guy that said he had some livestock?"

"Yes I do. He was large."

"Maybe you and I can pay him a visit in a day or two. See what he's up to, see if we can set up some trade or barter."

"Good idea. If I remember correctly, we need fat to create soap."

"Soap! I just remembered - I have something to show you. Follow me into the house"

Back in the dining room, I spread all of the *Foxfire* books on the table.

She gasped. "Oh my God." Picking up one book, she thumbed through the pages. "This could change everything."

"We have a complete set," I explained. "These books tell us how to make practically everything we'll need to survive."

"You found these in town yesterday?"

"Uh-huh. Years ago I remember seeing these books in a bookstore or library. At the time I thought they were quaint – they were only for those crazy 'back-to-nature' types. Let me tell you, I was shocked to find them in our local library."

"We need to take good care of these," she said with conviction.

"Maybe you should be the only one who handles them," I answered. "We don't dare damage or lose them."

She thumbed through *Foxfire 3: Animal Care, Banjos and Dulcimers, Hide Tanning, Summer and Fall Wild Plant Foods, Butter Churns, Ginseng, and Still More Affairs of Plain Living.* "The information in here... if we use it correctly, gives us a chance for long-term survival."

*****

We decided to celebrate Mike's reunion with his family with a bonfire. We made a huge pile of sticks and branches, improvised some outdoor seating, and feasted on MRE energy bars for supper. As dusk began to envelope us in darkness, I lit the sticks and sat back to watch the flames.

Since the beginning of the plastipocalypse, we hadn't taken the time to celebrate our survival. We lived in the moment, literally living hand to mouth. We were dirty. We were hungry. But we were adapting.

Declan sat between Trixie's legs and poked a stick at the flames. He seemed perfectly content with our situation. Josh, the other boy in our group, was also enjoying this adventure. After all, what 10-year-old wouldn't want to live a life without school, rules, and schedules? His sister, Hailey, wasn't quite as resilient. She sorely missed her iPhone and her classmates. Yet she was pulling her fair share, and never complained about the tasks we set her to.

We had to build a future for these young people. We also needed to find more young people – for there would surely be illness and disaster. Continued survival was not guaranteed.

I had a surprise for everyone. After disappearing for a moment for a "call of nature," I returned holding a beautiful, fully intact acoustic guitar.

"Well look what Coppa found!" Emily exclaimed, using the nickname that her children had bestowed upon me.

I sat and tuned the instrument. "Evidently, this one was made with wood, bone, and brass."

I played a quiet melody and stared at the fire.

Miranda was the first to speak. "This is nice. It's the first chance we've had to really relax since this whole thing began."

"Amen!" It was Mike. "I'm not much at speeches, but just let me say that right here, right now, I am content."

Connie gave her husband a smile and a hug.

"We have a lot to be thankful for," Trixie added. "We are all here and we are safe."

"Plus," I interjected. "No taxes!"

Everyone laughed.

Miranda said, "No cable or cell phone bills!"

One by one we all added things to the list that we were happy were gone forever.

"No traffic! No politicians! No computers!"

After a bit we ran out of things to list, and we each began to remember that there would be things that we *would* miss.

"I miss hot showers," Trixie said. "And roasted chicken."

"I miss Cap'n Crunch," Josh added.

"I miss daddy," Declan whispered.

I looked into the fire and said softly, "And I miss our son, Graham."

*****

It didn't take long for us to recognize that having Mike back home would be a game changer. The very next morning he went hunting and returned with a good size whitetail doe. First, he showed everyone how to skin and cut the meat, and then he built a homemade drying rack, relit the bonfire, and set about drying the venison. We worked together to engineer a more reliable water storage system. After three days we collected enough water from the frequent rain showers to

166

each take a quick bath. Mike and I each went on foraging missions, and one afternoon I hit pay dirt.

As I cautiously examined an isolated, burned-down farm, I was overjoyed to find live chickens feeding in the yard. Evidently a feed bag had spilled somehow, and there were several birds strutting about the property. Mike and I built some homemade cages from sticks and with the help of the children, caught the chickens and brought them back to our home. We were able to salvage quite a bit of chicken feed also, but I had no idea what we'd feed them when it ran out.

One damp afternoon, Mike and Josh returned home, pulling three goats behind them on leads.

I grimaced and muttered, "Great. Goat milk. And feta cheese." I was not a fan.

"Oh shut-up," Trixie replied. "You'll learn to like it."

I had to admit that the goats were comical to watch. And useful — they quickly cleared out the weeds that were beginning to overtake the yard. We'd have to watch these horned devils later, after our yet-unplanted garden began to grow.

Since we now had water, eggs, dairy, and dried venison, it was time for us to begin planning for long-term survival. The *Foxfire* books were a fantastic wealth of knowledge — imparting information on how to weave cloth, make gunpowder, find herbs in the wild — really just about everything a pioneer would need to know. But to really get a society up and running again, we needed a real expert.

I announced to the group that night at our campfire (which had become a ritual) that it was time to go back into town.

"I want to recruit that scientist I met, John Burns, to come join our family."

Mike looked at me with concern. "Do you really think it's necessary? We've been getting along just fine without him."

I nodded in agreement, but added, "For now. But what about winter? And what about long-term?"

Mike bristled. Up to now, our leadership had been shared. Even though we all verbally stated that the women were in charge of things as much as he and I were, the truth was, Mike had the best wilderness survival skills. Our group relied upon his ingenuity for preparing game and taking care of our animals.

"If we want to continue to live like 10th century peasants," I said, "I imagine we could survive quite a long time. But isn't it our responsibility to try to recreate a society that has commerce? Culture? Education?"

"As long as we get it right," he answered. "But I think I speak for all of us here – we don't want to go back to what we had before."

I had to agree that Mike was right. American society had become twisted into a religion of angry consumerism.

"Maybe we should vote," Trixie suggested. "Show of hands! Who thinks we should try to bring the scientist into our group?"

One by one, the adults began to raise their hands.

Connie, who had been sitting quietly, also raised her hand. "I think we need to give ourselves every possible advantage. For the children. For *their* future."

Finally, Mike raised his hand and shrugged. "Okay, I'm with you guys. I just wanted to make it clear that I don't want to go back to the old ways."

I laughed. "Hell Mike, even the Amish use machinery!"

Chapter 16

"So what form of government do you think we should adopt?" I asked as we walked towards town. We both carried weapons – me with my trusty Sig and Mike with his 30 caliber hunting rifle.

Mike walked beside me for a bit, considering his answer.

"Historically, agrarian cultures had a chief," he said. "And probably a council of elders."

"I suppose that is the normal course of things," I replied. "Right now we are a very small tribe. We have two 'warriors,' four women, and four children."

Mike gazed into the distance. "From what I can see, there aren't other tribes competing for our resources."

"Yet. But you know how people are. We reproduce at a very rapid rate."

"But it will take generations to repopulate the planet to even something like pre-Roman times."

"We need more people, Mike. Good people. We need to dilute our gene pool. Plus, we need people that know stuff. Like how to generate electricity or forge iron. I'd like to have the simple luxury of a hand pump, for God's sake!"

"We can probably salvage a pump from somewhere."

"Sure, but what about later? Parts break. Nothing lasts forever. Look, I agree with you that this is our chance to rebuild a new society – one that uses only the best things from what we had before. But you're kidding yourself if you think we can keep it pure. There *are* assholes that survived the plastipocalypse. We will need to make sure that anyone we accept into our group is a good fit."

"You mean our 'tribe.'"

"Okay. Tribe. But even Native Americans welcomed new people into their tribes."

"As long as that person had value."

"Yes. Value. But I don't think we'd turn away a starving child. Everyone has value, Mike. We need to keep our eyes and hearts open to everyone."

He stopped walking and looked me straight in the eyes. "We are not going to let 'everyone' into our tribe."

"My choice of words could have been better. Sorry. But let's see what happens with John Burns. He did me a good turn with those MRE's. I have a feeling he's a decent human being."

As we entered the city, we couldn't help but notice an overwhelming, nauseating odor.

"Smells like decaying bodies," Mike said.

The extreme heat and humidity had taken a toll on the hundreds of unfortunate souls that did not survive the first week of exposure, fires, and superstorms. Hopefully, the prevailing winds wouldn't blow the stench towards our home.

"Yup," I agreed. "Not much you and I can do about it."

"It's amazing that everything fell apart so quickly."

"I really can't get my mind around it," I replied. "Take away power and synthetic fabrics and the whole world goes to shit. Thousands of years of advancing civilization, and 95% of the population is gone in just a few weeks."

Wrapping cotton bandannas around our faces to ward off the smell, we continued our trek.

We walked silently until the National Guard armory was in sight. In the distance, the "Corporal" or "Sergeant" was taking a piss against a tree.

"Now that guy?" I whispered. "Not welcome in our tribe."

*****

Mike and I lurked in the shadows for over an hour, waiting for Burnsy to emerge from the Armory. We watched the two para-military men, who seemed preoccupied with something that was hidden under a tarp near some trees. The "Corporal," who was about 50 yards away from us, crouched and inspected whatever was underneath the tarp. He poked at it and laughed.

"What do you think that S.O.B. has there?" I whispered to Mike.

"No idea. If we get a chance, let's check it out."

The "Corporal" disappeared back into the building. Using hand signs, Mike gestured for us to creep closer to the building, which also brought us closer to the tarp. Without difficulty, we were able to find a decent hiding spot behind some 30 gallon drums that were labeled "motor oil." The Corporal and Sergeant both appeared from the building together. Burnsy walked behind the two men.

I gave Mike a nod and mouthed, "That's our guy."

The Sergeant was angry about something. He kicked the tarp and said, "You had enough yet? Or do you want to stay out here a while longer?"

The Corporal sniggered, reminding me of a stereotypical bully's sidekick. "Give her some more, Boss!"

Mike and I shared a look of concern. These wannabe "soldiers" had a prisoner. A *female* prisoner.

Burnsy stepped in front of the two thugs and plead, "Please. Allow me to see if I can convince her to cooperate."

The Sergeant let out a mocking laugh. "'Allow me', he says! Like he's a fuckin' butler or something."

The Corporal snickered. *Muttley!* That's who he reminded me of! That stupid cartoon dog from my childhood. I had always hated that cartoon, and now I hated the Corporal.

The Sergeant gave the captive another solid kick and then turned and headed back into the building, with Muttley hot on his heels. "Let's see if the Butler can convince her to do what we want."

Burnsy crouched and spoke softly to the prisoner. We couldn't hear what he was saying, but we could tell from the tone that he was pleading.

I decided it was a good time to get Burnsy's attention. I found a pebble and tossed it towards him, striking him on the upper arm.

He looked up, startled. As he stood, I could tell that he was considering his situation. He nodded and then slowly walked in our direction. He stopped next to the barrels where we hid and pretended to take a leak.

"Is that you, Greg?" He whispered.

"Yes," I replied. I brought a friend along this time. We are here to see if you want to come back to our place to live."

"That is a generous offer," he replied quietly. "But my two 'friends' inside might have a different perspective."

He finished his pretend urination, but as he turned he said, "Wait here ten minutes, but be ready!"

He walked back into the building.

Mike looked at me and asked, "Do you trust this guy?"

If I were being honest, I'd say no. But sometimes you just need to go with your gut instinct. "I do."

We continued waiting. Suddenly there was a lot of yelling. "FIRE! HELP! The building is on fire!"

Running, Burnsy emerged outdoors. He immediately removed the tarp from whomever it was covering and used a knife to cut the ropes that were being used as restraints.

He pulled the person up and we were surprised to find it was a tiny, half-naked teenage girl. She wore some ill-fitting trousers but no shirt. She covered her chest as best as she could as she ran to our hiding place with Burnsy and crouched near us. Even though it was a steamy day, I wore a long-sleeved cotton shirt, which I removed and handed to the girl without comment. She nodded and immediately put it on.

"I created a diversion," Burnsy explained. "Those two buffoons will be busy for a while. Let's go!"

Before we could get to our feet, Mike spoke. "Wait! Is there more food in the building?"

Burnsy, who was only thinking of escape, was surprised by the question. "Uh, yes. There are several cases of MRE's in the kitchen."

"Show me where the kitchen is," Mike demanded.

"You won't have time! Those assholes will figure out what I did quickly enough and then they'll come looking for me!"

"Show me!"

Resigned, Burnsy drew a layout of the building in the dirt. Mike jumped up and said, "Give me the Sig."

I handed him the pistol and took possession of his rifle. "Watch the doorway," he commanded. "If they come out chasing me, take them out!"

He turned and ran before I could reply. "Take them out?" I don't think I could do that!

Smoke began to emerge from the front of the building. I suddenly had an idea.

"Stay here!" I said to Burnsy and his young companion.

I ran over to the back doorway – the one that Mike had entered – and waited. After what seemed like an eternity the door slammed open and Mike emerged from the building, pushing several cases of MRE's on a hand cart. He saw me lurking on the side of the door and said, "Let's go!"

Just as I began to move a second body emerged from the building. It was Muttley, and he was in a rage.

"Come back here you motherfucker!" he yelled. "You do not fuck with me!"

Without a moment's hesitation I cold cocked him with the butt of the rifle.

Mike looked at me and laughed. "Well done, Greg!"

I chuckled. "I've wanted to do that from the first time I laid eyes upon him."

*****

Needing to get as far away from the Armory as possible, we moved quickly – half walking, half running – whatever we could do to separate ourselves from Mutley and the Sergeant. Burnsy, who was in his mid-60's and not in optimum physical condition, had trouble keeping up with Mike, who was pushing the cart of MRE's, the girl, and me.

"Come on, Burnsy," Mike yelled.

Burnsy reached us and bent at the waste, put his hands upon his knees, and fought to catch his breath.

I looked at the girl and asked, "What do we call you?"

She looked away and did not reply.

"She doesn't talk," Burnsy gasped.

"Deaf?" I asked.

"No. Trauma."

I nodded and smiled at the girl. "We are going to help you," I said. "Let's go."

We walked quickly through the city and did not relax until we reached the country road that lead to our home. After an hour, and no sign of the Sergeant or Mutley, we relaxed our pace.

"Do you think they will try to find us?" I asked Burnsy.

"Those two? They aren't the sharpest tacks in the drawer. But they are stubborn a-holes. I think they won't rest until they get revenge."

Looking at Mike, I asked "What did you do to the Sergeant when you stole the MRE's?"

He laughed. "I found a pile of newspapers and quickly started a fire as a distraction. Then I ran from the room and yelled "FIRE" and waited for those two buffoons to come running. The Sergeant showed up, and as he ran into the room, I tripped him and sent him into a wall, head first. Your pal Mutley must have been jerking off somewhere, because I never saw him until you cold-cocked him outside the building."

"They'll both have headaches for a while," I said.

The heat was stifling. "Damn, the humidity must be 99%," I complained. I took a swig of water from my canteen and offered it to Burnsy. "Here, have a drink. Please share it with the girl."

We trudged on, taking turns pushing the cart with the MRE's. The sky was darkening – another storm was approaching from the west. Finally, we reached the intersection that marked the last mile to our home. "Just a bit more," I said to Burnsy and the girl.

As we walked, Burnsy asked, "What exactly are your plans for me?"

Mike looked at me and spoke with lightly veiled sarcasm in his voice. "We needed an old guy so we could elect a President."

"He's joking," I interjected. "Just before we liberated you and the girl, Mike and I were discussing what sort of government we'd form in this new world."

"Interesting topic!" Burnsy exclaimed. "What did you come up with?"

"I don't think we came up with anything."

As the gravel crunched beneath our feet, I said, "You told me you were a chemist at Michigan State University."

"I was."

"I convinced our little tribe that we needed to add new people to our community. People who know stuff. You seem like you might be able to help us with problem solving."

"Thank you for your effort," he replied.

"Well, you did give me that box of MRE's. It was the least I could do."

We smiled and looked east across hundreds of acres of unplanted fields.

"There it is," I said, pointing at a mangled mess of trees in the distance. "That's our place."

*****

Our timing couldn't have been better, because we made it to the driveway just as heavy rain began to fall. The four of us each grabbed a corner of the cart and pushed the valuable food towards the house before the boxes could get soaked.

Trix and Connie, who had been sitting on the front porch, ran to join us.

"Quick, let's get these boxes out of the rain."

We all pitched in and unloaded the cart. Then I directed Burnsy and the girl to the porch and suggested that they sit and rest wherever they could.

Trix look at our two new guests and smiled. "Hello! I am Trixie. Welcome to our little survival group."

"Forgive me for not standing," Burnsy said, offering a handshake to Trix. "I am exhausted!"

She laughed and looked at the girl. "And who do we have here?"

The girl looked away quickly and refused to answer.

"She does not speak," Burnsy said.

"Oh," Trixie replied. "Such a dear little thing! She took the girls hand and said, "Come with me, honey, let's get you cleaned up!"

*****

The storm passed quickly, leaving the landscape drenched and steamy with humidity. Oh, how I longed for just one dry, sunny day!

We went back outdoors, where Mike and I put a sheet of plywood on a couple of salvaged saw horses and made an improvised table, which the women piled with a MRE smorgasbord.

We all gathered around the bland but abundant food. Wanting to make this a fun affair, I said to everyone, "Oh, the reconstituted potatoes look delicious!"

I heard a few laughs.

"Who will say grace?" Trixie asked.

There was a moment of silence, then Connie spoke.

"Thank you Lord for this wonderful meal." (I sort-of grimaced). "We welcome our new friends to our meal and our family. Please Lord, look over us and save us from further trials and tribulations. (Great. Now I'm thinking about *Jesus Christ Superstar*, one of my all-time favorite musicals). "Lord, we all trust you to lead us to salvation as we work to build a new community. In Christ our lord, Amen."

We each said our "Amen" and then began passing around the food. While it wasn't exactly Thanksgiving, we did have variety.

"The canned beans and franks are actually pretty good," Emily stated. Her little guy, Declan, was happily shoving the sweet and savory beans into his mouth.

I looked at our newest female family member, who sat quietly between Trixie and Emily. With clean hair and clothing, she was a beautiful young lady. I guessed she was a 14 or 15 years old. Sitting directly across the table, I tried to make eye contact with her and smile, but she kept her eyes down.

Trix gave me a knowing nod – indicating that we needed to be patient with the girl. After the way she'd been treated by Muttley and the Sergeant, it could take weeks for her to begin to trust us.

"Mr. Burns," Emily said, "Please tell us about yourself."

He took a swig of powdered orange drink and told us his story.

"Before the plastic began to disappear, I was a chemist at Michigan State University. I married late in life, and my poor wife, Susan, was diagnosed with ovarian cancer just one year into our marriage. She passed one year later, and I've been alone ever since. Still, we did enjoy our brief time together."

A sad moment passed between us all. "Anyway," he continued. "I commuted daily to MSU. I taught advanced chemistry and a few math classes to underclassmen. My career at State was steady and unremarkable. I guess I flew under the radar."

"So you never had any children?" Trixie asked.

"My one regret! I love children, and as I see you here with your children I am very, very happy."

"Our children need a new grandpa," Connie announced.

He smiled and nodded in agreement. "I would be honored!"

"Hey wait," I laughed. "Until today I was the honorary grandpa around here!"

"Sorry pal," Burnsy replied. "I win by default of my advanced age."

"Are you able to explain to us what happened to the plastic?" Mike asked. "It would be good to hear this from a scientist."

"You flatter me! I simply taught science. I wasn't fortunate to have the opportunity to work on many research grants."

"Still," Mike continued. "You must know more than the rest of us."

He nodded in agreement. "I'll tell you my theory."

We excused the children from the table to run off and play as Burnsy spoke. Our rescued girl sat quietly in her chair, perhaps listening to our conversation, more likely lost in the nightmare of her recent existence.

"First, I have no idea what actually caused the plastic to sublimate. I imagine something went wrong in a lab somewhere, and well, here we are. But the plastic did sublimate..."

"Please explain "sublimate," Mr. Burns," Trixie asked.

"Sublimation," he explained, "Is the process in which a solid turns into a gas."

"Hence the explosions," I stated.

"You are right," he continued. "Plastic turned into gas – methane– and left us with exploding buildings and burning roads. Even I was confused about what was happening at first, but I soon realized that *visible light* was causing plastic to sublimate. So unless we keep all remaining plastic in complete and utter darkness, it will sublimate."

Miranda, who up to now had been quiet, asked "Do you think we could ever create something like plastic again?"

"I've wondered about that," he replied. "At first I thought only plastics derived from fossil fuels was subject to degradation, but nowadays a lot of plastic is made from vegetable oils too. And that is also unstable."

We all sat quietly and pondered our uncertain future.

Trixie spoke first. "Our ancestors created a modern world before plastic was invented. We will have to persevere and invent our own world. We will learn to make things again." She smiled and looked directly in Burnsy's eyes. "With Mr. Burns help, of course."

He laughed, "Of course! How could I ever say no to such a persuasive and beautiful woman?"

"So now you know what I've been dealing with for almost 40 years!" I shared, laughing.

At the end of an exhausting day, we were all happy to have full stomachs and a chance to relax. With low clouds hovering overhead, darkness fell and we headed back inside the house to sleep.

Chapter 17

The next two weeks were a busy and happy time for our entire extended family. Our new teenage female eventually felt safe among us, and while she was eerily quiet, we did learn her name: Alex.

We enjoyed our nightly campfires, with everyone relaxing and telling stories. I entertained everyone with a variety of classic rock songs played on my old guitar. Sometimes the group joined me on the choruses, and Trixie, who never forgot *anything*, was always ready to help me remember half-forgotten lyrics.

The ground was finally drying, so we used shovels and hoes and worked the soil and planted our first garden. The goats, with their happy yet destructive disposition, were a constant threat to our plantings, so Mike and I built a fence from scavenged chicken wire and metal fence posts. I was also able to find the fittings I needed to connect the huge propane pig to our propane grill. Now we could heat water and cook as much as we wanted. The plan going forward into the next winter was to find as many small canisters of propane as possible to use when the large tank eventually became empty.

Our group enjoyed fresh eggs from the chickens and milk from the goats. Miranda was experimenting with goat cheese, but so far all she could show us was some nasty looking curds.

In response to look of disdain on my face she said, "Relax. These things take time! We'll be eating cheese sooner than you think!"

Mike and I kept our eyes constantly looking west, as we both suspected the Sergeant and Muttley were looking for us. Hopefully they were too lazy to strike out as far as our little commune. After all, there were plenty of easy pickings in town.

When real trouble came we were horribly unprepared.

I must have been struck in the head as I slept. When I awoke, probably two days later, I had a raging headache and a probable concussion. I remained on the floor and felt dried blood on the top of my head. Flies buzzed around the room, attracted to whatever it was that smelled like rotting meat. As I began to sit up, the room spun out of control and I passed out again. It was night when I awoke, and this time my head was clearer. The room was silent. I reached towards Trixie's sleeping pad only to discover that she was not there.

"Trixie?" I gasped with a throat that was desperate for water.

"Mike? Anyone?"

The room remained silent.

I crawled towards the table and gasped as my left hand touched a stiff, cold human body. Using all of the strength I possessed, pulled myself up into a chair. In the darkness I was nearly blind, so I carefully felt across the table until I found what I was looking for: matches.

The light from the small fire nearly blinded me, and with blurry, spinning vision, I was able to locate and light a candle.

I will forever wish that I had never lit that candle. Actually, I wish I had not awoken from my concussion-induced sleep, for the carnage in the room is something that once it is seen cannot be unseen. It was the sort of destruction that is only found in horror films or in far-away places on the evening news. Mike had been brutally beaten. The top of his head was caved in, his face was virtually unrecognizable. His legs and arms were splayed in unnatural directions. I could only surmise that Mike had fought the intruders and lost. I guess it was my good fortune to have only been struck hard enough to cause me to pass out. The intruders may have believed that I was also dead, so they left me as I lay.

My thirst was overwhelming. I carefully stood, candle in hand, and went in search of water. In the kitchen, which looked as if it had been completely ransacked – all of our utensils, pans, cans of spices, towels were scattered throughout the room. I found a metal water bottle lying upon the countertop, half-buried in a pile of cotton towels. I lifted the bottle and was relieved to find it still contained water.

I urgently took a swig. My head throbbed like crazy, and the room began to spin again. I closed my eyes and tried to concentrate on breathing. Slow breath in, slow breath out. After a moment my equilibrium recovered a bit and I resumed my inspection of the carnage. I moved toward the door that led outdoors and nearly stumbled over the prostrate body of Burnsy. His stiff body lay across the steps that separate the kitchen from the mud room. I didn't need to take his pulse to know that the old man was dead.

I still hadn't found Trixie, Emily, my grandchildren, or any of Mike's family. Miranda was also missing. Whoever it was that had invaded our home had evidently planned on killing the men and stealing the children. I collapsed onto a wooden bench, placed my aching head into my hands, and cried like I had never cried before. Just when we had begun to feel as if we were going to survive and foster a new community it was all taken away in a heartbeat. My sorrow for the loss of my dear friend Mike was intense and painful, but even worse was my grief over losing my wife, daughter, and grandchildren. Maybe I would have been better off dying in the initial methane explosions. Maybe we should have all died last spring, when this whole mess began.

I rose and looked into the darkness outdoors. It was still night, but I had no idea how many hours until the sun rose. I went back into the house and curled up onto a ball and slept, knowing that in the morning I would be leaving to find my family.

*****

Upon awakening my first thought was, "Boy, what a horrible dream!" But as light crept into the dining room I could see that my experience the night before had been real. Mike's body still rested on the floor. The women and children were still gone.

I carefully rose from my sleeping pad, testing my balance and equilibrium. The room remained steady and I slowly walked into the kitchen, where I found my water bottle.

As I took a swig of cool water, I looked towards the kitchen door and saw the feet of Burnsy poking through the doorway. I would have to take care of the old man and Mike before I could leave to find my family.

I walked towards our coat rack and was surprised to find that the canvas backpack that I used to carry my Sig remained unmolested.

181

Evidently, the intruders were after people, not possessions. Ignoring Burnsy, I went down into the basement to see what food remained for me to take on my journey. I found a dozen or so foil-wrapped energy bars, which I threw into my backpack. There were a couple of glass bottles of tea and several glass jars containing MRE entrees. I took the tea and left the MRE's, which were too heavy for my light pack. I returned upstairs with enough food to last me a few days at most. Scavenging for food was definitely in my future.

I wondered, how had the bastards found us? Were they the same guys that had seen Mike over two weeks ago as he trekked home from Clare? Maybe they spotted the smoke from our nightly campfires. Fuck, I was personally responsible for this. We should have increased our security, left someone on nightly watch. Hindsight is hell and I was beating myself up. With rage burning through my veins I turned and smashed my foot through the kitchen door. My head, which still heart like hell, pulsed and throbbed where I had been struck by the intruders.

"Son of a bitch!" I screamed, "You motherfuckers will PAY for this.

Shaking with anger, I pulled on my boots and dragged Burnsy and Mike's bodies outdoors. I was surprised to find hoof prints all over my front yard. Evidently, the intruders arrived and left on horseback.

"Damn," I muttered. The intruders were leaving easy-to-follow tracks, but they would be able to travel much faster than I could on foot. That meant that I'd need to use my bicycle – which would work fine as long as they stayed on roads.

I returned to Burnsy and Mike and dragged the bodies to the back side of my property, well away from the house and garden. Taking time I did not have, I quickly dug two shallow holes and buried the men. I would return and do a better job later.

Without fanfare and with grim determination I mounted my bicycle and left, following the hoof prints. Taking one glance back, I saw the goats munching away at weeds in the front yard. Mike's dog Radar was nowhere to be found. Em's two small pooches were sniffing around a pile of garbage on the corner of the property. I looked at the dogs and exclaimed, "You guys are no help at all!"

I put effort into pedaling and rode into a stiff headwind on what remained of the road.

*****

Evidently the intruders felt that there would be no survivors left to track them, as they made no attempt at evasion. Their hoof prints lead straight north, and as I rode I recalled Mike's story of encountering a group of horsemen as he walked south from his trapping adventure in Northern Michigan. Were these the same horsemen?'

My bicycle held up surprisingly well, considering the road surface was nothing more than rocks and dirt. With no spare tire or pump, a flat would mean that I'd have to walk. The wind had shifted from the south, so I had the benefit of a tailwind. The perpetually cloudy sky dripped occasional raindrops upon my sweaty head. The landscape was totally devoid of human presence. I passed empty, burned-out homes and rode through ghost towns. Was everyone dead? Or had the intruders gathered them all up?

I pedaled with urgency, not caring about my own safety. My only thoughts were on finding my family before they could be harmed.

As darkness fell I began to look for a place to spend the night. On my right I saw a rural school building. I rode up the drive and stashed my bicycle in the rear where it wouldn't easily be spotted. I munched on a stale energy bar as I inspected the building. The main doors to the school were open, the latches broken by someone with a crowbar or other implement. I found a quiet room, spread out a wool blanket, and lay down to sleep. I'd ridden about 60 miles that day, which meant I was close to where Mike had seen the horsemen. With luck I'd find them soon.

*****

I woke, ate another stale energy bar, and hit the road. After a few hours of uneventful travel I came to a crossroad, where the hoof prints split and went in opposite directions. Since the majority of prints headed west, I also went west.

183

Up to now the rain hadn't amounted to anything more than annoying sprinkles. Without warning, the sky released a massive downpour, making the road a quagmire of mud that my skinny tires could not handle. Worse, the hoof prints were disappearing. I pushed my bicycle into the remains of a barn to sit out the storm. Finding a comfortable spot among hay bales, I relaxed and pondered my situation. I must have dozed, because I was startled awake as I felt something pulling on my pack, which rested under my left arm.

"Hey," I yelled as I jumped to my feet. "Leave my bag alone!"

A small child ran away quickly and disappeared into the back of the barn.

"OK," I said, as calmly as possible as I walked towards where I saw the person disappear. "I am not here to hurt you. Come out of there."

After a moment of waiting, I had an idea. I removed an energy bar from my bag, unwrapped the foil, and set it where it would be easily seen.

"I have food. I will share."

I went back to the hay bales and sat, watching the energy bar. After a minute or two a shoeless, filthy boy, with wild, unkempt hair and tattered clothing emerged. The child walked towards the food, never taking his eyes from me. In a flash, he grabbed the food and disappeared back into the shadows.

I decided to be coy and ignore the child. I doubted I could get any information from him anyway. I rested and dozed for another hour or so as I waited for the rain to stop.

I could feel the eyes of the child staring at me. How had this little person survived? Was he all alone out here? Did he belong to anyone? Or had he escaped from the horsemen?

The rain stopped. I pushed my bicycle outside but quickly found the road too muddy to use.

"Dang," I complained. As I turned to push the bicycle back into the barn I spotted the child, who was staring at me with huge, blue, fearful eyes. He raised his arm and pointed. I turned and saw a group of five horsemen crest a hill about a mile away, heading towards us. Without thinking, I sprinted with my bike towards the barn. Hopefully they hadn't seen us. If they had, I needed to set up a defensive position.

*****

The horsemen rode up to the barn and stopped to argue among themselves.

"Damn it all Jenkins, there is no one here."

"Fuck you, James. I know what I saw."

Crouching in the darkness behind metal machinery at the rear of the barn, I could see the figure of a tall man standing in the doorway. With caution, he walked into the building and stopped directly in front of the hay I had been sitting upon. Cripes, I hoped that I hadn't left anything laying there!

Evidently there was nothing to see, for the man turned and abruptly left the building.

I heard the first man speak again. "See, I told you there was nothing in there."

"Fuck you, James."

After a few moments, I emerged from the darkness and crept to the front door. The riders, which appeared to be all men, rode away, heading east.

I went back to the hay bales and was surprised to find a wad of tin foil lying on the floor.

"It's a good thing that guy didn't find this," I said to myself.

I sat for a bit and waited for my young friend to join me. I took a pull from my water bottle and relaxed. Maybe this youngster knew something about the riders. The last thing I wanted was to be responsible for another person, but I needed information. Hopefully, this little person could help.

*****

I was fairly confident that I had found the horsemen that had abducted my family and friends. The question was, what was I to do about it? For the last couple of days I had been consumed with the

185

idea of finding them but had not considered the end game. I couldn't kid myself – I was no lone vigilante. While I had a good handgun and knife, I knew that any direct attack upon their group would end in disaster for me.

I walked to the rear of the barn to take a leak and thought about my situation. I could try to infiltrate the group. Maybe they'd accept me and then I could sneak my people away after a few weeks.

No, that wouldn't work. They'd come after us for sure. The grim fact was that I needed to get my family away safely *and* eliminate any future threat of retribution.

I returned to the barn and found the child munching on another of my energy bars.

I laughed. "You must be hungry! You are going to eat everything I have."

Without responding, the child ate and stared up at me with a filthy face.

"What is your name?" I asked.

No reply.

"Are you all alone?"

The child continued to eat. I sat and took a pull from my canteen. While I held my head back and drank, I felt a tug on the canteen's strap.

"Easy there, little one! Are you thirsty?"

The child pulled at the canteen with surprising strength and said, "Drink!"

"Oh, so you can talk!"

After a long drink the child replaced the cap and placed the canteen on the hay bale.

"What is your name?"

After a few moments of silence, the child responded.

"Etan."

"Ethan?" I replied?

He nodded. "My name is Etan."

"Well, Ethan, my name is Greg."

Thinking that Ethan might have information that would help me find the horsemen's headquarters, I considered how I might extract the intel without further traumatizing the child.

"Ethan," I asked, "Do you have a mommy?"

A look of sadness came upon his little face. "Mommy is gone."

"Did the men on the horses take her?"

He nodded, yes

"Did they take you with them too?"

Another answer in the affirmative.

"Do you know where they live?"

He sat quietly for a bit, but finally responded with a hesitant "Yes."

"If I go with you, will you show me?"

He stood and walked across the dirty barn floor. He picked up a small rock and looked at it with 5-year-old curiosity.

"I will show you. We need to get my mommy."

I was extraordinarily relieved. Knowing where the horsemen lived was a huge advantage for me. My other advantage was that they had no idea that I even existed. If I could muster the courage, I just might be able to turn this situation around.

I reached out and stroked the boy's tangled and filthy hair. "We will find your mom, Ethan. I promise."

*****

Since it was late in the afternoon, I decided to rest for a few hours until dark. Then I would ask my little friend to take me to his mother. We napped, Ethan lying snugly next to me. Upon waking we shared my last remaining energy bar and bottle of Snapple.

As dusk fell, I gently took Ethan's hand in mine and led him outdoors. I crouched on one knee and looked him in the eyes.

"Which way do we go to find your mama?"

He pointed west.

"Is it far?"

He shook his head, no.

I stood and returned to the barn to grab my pack. If I was going to do this, it had to be soon. I was out of food and didn't want to even consider what happened to my female family members and friends at the hands of a bunch of dangerous, wild men.

Back outdoors, I took Ethan's hand and said, "Show me the way."

Chapter 18

The relentless low overcast provided excellent darkness to reconnoiter enemy territory. It was a steamy night, and I quickly saturated my wool shirt as Ethan and I trekked through the empty landscape. I was astounded at the boy's ability to lead me to the horsemen. I doubted I could have remembered the route when I was five years old – and I hadn't suffered anywhere near Ethan's trauma when I was a child.

I tried not to think too hard about what I would find when we reached our destination. While I doubted that any substantial harm had come to the children, I was not so sure that the women would have been left unscathed. I thought back to conversations I'd had years before, when civilization was still intact and plastic was something you rarely thought about.

My friends all knew that I was about as non-violent as a person could possibly be. I did not hunt, and with the exception of one minor altercation (I punched a small-time thug who had tried to steal my bicycle), I had led a peaceful life. But due to recent circumstances, I had resorted to violence, and I was afraid that I might be getting a little too comfortable with the act of hurting others.

"There must be a situation where you'd harm someone," my friend Tony asked years before as we drove north for weekend of skiing.

"I get angry just like anyone, Tony. Like the time my bike was stolen. I caught the guy before he could make his getaway, and the second he opened his mouth to spout off, I popped him."

"I didn't know you had it in you," Tony laughed.

"Me either! But I imagine the one thing that would set me off would be if someone intentionally harmed my family. I suppose I'd lose all control and go all Clint Eastwood on their sorry ass."

So here I was, years later, thinking about the violence that was sure to occur in the next few hours. With luck I could use stealth to my advantage and rescue my people. But I would not hesitate to strike first.

Ethan led me west about a mile, then we turned north on what used to be a fairly major state highway. The outlines of former gas stations, hotel chains, and franchised restaurant chains loomed in the darkness. Even though I couldn't be sure, I was fairly confident that we were nearing the southern outskirts of Clare, the same town where Mike had been checking his traps two weeks earlier.

After walking another ten minutes or so, Ethan stopped.

"What's up, buddy?" I asked. "Are we here?"

He nodded. "We are here."

In the darkness I had difficulty telling what "here" meant. I walked to the side of the road and saw a weed-covered chain-link fence. Ethan grabbed my hand and pulled me into a small cluster of pine trees.

I understood his intent immediately – we had to stay out of sight. The horsemen would have sentries, and without Ethan, I would have stumbled right into them.

I figured it was about midnight. We had walked about six miles from the barn to arrive here. Ethan was tired, and I watched as he curled up beneath a pine tree and quickly fell asleep. Sitting still during a crisis was never my strong suit, so I decided to investigate the property.

Cautiously, I walked along the fence. Fortunately, thick weeds and trees helped to conceal me from anyone who might be watching. I followed a two-track path towards the rear of the property until I came to a locked gate, with a sign overhead proclaiming "Clare County Fairground: Vendor Entrance".

Aha! It made perfect sense now. Suppose you've got a gang of 10 or 20 guys, and each of you has a horse. A fairground would provide shelter for you and your animal, plus some basic security. They probably had access to water and ample room to grow crops too. Plus, they'd been really lucky, they might have some livestock.

I didn't see any human activity at all on this corner of the property, so I continued to move along the fence. In another 50 yards I reached the rear of the grounds and made a hard left turn and continued following the fence. I had entered a thickly wooded area, and was surprised to find that one of the frequent storms had blown a tree onto the fence. I climbed the tree and easily used it as a bridge to gain access to the other side of the fence. Once I found my people, I could lead them back to this spot and we could escape through the forest.

I crept quietly forward in the darkness, moving from tree to tree. The night was eerily silent. It seemed like everyone must be asleep, for I could hear nothing.

Reaching the end of the wooded area, I encountered a clearing. Sitting in the middle of 20 acres of unkempt grassland were three or four outbuildings. If this fairground was anything like the one back home, there would be a couple of pole barns for animals, a commercial building, and a main fair office. Staying in the darkness, I waited and watched.

Sometime deep in the middle of the night I awoke, startled, surprised that I had allowed myself to fall asleep. I heard a door open and could just barely see a person emerge from the smallest building.

It turned out to be a man who was outside to relieve himself. After taking a very long piss, he zipped his trousers and returned inside. I concluded that this small building was the main office, which would be where they slept. Would the women be in there with them, or were they kept somewhere else?

I moved slowly and carefully towards the buildings, crouching, keeping low in the grass so I would not be discovered. At one point I reached a dry ditch, which I easily crossed. I climbed up a small hill and was back on the main grounds. I crept forward until I reached the back of a large pole barn. My heart pounded and my hands broke out in a cold sweat. No messing around here, Greg, I said to myself. This is for real. Get a grip on yourself!

I pulled off my backpack and retrieved my knife and the Sig. I had just two clips of bullets – one in the gun and one spare. The knife, which had belonged to my good neighbor Mike, was potentially lethal.

I held the knife in my right hand and put the handgun in the rear of my trousers, just like I'd seen in countless television shows.

I continued moving along the side of the building. Eventually I reached the front, where two huge sliding doors stood, partially opened. This was fortunate for me, for I certainly would have made a lot of noise opening these doors. Once inside, I was enveloped in near total darkness.

I crept forward, holding the knife in attack position. I almost shrieked at the sound of a horse snorting. Laughing at myself, I knew that I'd have to be a whole lot more mentally strong if I were to have any chance of perseverance.

After several moments of carefully reconnoitering the barn I was confident that it held horses and nothing more. I continued my search in the next building, which as I suspected, contained a small assortment of livestock. They had one cow, a steer, and a few pigs and rabbits - slim pickings for such a dangerous crew.

The next building would most likely be a commercial building. This is probably where they kept their captives. I also assumed it would be guarded.

Thinking about how I might improve my chances of survival, I crept slowly around the building, looking for some dark dirt to smear upon my face. The clouds broke and I spotted some barrels about 20 yards away. At that moment I realized that I was dying of thirst, for I had left my canteen back with Ethan – and if the barrels contained water I would enjoy a drink. I could also use the water to make mud, which I would smear on my face.

I tiptoed to the barrel and removed the lid. Yes, it was water! I set the knife on an adjacent barrel and used my hands to cup the cool, refreshing water.

"Can't sleep either?"

It was a man's voice. Someone who, in the darkness, probably thought I was part of the gang.

I don't know why, but it made sense to try to disguise my voice. "No," I said, in a low, raspy tone. "Too damn hot."

The other man sauntered next to me and found a metal ladle that I hadn't discovered. He took a drink and sighed. "Yea, the heat is a bitch. But the women almost make everything worthwhile."

I guess I should have laughed along with him, because when I failed to reply, he looked at me closer. "Hey, who the hell are you!"

They say that killing a man with your bare hands is something you will never forget, and let me tell you, they are right. Relying entirely on instinct, I found my knife and in one fluid motion, drove it straight into the man's neck. I continued pushing as the warm, sticky blood poured over my hand. After a few moments, the man fell forward to the ground, lifeless. The entire event took less than ten or twenty seconds, but it felt much, much longer. I knelt on the ground next to the dead man and waited, listening carefully to see if anyone else had been alerted.

After several moments I realized that, for the time being, everyone was still asleep. I looked at the dead man and said quietly, "Sorry, pal. But you reap what you sow." I wiped my hands and the bloody knife on the man's trousers and returned the knife to the sheath. As quietly as possible, I dragged the sentry back behind the livestock building where he would not be easily discovered.

I returned to the commercial building and found a small entrance door, which was half-open and unlocked. The man I had just killed had probably been on guard duty, and he left the door and building open for me. I had been very, very lucky. But sometimes luck is better than skill.

I entered the building. A narrow hallway led to my left. A chair, probably where the guard rested, sat on my right. Using extreme caution, I stealthily moved down the dark hallway and entered a larger open area. The darkness was all-consuming here, and as I felt along the wall I found a door.

Locked. Damn it, there must a key somewhere! I felt along the wall and was not able to find a key. Then I realized that the sentry would most likely have the keys on him. So I backtracked to the livestock building and found the dead guy. I searched his pockets and found a small key ring, holding just two keys.

Back inside the commercial building, I found the locked door and nearly freaked out when neither key would work. I took a deep breath and tried the keys again. With satisfaction, the lock clicked and the door opened.

The room was extremely quiet. In the darkness I could see very little, but I could tell it was a very large space. If the women and children were in here, they were all asleep (or pretending). I crept through the room and whispered, "Trixie... Emily..."

I heard a muffled sound and was struck square in the back by a heavy object. I fell to the cold cement floor and gasped for breath as the wind was completely knocked out of me. Sensing danger, I rolled and retrieved my knife and swung out in a wide arc.

"Gaaaah! You sonofabitch!" With my breath slowly returning, I lunged forward at a large shape and drove the knife upward into soft tissue.

Another heavy blow fell against the top of my head, but I barely registered the pain. Adrenalin and anger fueled my rage as I twisted the knife loose and plunged it once more into my attacker. I heard another gasp of pain as the large man collapsed to the floor, his lifeblood rapidly leaving his body.

I sat on the floor, stunned. After a few moments, heard a voice – a voice that I had almost believed I might never hear again.

"Daddy! Is that you?" she whispered. Following the sound, I found the body of my daughter and wrapped my arms around her. She was naked beneath a blanket, holding the baby Cora tightly. "It's alright, Em. I am here now."

I embraced my daughter and granddaughter for a very long time, yet I kept my ears open for the sound of any more male adversaries.

I released myself from Emily's grasp and asked, "Where is your mother? Is she all right?"

Emily's silence told me much more than words ever would. I knew right then that Trixie had not survived.

*****

I lit a candle and surveyed the room. Emily, Miranda, and Connie Foster sat on the floor, each of them naked except for the blankets they sat upon. Anger consumed me as I realized what horrors these women had been subjected to, and my rage intensified as I saw that they each had a chain running from their ankle to a wall beam. There were also three additional women that were captives. As I fought to recover my senses I nodded at them.

"Hello. My name is Greg. I am going to get you out of this." Looking at the women, I asked, "Is one of you Ethan's mother?"

I heard sobbing in the darkness. Under the dim candlelight I saw a filthy, naked woman bury her face in her hands. "You have my baby!" she cried. "You have Ethan?"

Crouching next to the woman I explained, "Yes, he is safe outside the compound. I will take you to him."

I found several children, including our newest family member, Alex, in an adjacent room that was opened with the other key on the keyring.

My grandson Declan looked up at me from the blanket he had been laying upon and said, "Hi Coppa."

"Hi, Declan. Time to get up. We are leaving this place."

I returned to the main room and inspected the lock that held the chain to my daughter's leg.

Miranda spoke, her voice barely above a whisper. "I think that asshole has the key." She nodded in the direction of the man I had just killed.

I found the key in his pocket and was able to unlock all of the women, who gathered the children and waited for my instructions.

I whispered to the adults, "I saw one other man leave the main building earlier tonight. He might be the only left."

"There were at least five other men here earlier today," said Emily.

"I saw them riding when I was holed up in a barn. They were heading east."

"Probably scavenging for more slaves," Connie responded.

"Okay, here's what I am going to do. I will go take out the other guy and make sure there is no one left here to follow us."

Emily asked, "What about the horses?"

"We will have to leave them," I replied. "Too easy to track."

With my knife in one hand and the Sig in the other, I left the commercial building and quietly walked to the main fairgrounds office. I tried peeking into the windows, but could see nothing. I reached the front door, and found it to be unlocked.

Opening the door as quietly as possible, I heard a rustling sound and then a tired, male voice spoke from a dark corner in the rear of the room.

"Must have had your fill of that young pussy, eh?"

It took a lot of effort, more than I can ever explain, to reply, "Yup. Pussy."

The man chuckled, but even though it was very dark, I could tell that he hadn't bothered to rise from where he had been sleeping.

"Here," he said, "I've got a bottle of Jim Beam."

"Jim Beam," I replied quietly as I walked towards him.

When I reached his dark corner, I could make out his arm reaching up to me with the bottle of whiskey. I reached down for the bottle, but at the last second I shifted my weight and drove the knife into his chest until I was stopped by bone.

"Arrrrgh!" he gasped. "What the fuck!"

Using all of my strength and pent-up anger, I extracted the knife and drove it hard into his heart, severing arteries with the cold steel that had been tempered and hand-built by my friend Mark.

"That is for Trixie, you bastard. I hope you rot in hell."

He looked up at me, and even in the darkness I could see the surprise and fear in his eyes.

I removed the knife, wiped it clean on his bedding, and stepped backwards. Since no one else had come to this creep's assistance, I concluded that for now, all of the raiders were dead. Striking a match, I found several boxes of canned goods – soup, vegetables, and fruit cocktail. Cases of Jim Beam sat nearby. There were also three backpacks, some clothes, and an assortment of firearms.

Returning to the women, I told them of my discovery and brought them back into the office where they dressed as best they could. They filled the packs with cans of food and distributed the firearms among themselves.

The sky was just beginning to show the slightest hint of daylight as we crossed the fallen tree and headed back into the forest.

We reached a small clearing and I told the women to wait while I retrieved something.

Running as quickly as possible, I returned to the stand of pines where I had left my newest friend, Ethan.

Carefully shaking the boy on the shoulder, I woke him and said, "Come on Ethan, you are going with me now."

We jogged back to the women, who were standing with their firearms ready to kill.

"Easy everyone," I whispered as I approached, "It's just me and my friend Ethan."

Just then Ethan's mother ran forward and smothered her son in hugs and kisses. "Oh, Ethan! I never thought I'd see you again."

"That's all right mama," he replied. "I've been taking care of myself."

In the dawn light the women and children, who all had haunted looks upon their filthy faces, looked at Ethan and nodded.

"Come on, everyone," I stated. "We've gotta get out of this place."

Chapter 19

Moving as quickly as possible, I led our group back to the barn where my bicycle was stashed. Without taking a break, we walked south, keeping to country roads and staying off the main highway. As I pushed my bicycle on the crushed stone and dirt of the road, I worried about leaving a trail that the remaining horsemen would follow. The sky to the west was darkening as another storm approached. With luck, rain would soon fall and obliterate our footprints.

Under a gloomy sky we marched, silent, no one saying a word about the experiences of the last week. With each step I longed for Trixie, and several times I felt she was walking along beside me. I'd catch a glimpse of her, dressed in the well-worn clothing of our survival, out of the corner of my eye. Then I'd turn to look and she'd be gone, nothing more than a memory.

I did not press Emily for details of Trixie's death, but eventually I learned the truth.

"She resisted. We buried her. I wish I could show you where it happened, but we were blindfolded."

Monstrous, bullying men had taken the life of my wife, a woman who was the kindest, most helpful person you would ever have the pleasure of knowing. I felt responsible for Trixie's death and the evil that had been forced upon the other women. I made a vow to myself that I would never let it happen again.

Enormous raindrops began to fall from the sky. We were exposed, on an open road, with no shelter in sight.

I shouted encouragement. "Come on! We've gotta find someplace dry."

We picked up the pace, with some of the women carrying the smaller children. Finally, after walking nearly two miles, we found an old farm that had one remaining structure – a cement block milk house. Six women, six children, and me, all clambered inside the 20 x 20 building.

"At least it's dry!" Emily exclaimed. She set about spreading the blankets we'd taken from the fairgrounds on the cement floor to make a comfortable spot for the children. Lightning crashed nearby, startling everyone. A long roll of thunder rumbled, and the wind picked up. Through filthy windows we could see debris flying by outdoors.

"This is going to be one hell of a storm," I said quietly. I moved close to Emily and whispered, "The rain will make it impossible for those men to find us."

As we waited out the storm, we shared our food and had a cold but filling meal. Emily and I ate refried beans and water. Declan was thrilled to have beans and franks, his favorite meal. The other children feasted upon fruit cocktail and canned spaghetti-o's.

For the first time in three days I had time to consider our options. I needed to get back to my home to retrieve the *Firefox* books, but the horsemen, seeking revenge, would certainly head there too. We were about 80 miles north-west of my house. Hopefully the remaining marauders hadn't yet discovered what we'd done and we had a head start. My bicycle gave me an advantage – with luck I could get home in just one day. Hopefully this storm would blow out overnight and leave me with a couple of dry days.

A massive blast of thunder rattled the windows. I stood and gathered the women near me.

"Who here knows how to handle a firearm?"

One of the women who had been quiet up to this point spoke up. With a stocking cap pulled tightly over her frizzy black hair and intense, deep blue eyes, she looked rather intimidating. Resting in the crook of her arm was the 12 gage she'd been carrying all day. "I used to hunt with my boyfriend."

"Good!" I exclaimed. "Anyone else?"

When I failed to receive a reply, I said, "OK. We'll find a way to get you all some training. But for now, get some sleep. I am going to take first watch." I pointed at the woman with the shotgun. "And you will take the second..."

"My name is Beth."

"Get some sleep. I'll wake you up in a few hours."

The storm raged outside for the entire night, but we were dry and secure in the little building. Once or twice I was freaked out, thinking I saw horsemen outside, lit by the frequent lightning strikes.

"Just your imagination," I said quietly to myself.

*****

The dawn was gloomy but the storm had stopped. Beth turned out to be a vigilant look-out, and she let me sleep much longer than I'd anticipated.

"You looked like you needed sleep more than I did," she explained.

I laid our arsenal on the floor and took inventory. We had my Sig, the Glock, two shotguns, and two additional Colt handguns.

The shotguns had limited use, since we only had 24 shells – 12 slugs and 12 buckshot, all made with paper instead of plastic covering. The paper ones had to be at least 30 years old, because I clearly remember switching to the plastic shells when I deer hunted as a teenager.

We had 2 full clips of shells for the Sig, one clip for the Glock, and one clip each for the Colts. I resolved to locate additional weapons as soon as possible.

The women and children were beginning to stir. Emily handed me a Balance bar.

I pushed the bar back at her, "No thank you. Please share it with the children."

"You need to eat, Dad. The kids are fine. We have enough food for now."

I bit into stale conglomeration of oats, honey, nuts, and protein. To be truthful, I could have eaten a dozen.

I finished chewing and said, "Listen up, everyone! We are going to head out soon. The goal is to find you all a safe place to hang out for a few days. As soon as we find you a suitable shelter, I am going to return to my home to retrieve some valuable items that will help with our continued survival."

Connie spoke up. "What about weapons training?"

"I'd love to let you all fire off a few rounds, but we don't have enough ammunition. But I will give you all a brief demonstration of how to handle a handgun."

For the next several minutes I had each adult handle the various handguns. I pointed out how to use the safety and how to arm and reload the pistol.

When we were finished, I said, "No one will ever mistake us for an army. But we won't be pushovers either."

I led the group away from the farm, with Beth and her shotgun providing rear security. We took turns pushing my bicycle and carrying the younger children. I figured we were averaging about two miles per hour. The older children, who were all getting used to tramping across the countryside, were all keeping pace.

Eventually we entered the outskirts of a village. The destruction here was just as complete as it had been everywhere else.

"Keep your eyes peeled for a solid, brick building," I announced.

I led the group around the center of the town, hoping to avoid confrontation with any lingering survivors. Not that there would be anywhere for them to live – the entire town had been leveled by the storms and fires. Some facades were all that remained. The "Sanford Community Library" and "Margie's Diner" were nothing more than brick storefronts. The backs were nothing but rubble. We walked over a quaint one-lane bridge that allowed vehicles to cross a small river. I looked at Emily, pointed at the river and said, "Water supply."

As we quietly walked down the center of what had been a residential street, Miranda, who had been walking on my left, said, "Will that do?"

A block to east, across from a city park, was the First United Methodist Church. The building was modern, but it was made from brick and glass.

"I like the location," I answered. "It's got good sight lines on three sides."

We walked across the park, where I instructed our group to remain while I reconnoitered the area. Beth, confident with her shotgun, remained to watch over her new family.

Em left little Cora with Alex and joined me as I began to look for a way inside the building. With my Sig in hand, I quietly walked the perimeter of the building. Em, demonstrating a complete lack of concern, walked right up the front door and announced, "Hey dad, the front doors are unlocked!"

I followed Emily into the building and was pleasantly surprised that the inside was clean and dry. Stained glass windows allowed ample light to stream across through the comfortable foyer area, which at one time had featured carpeting and seating for visitors. Even in the condition it was currently in, it would be quite livable for our group.

While Emily looked around the church offices, I entered the main worship area. Walking slowly towards the altar, I recalled the many times I'd been in churches with Trixie. A wave of emotion rippled through my body as I came to a stop at the foot of the altar. Jesus looked at me, suspended above me on the back wall, his hands welcoming me to join him.

Tears began to flow from my eyes. I wept. I wept for the loss of Trixie and I wept for the hardships we had been forced to endure. I wept for Graham, my son that I may never see again. I wept for Jory, the father of my grandchildren.

"Jesus," I cried. "Why do You allow such evil to prevail upon Your world?

I waited and listened, my tears subsiding, and was not surprised that no answer was forthcoming. Such was the way of faith. You had to believe that everything happened for a reason. That God had "other" plans.

I prayed. "I don't know why Trixie was taken from me, Lord. But I will ask you plainly to keep those that remain safe. Please look after my grandchildren. And if Jory and Graham are alive, show me the way to them."

I turned and there was Emily, quietly sitting in the third row of pews.

"It feels good to be in here," she said.

I nodded in agreement. "It will do."

*****

While the church was a solid structure, all was not perfect. Emily and I searched the remainder of the building and discovered the basement. The room had most likely been used to serve after-service donuts or post-funeral meals. Metal folding chairs lined old wooden tables. The air reeked of decay. In the back of the room, resting on the floor, we found seven dried-out bodies.

Even though the room was quite dark, enough light streamed in through the windows to allow us to see that these people were elderly.

"Maybe they asphyxiated while waiting out a storm," Emily stated.

"Yeah, that's all I can think of. We'd better get them out of here.

We rummaged around and found a stack of cotton tablecloths, which we used to wrap the bodies.

"Help me lift this guy," I said to Em.

She took his feet and I took the upper half. "He's lighter than I expected," she proclaimed.

"Dehydration. These folks have been dead for at least two weeks."

Working quickly, we hauled the bodies outdoors. I opened the basement windows to allow fresh air into the building.

At the back of the basement we found a kitchen and began rummaging for food.

Emily opened a door. "Here's the pantry! Looks like we will have plenty of creamed corn, green beans, and dill pickles to eat while you are gone."

"At least you won't starve!" I laughed, realizing that it was the first time I'd laughed in days. Maybe being in church was good for me in some sort of unexplainable way. Ah, the mysteries of life!

We were also happy to find a door that led directly outdoors. A small set of outdoor steps headed up to ground level.

"I suggest you keep everyone down here while I'm gone."

Emily wrinkled her nose.

I added, "Hopefully, the stench will subside soon."

Chapter 20

It was late afternoon before I began my journey home. I had a ride of about 70 miles before me. The wind, which was blowing quite stiffly from the south, was not helping. I figured that I could average 12 to 15 miles per hour on the bicycle, which would put me near home at around 10 PM. If the rain held off, I would make it in one push.

The sky darkened and I heard far-off thunder, but it was a dry storm. In the blink of an eye, the wind shifted from the north-northwest, which pushed my speed a tolerable 16 or 18 MPH. I had to make it home to set up an ambush for the remaining horsemen, who were certainly on their way to exact their revenge.

I was confident that the group of women and children would be safe enough without me for a few days. Beth was a strong young lady who had recently lived through hell. Plus, she had a gun.

The group had more than enough canned goods to survive for weeks, and the river was just a few blocks away from the church.

The sun was laying low on the horizon as I reached familiar territory. I turned the pedals with urgency, as I suddenly possessed a strong desire to be home. As the last hint of twilight left the sky, I turned onto my road. When I was several hundred yards away from the house, I stopped and stashed my bicycle behind a fallen tree. With extreme caution, I crept to my home and watched from the boundary of the property. In the early evening darkness it was difficult to make out detail, but it looked as if everything was where I had left it nearly a week earlier. I watched and waited, not willing to expose myself to unnecessary danger. The goats were still there, and they had eaten all available greenery within their fenced-in area. I resolved to let them loose when I left.

Where were Emily's two dogs? Where was Mark's pooch, Radar?

I sat down on the ground and leaned against a fallen maple tree and made myself reasonably comfortable. The air was humid, and as I ran my hands through my sweaty hair, I thought about what a sight I must be. Damn, I could use a shower!

An hour or so after darkness I began to get sleepy. I rose to my feet and continued to watch the house. After another hour or so I concluded that the place must be empty. Quietly I approached the back door, but was suddenly stopped when I saw a flash of light shine between the boarded up windows.

In panic, I turned quickly and banged my shin on the children's Western Flyer wagon, which I hadn't seen in the darkness.

I fell to the ground as the wagon tipped over and crashed loudly on the paving stones that made up the sidewalk.

"Fuck!" I exclaimed to myself as I jumped to my feet and sprinted back to the safety of the fallen trees.

As I ran I heard the barking of one of Em's dogs, Cocoa.

I dove into the sticks and brush and lay as quietly as possible, despite the throbbing pain in my shin. There was someone in my house!

The back door to the house opened and the two dogs sprinted forward towards me. While both animals were noisy as hell, neither of them was aggressive. They stopped about 10 yards from my hiding place and continued barking. I had to wonder, where were you two yappers when my family was attacked and abducted?

A large body followed the dogs and stopped. I couldn't make out any details – was he holding a firearm?

"Who is out there?"

It was a friendly voice from the past!

"Jory!" I cried. "It's me, Greg!"

I stood and raised my hand. With caution, Jory walked forward several yards. He stopped and said, "Dad, is it really you!"

I ran forward and smothered him with a bear hug. "Yes it's me! I am so glad you made it!"

Tears poured from his eyes. "I never thought I'd see you again." He hugged me tight, and added, "Where is Emily? Where is Declan? Where is Cora?"

I nearly broke down myself. I was not yet ready to tell him about what happed to Trixie. "Your family is okay! They are in a church in the village of Sanford. I'll tell you everything, but we have a more urgent problem to take care of first..."

*****

I explained to Jory that raiders on horseback had taken everyone north, to be used as hostages and slaves.

"Motherfuckers!" he screamed. "I will make them pay."

"Well," I replied. "About half of them have already met their maker. But five or six are most likely on their way here, right now."

In the blink of an eye, Jory transformed from concerned father to United States Army Infantryman. His entire demeanor changed as his warrior instincts took over.

He had been holding a rifle. I pointed at it and asked, "What do you have there?"

"M-16. I was lucky to find it in the armory commander's office. All of the M-4's were made from plastic."

"How many rounds to you have?"

"I have ten 30-round magazines. Plus I have a Beretta M9 pistol, and five 17-round magazines." He reached down and pulled a huge knife from a sheath that was attached to his belt. "Plus I have this pig-sticker."

"Good!" I pulled the Sig from the small of my back, where I had been keeping it ready for fast retrieval. "I have this Sig Sauer pistol. It uses 10 millimeter bullets, and I have two 8 round magazines. I also have an excellent knife."

"Not bad. What do you know about the horsemen?"

"Not much, to be honest. My neighbor, Mike, met them the first time when he was hiking home after everything went to hell. Mike said they left him alone, but I guess they had second thoughts and eventually tracked him to this place."

Jory walked slowly towards the road, and I followed. After looking around, he said, "Okay, this is what we're gonna do."

*****

I sat in a hastily-made hiding place. Large branches provided cover and protection from the front, while additional branches provided camouflage. I faced east, but I could also see north and south. I leaned against a tree stump. If the marauders approached from the west, I'd be exposed but at least I could fire my weapon. I had a nice pile of large rocks ready to use as projectiles at my side, and lying across my lap was a ceremonial Mason's sword that had been given to me from my grandfather. It wasn't a weapon of war, but the point was sharp and it made me feel less vulnerable. Jory, with his military training and M-14 assault rifle, would lead the attack. He was our ace in the hole. The attackers would not expect organized resistance, and we had the element of surprise to our advantage.

As Jory and I built our forts, he told me that he had arrived at our home just hours before my return from the north. "I found the note that Emily left at my house, and then immediately began my hike over here."

"To find an empty house."

"Yeah, that sucked. I was so ready to see my kids and Emily! After everything I'd been through to get here, all I found was two dogs and a bloody dining room."

"Sorry about that," I replied. I had to leave in a hurry."

Sweat dripped from my forehead and armpits in the warm evening. The cool north wind had stopped sometime during the night and the humidity had returned.

Jory explained to me that the bad guys would most likely approach from the east, just before dawn. That way the sun would be in our eyes. If they came from the west, we would have the same advantage.

He built a similar shelter about thirty yards from mine, using salvaged cement blocks and stones from the foundation of our grainery building, which had been destroyed in the storm. He had 360 degrees of vision, but he was focused upon watching anyone who approached from the west.

We had agreed that whoever spotted the raiders first would signal the other with a mourning dove call.

Jory had suggested that we leave the dogs outdoors, as they would surely bark at anyone lurking in the darkness. We also lit some candles and placed them inside the house where they would be visible from the windows. Hopefully the raiders would see the candles and assume we were inside, unprepared for attack.

Looking at the old farmhouse in the darkness of the night, I thought back to all of the memories Trixie and I shared there. We were in our early 20's when we acquired the place, and at first the maintenance took a staggering amount of work. Working together, Trix and I repaired plaster, removed carpeting, sanded floors, and stripped wallpaper. The large lawn, which was home to almost 200 trees, required continuous care. Winters could be brutal too. Deep snow plugged the driveway and howling winds sucked the heat from the structure. Trixie and I raised both of our children here. We celebrated holidays and birthdays here. We mourned the losses of our grandparents and parents here. As grandparents ourselves, we played with Declan in the yard and enjoyed the company of our growing family. Everything had gone according to script until one day, out of the blue, plastic had become unstable. I wondered how the nation – no, how the world – had become so dependent upon one technology. When you look at all of the technological advancements that had taken place over the last century, one could argue that the adoption of plastics was the most ubiquitous. I couldn't conceive of any other technology, that if suddenly taken away, would be so disruptive to daily life. A lot of "preppers" worried about the grid going down. Losing electricity would be catastrophic, for sure, but people would not suddenly find themselves naked! They'd still be able to use plastic bottles, sleep on mattresses, and live in their homes. I would happily trade any other technology to have plastic back. The Internet? You can have it! All it did was divide everyone. While the Internet *did* provide effortless access to information and technology, it also fostered the invention of Social Media. It didn't take long for everyone to figure out, by using Facebook, Twitter, and Instagram, that their co-workers and neighbors were assholes! Take the Internet! But give me plastic back!

This old house, with part of its roof blown off in the storm and half of its windows gone, represented nearly 120 years of human progress. The first people to live here did not use plastic. Their daily lives, which lacked what modern people called "modern conveniences," were fulfilling. They worked hard, but they also socialized, went to shows, and traveled. If the human race was to survive, we would have to return to the way of life that our grandparents enjoyed.

If Jory and I survived the upcoming battle, I resolved to see that my grandchildren would enjoy a rich and rewarding life. Trixie would be there with me, her spirit shining down upon us, lighting the way.

As the night dragged, I became very, very drowsy. I had been awake for over 20 hours, and the long, painful bicycle ride had taken a toll on me. I fought to remain alert. My head sunk into my chest a few times, and I probably did doze, but I managed to keep myself from falling into a deep sleep.

I startled awake to the sound of a mourning dove call. Suddenly alert, I looked towards Jory in the pre-dawn light. I was just able to see him signal with this hands that there were four people approaching from the west. I turned and looked, but saw nothing. Thank God my son-in-law was there, with his young eyes and excellent hearing! I turned back and looked east. The sky was brightening, but the road was clear. Unfortunately, there were plenty of brush piles, destroyed trees, and storm-ravaged buildings that someone could use for cover.

The two dogs, which had been milling about the house, let loose with a cacophony of barking.

Once again, Jory used the mourning dove call to alert me. I felt extremely vulnerable in my hiding place, with nothing more than heavy branches to protect me. The idea was that Jory, who was better protected with concrete blocks and stones, would draw the initial fire. When the attackers got within range, I would attack with my Sig.

I continued looking east. The sun was just beginning to become visible, but it would soon disappear behind a low cloud bank. Watching the trees in the distance, I caught a flash of movement. A man suddenly dashed from behind a tree and ran to a deadfall, where he hid. Two more men followed him. Alerting Jory with the call of the mourning dove, I signaled that three were approaching from the east.

Seven against two. I did not like these odds at all. But the bad dudes had no idea we waited for them – and we had decent firepower.

As I waited for the attack to begin the nervous tension became unbearable. My hands were freezing. I desperately needed to cough. Only the thought of seeing my family again kept me from jumping to my feet and running as fast as I could away from the pending carnage.

Bang! Bang! Bang! Jory's gun fired three times in quick succession. I burned with the desire to turn and see the results, but I had my own problems. The three approaching men, who had been lurking behind a fallen oak tree, returned fire towards Jory's little fort.

Bang! Bang! Sparks flew from the stones that guarded Jory's back. Bang! Bang! Bullets struck the stones at Jory's front. He was surrounded.

The dogs, frightened by the gunfire, ran away and cowered under a large piece of plywood.

The attackers had no idea that I was hidden nearby. As long as they were occupied by Jory, I might be able to make a move on my own. Jory returned fire and dove back behind the cement and rocks.

Using extreme caution, I extracted myself from my hiding place. With my sword in my left hand and pistol in my right, I slowly crawled out of the field of vision of the eastern attackers. I ran around the north side of my house, and sprinted to the propane pig. I rested for a few seconds, and counted at least ten gunshots. Jory was holding his own, but it was time for me to step up and join the party.

I ran to the porch of my house, climbed the stairs, and was shocked to see a man standing before me, facing away as he fired his handgun at Jory. He hadn't noticed me yet, so as quietly as possible, I slid along the shadows until I was within arm's reach. In one hard, continuous thrust, I drove the ceremonial Mason's sword through his back, puncturing his left lung and probably striking his heart. As he fell to the floor, I yanked back hard on the sword, ready for another strike.

I looked at the man's face for the first time, and recognized him as one of the two men that had argued back at the barn, where I hid with Ethan. It was Jenkins. Or James.

I had no idea if the man was dead or not. I crouched behind the porch railing. The two remaining raiders were arguing. Holy shit! It was the Sergeant! And Muttley! Had they been with the horsemen since the attack upon my house? Had they tracked me, Burnsy, and Alex back here? I was furious – at them and at myself. Those assholes probably led the horsemen to us. Anger seethed through every vein in my body. I was going to crucify these motherfuckers.

The Sergeant, who was unaware that I lurked on the porch, ran around the corner of the house and crouched next to the stone foundation. Jory fired at him and hit the house with four or five shots. Stone chips struck the Sergeant's face, and he reflexively stepped backwards to find a safer position. He stood about ten yards away, an easy shot with the Sig. But I didn't want to alert Muttley to my presence. Suddenly, the Sergeant got the idea that he would be better off on the other side of the house. He ran up the stairs and nearly tripped over his dead companion. Spotting me, his gun fired and I felt a searing pain in my right hip. As I fell against the railing, I raised the Sig and fired two quick rounds, striking him square in the chest. He fell to the floor, but before I could assess the situation, bullets struck the porch woodwork. I dove to the floor, and crawled back towards the rear stairs. Rolling to my left side, I could see that the Sergeant's bullet had grazed my hip. "Only a flesh wound," I muttered. "You're gonna have to do better than that to take me out!"

Muttley continued firing at the porch. I could hear gunfire from the other side of the property, where Jory was still engaged in fighting.

Ignoring the pain in my hip, I descended the porch stairs and crawled in the dirt and weeds to find a place where I could get a bead on Muttley. Shit, I forgot the sword! Muttley fired two more shots at the porch and then stopped. Was he running out of ammunition? It was suddenly very quiet. Jory was no longer firing.

I crept around the corner of the porch and looked to where Muttley had been hiding. He was gone! Forgetting my own safety, I sprinted across the yard, looking east as I ran. There he was, running across the field near a row of downed trees. Far ahead I could see their horses, where they had been left before the fight began.

Muttley wasn't much of a runner. He stumbled in the muddy field and nearly fell, which allowed me to easily catch up with him. When I was about 30 yards away, I yelled, "Stop!"

He ignored me and continued towards the horses. I fired my pistol into the air. "I said STOP!"

Oh, he must have been so disappointed! He only had about 10 more yards to the horses and freedom. He turned slowly and looked at me with his nasty, scowling rat face. He held a handgun at his side. "Who the FUCK are you, anyway!"

I lifted my arm and pointed the Sig directly at him. "I am the man who owns that house. I am the man who helped Burnsy and Alex escape from the armory. I am the man who took the women and children back from the evil bastards at the fairgrounds."

I walked slowly towards him, keeping the gun leveled at the center of his chest. "Tell me this," I said. "Were you with the men that attacked the house and took my family?"

I could tell from the look on his face that he was a shifty bastard. His eyes squinted, as if he were trying to channel Lee Van Cleef in *The Good, The Bad, and the Ugly*. I laughed. He looked more like Don Knotts.

When he did not reply I walked closer. I was watching his gun, and did not consider that he might have another weapon. When I was about a yard away, he lunged at me, an eight-inch knife in his left hand. I turned just in time as the knife slid across my chest, doing little harm. I brought up the pistol and fired, but he fell to the ground and slashed at my legs. I jumped and fell directly upon his prone body and pinned his knife arm to the ground. With the Sig still in my right hand, we wrestled until I struck him hard with the butt of the pistol.

"Stop it!" I yelled. I hit him again and stunned, he finally let the knife fall from his hand. Carefully, I picked up his knife. I backed away, my eyes never leaving him, and retrieved his pistol. I fired it into the ground. Nothing happened. He was out of shells.

I walked towards and gave him a swift kick in the ribs.

"Arrrrggg," he complained. "Okay, okay, I've had enough. You win."

"You've had enough?" I was fuming with rage. "You have had ENOUGH? What about my family? And all of the other people you and your buddies have hurt!"

He sat up and shook his head. "I wasn't there when they killed your friends! I wasn't there when they killed your wife!"

Just then I understood. He had just sealed his fate and left me with no choice.

I fired two 10mm rounds into the center of his forehead. "I never told you that my wife was dead, asshole."

*****

I sat with my back against a lone remaining tree, crying. Oh Trixie, I have avenged your death. Those men would never again harm another human being. I wondered, was I as bad as them? I have killed so many men. Oh God, will you forgive me for my sins? I have lived a long time and never ever killed until the last few weeks. What was I becoming?

Hearing footsteps, I looked up to find Jory walking towards me. "Hey Dad," he reached my resting place.

"Hey Jory. How's it going?"

It was an asinine thing to ask, but in my exhaustion it was all I had.

"Uh, it's going better for us than it is for the other guys."

"Are they all taken care of?"

"Yes. I had four on my side. They put up a pretty good fight, but they lacked discipline."

I nodded. "It wasn't quite so easy on my side of the house."

He walked over to Muttley and nudged him with his boot. "I found the other two. Saw some blood on the porch."

I stood and showed him my injured hip. "The blood was mine. Nothing too serious."

"Good." He walked over to the horses, which were lathered from their hasty journey. He untied them and led them back towards me.

214

"Let's take these guys back to the house and get the hell out of here. I want to see my family."

Chapter 21

Immediately upon returning to my house after the gunfight I retrieved my ceremonial Mason's sword (which was now battle tested). I went inside the house for the first time since leaving a week earlier. Memories and emotions washed over my body as I saw remnants of our former lives, before and after the plastipocalypse. I stuffed my backpack and salvaged photos of my children and grandchildren. I found the *Foxfire* books and put them into the pack. I also found several packs of unused garden seeds, which I knew we would need.

The last thing I took from the house was our wedding photo. Two twenty-year-olds, ready for everything life would throw at us. I put the photo in the pack and left the house, probably for the last time.

Jory and I rode north together under a perpetually gloomy sky. The two dogs ran beside us, fearful of being trampled by the horses. Every two hours or so we switched horses with the other five that we had taken from the raiders. The goats followed us, tied to leads, occasionally braying at the dogs, who they definitely did not appreciate.

*****

As we rode, I told him our story, beginning with Trixie and me hiking to rescue Emily and the children. I left out the part about Emily getting shot (there was no point in getting him even more worried!). I told him about Burnsy and Alex, Mike, and the two assholes at the armory.

"There are plenty of those guys left," he said. "It seems like assholes always survive."

"Present company excluded," I laughed.

"Present company excluded."

"Jory, I have something to tell you that is very, very painful." I choked back tears, but my wavering voice made it obvious that I was in anguish. "Trixie was killed."

"No!" He stopped the horse shook in rage, his hands clenched in fists at his side.

My horse, startled, bucked around a bit. I had ridden horses several times in the past, but I was no horseman! Fortunately, I calmed the frightened animal and continued. "I don't know the details. While I was unconscious, the men we just had the firefight with attacked our property. My friend Mike and I had let our guards down, and we paid. Dearly."

All he could do was stare into the distance.

"The men were gathering women and children. Probably to use as slaves. Some of the women were..."

I choked... I was unable to say the word.

"Was Emily...?" he asked, hesitantly.

"I don't know. I don't think so. She is a strong woman, and she stepped up and helped keep everyone safe after her mother was murdered."

He relaxed and let out a huge sigh. "I am so sorry for you... losing Mom." He began to sob, so I rode closer and put my arm around him as his grief poured out.

He eventually controlled his emotions and spoke. "I've seen the worst of humanity over the last few weeks. But once or twice I ran into guys that made me think, damn, that guy is just like Emily's dad! Or that lady is just like Trixie! They are going to make it. They are going to help other people start over."

"We are going to have to carry on without Trixie. Now I have both you and Emily to help."

We stopped talking. I gave my horse a nudge and we began moving again. "What is going to happen now?" he whispered.

"We are going to rebuild. Look, it was only a little more than one hundred years ago that people lived without plastic and electricity. We just have to figure out how to do what they did. We will farm. We will weave. We will hunt. And we will survive."

We rode quietly for a few miles on the dirt road, passing one deserted or burned-out farm after another.

"I have a question for you, Jory. At the National Guard Armory, did you have any sense that this 'plastipocalypse' was global? Or was it just regional?

"*Plastipocalypse*?" he laughed. "That's what you call it?"

"I guess I used to read a lot of sci-fi."

"No, it's a good word. Plastipocalypse."

I asked again, "While you were with the Guards in Marshall, did you learn anything about what is going on? Is this global or local?"

He paused for a long time before replying. "I think it's huge. Bigger than just Michigan or even the entire Great Lakes region."

"Shit," I muttered. "I had a feeling..."

"Look," he continued. "I don't have any proof, because there were no communications at all from the U.S. Army. But from what I've seen... no aircraft overhead, no police or coordinated crisis response now for what is going on four weeks..."

"Yeah, I've been thinking the same thing. I haven't seen a single policeman or authority figure since this began. We are on our own now."

We had a long ride before us, so I asked him to tell me how he made it back to Lansing, then here, to my home.

He thought for a moment before replying. "I'll start at the beginning. I was at the juvie center. My shift was about half-way through, and this punk, his name was Jimmy, was acting out. He was shouting at another kid during lunch and I had to put him in lockdown for the afternoon. The inmates were all bitching about their plastic silverware. Jimmy shouted "This shit is fucked! The fuckin' forks are fucked." He noticed that one of the other kid's shirts was ripped, and he grabbed it and the entire shirt just fell apart. The other kid was pissed off, and he said something to Jimmy, which caused Jimmy to retaliate. I had to put Jimmy into restraints and walk him back to his cell. I put him in lockdown, and luckily for me, I decided return to my section by cutting across the courtyard. Just then, WHOOSH, the entire south wing exploded. Fortunately there isn't much glass in a

218

juvenile detention center, or I would have been cut all to hell. I hit the deck and the other three wings blew to smithereens.

"I laid there for what felt like hours. When I finally got up the whole place had gone up in flames. The power was out too. There were a couple of other guards that survived and I saw one administrator walking around in a daze, but no one seemed to be in charge. I worked my way through the destroyed remains of the building and found myself standing in the parking lot. One of the other guards staggered by, and I said, 'Hey, shouldn't we do something?' and he was like, 'Fuck that. I am getting the fuck outta here.' Right then I noticed that my shirt and pants were beginning to fall apart. I had no choice, so I went back into the building. The smoke and stench was horrible, but the screaming... the screaming was worse. There were boys stuck in their cells, still alive. Even though cell locks are operated remotely by an electronic system, I could still use my keys to open individual doors. At this point I thought that the explosion had only happened to the juvie center, I had no idea that shit was blowing up all over Michigan.

"I wanted to follow protocol, which was to evacuate the boys to the outside recreation area, where they would be contained by fencing. But there was only me! I had no help and there are over 250 boys in that juvie center. I am not proud to say this, but I bailed."

"You left the boys locked up?" I was incredulous. "They surely needed help!"

"Listen, Dad. Don't believe for a minute that I haven't thought about what I did. I know that a lot of those young men are just the products of shitty parenting and a failed system. But I had children at home that had *good* parents: Emily and me."

I considered this as he continued his story. "I decided to leave the premises and seek assistance. Since the phones were all out, and my cell phone had turned into a soft blob of goo, I had no other choice. I made my way into the locker room, and even thought it was dark as hell in there, I managed to find some pants and a jacket that fit me. It's a good thing too, because otherwise I'd have been forced to wear inmate coveralls – which are made from cotton, but have "Marshall Juvenile Inmate" stamped in red on the front and back."

"That wouldn't have helped you on the outside."

"No, they wouldn't. But I did eventually make it back outdoors. I was in a bit of a daze, but somehow I made my way to the Marshall National Guard Armory. The place was fucked just like the juvie center. Smoke poured from the windows, the roof had caved in. I saw a bunch of guys in the yard, just staring at the carnage. I don't belong to this unit, but one of the guys, an instructor that travels between units, recognized me. He introduced me to the unit and we all agreed that we'd see what we could do to help the locals."

"You didn't try to head home as quickly as possible? I asked.

"My job as a Guardsman is to help. I spent the next week trying to find water and food for the people who came to the armory, looking for the government or *any* authority to help. But each day one or two of the guys would just disappear. I think they went home. Eventually I came to the same conclusion. My family might need help also! So the first chance I got, I deserted my post and headed north, to Lansing. When I finally arrived there and found the empty house I had a bit of a meltdown. But the note led me to you, so well, here we are now."

"I am glad you made it back." I smiled at him and added, "By this time tomorrow you will be with your family!"

*****

We spent a quiet night sleeping in an old stone house and left at sunrise the next day. Jory and I were both anxious to see Emily and the children.

It was late afternoon when we rode into Sanford. As we rode towards the church, we spotted a young woman in the distance. She had been carrying a metal bucket of water, which she let drop as she ran at us in a full sprint.

"Jory! Daddy!" You made it!"

Epilogue

Even though we had survived difficulties that we had never expected, the next months were much harder. I missed my Trixie every waking moment and I dreamt of her as I slept alone at night. My grief, exacerbated by the loss of my wife of nearly 40 years and not knowing exactly where her body lay (Emily said that they'd all been blindfolded during their captivity), was an enormously heavy weight on my heart.

Evil, bullying men had taken the life of my wife, a woman who was the kindest, most helpful person you would ever have the pleasure of knowing. I felt responsible for Trixie's death and the evil that had been forced upon the other women. I made a vow to myself that I would never let it happen again.

After weeks of constant movement we eventually found a small rural hospital and turned it into our home. The building was easily defended by raiders, and having learned from previous mistakes, we were never without armed watchers.

With the horses, we could range for miles to scavenge. But we also had to feed the animals. One day Jory returned home from a hunting trip with good news. He'd found a barn full of oats.

We were faced with hunger each day, but we didn't have to eat the goats. Miranda eventually perfected cheese making (thanks to the *Foxfire* books!).

The first winter was brutal, but by the next summer we had established a working community that grew crops, raised livestock, taught children, and first and foremost: treated each other with respect.

Even though there weren't more than 40 or 50 people living in our vicinity, word must have got out that we were building something that offered security and a future.

We welcomed three new "families" into our midst, and resurrected some of the lost technologies that our grandparents had relied upon.

The *Foxfire* books gave us a real head-start. By using common sense and shared knowledge, we lived. We ate. We survived.

There was one last journey that remained before me. I sought out Emily, who was in the section of the hospital that we had turned into classrooms. She was reading *Pinocchio* to a group of youngsters, and she smiled as she saw me standing in the doorway.

"That's enough for now," she told the children. "You may go play."

The children all jumped from the wooden benches they sat upon and ran from the room, laughing and carrying on as only children can.

"What's up, Dad?"

I took a deep breath and hesitated. These words were not easy for me to say and would not be welcome to Emily's ears.

"I am going west. To find your brother."

Acknowledgments

I came up with the idea for this book entirely on my own. I don't recall the exact moment that I wondered about a world that was suddenly without plastic, but once I had the idea I couldn't let it go. Carol, my wife of nearly 40 years humored me and listened to my wild rants as I created a world that was suddenly without one of the most ubiquitous materials known to modern man. Carol also edited and re-edited this story – finding the simple mistakes in punctuation and spelling that are almost impossible for an author to spot.

I am very fortunate that my friend Dr. Shaun Bruno, who has a PHD in Chemistry, lives just down the road. When I presented the idea of the book to Shaun, he jumped right in with many suggestions, including the idea that plastic would sublimate and turn into methane that would create massive fire storms and disrupt the planet's climate in ways we've never imagined.

I also need to acknowledge my daughter Caitlin, my sister Kim, and my Nordic skiing travel buddy and teammate Tony Percha for their ongoing enthusiasm and support for this project.

Brent Jones invested a considerable amount of time and energy editing this story. Brent provided honest criticism and helped me make the book much, much better than it would have been had I edited it myself.

And last but not least, I would like to acknowledge Andy Weir, who with his book *The Martian*, has inspired me to "work the problem" in every aspect of daily living.

About Douglas Cornell

As a lifelong resident of rural Michigan, Douglas Cornell has carved a life that involves information technology problem solving, wilderness backpacking, Nordic skiing, bicycling, rocking out on his guitars, and playing with his three grandchildren.

Made in the USA
Middletown, DE
01 April 2018